None of them had ... g perfectly still behind o... r-greens listening attent... ...nversation. He'd seen Jimbo and Liz disappear and thought they'd be together in the garden talking about him, but instead he'd overheard that daft old bat Muriel telling Liz to be wary of Titus Bellamy. He hoped Muriel didn't think she was right in this ridiculous assumption, because she wasn't, Liz would never ... A cold chill ran down his spine and made him shudder. He remembered that look Titus gave Liz when he toasted her ... Hang his investment! He'd strangle the man for his boldness. Liz was his wife! He'd damn well teach him a lesson.

Educated at a co-educational Quaker boarding school, Rebecca Shaw went on to qualify as a teacher of deaf children. After her marriage, she spent the ensuing years enjoying bringing up her family. The departure of the last of her four children to university has given her the time and opportunity to write. *A Village Deception* is the latest in the highly popular Tales from Turnham Malpas series. Visit her website at www.rebeccashaw.co.uk.

By Rebecca Shaw

The Village Green Affair

Rebecca Shaw

An Orion paperback

First published in Great Britain in 2008
by Orion
This paperback edition published in 2008
by Orion Books Ltd,
Orion House, 5 Upper St Martin's Lane,
London WC2H 9EA

An Hachette UK company

A CIP catalogue record for this book
is available from the British Library.

Typeset by Deltatype Ltd, Birkenhead, Merseyside

Printed and bound in Great Britain by Clays Ltd, St Ives plc

The Orion Publishing Group's policy is to use papers that
are natural, renewable and recyclable products and made
from wood grown in sustainable forests. The logging and
manufacturing processes are expected to conform to the
environmental regulations of the country of origin.

www.orionbooks.co.uk

INHABITANTS OF TURNHAM MALPAS

Willie Biggs	Retired verger
Sylvia Biggs	His wife
James (Jimbo) Charter-Plackett	Owner of the Village Store
Harriet Charter-Plackett	His wife
Fergus, Finlay, Flick and Fran	Their children
Katherine Charter-Plackett	Jimbo's mother
Alan Crimble	Barman at the Royal Oak
Linda Crimble	His wife
Lewis Crimble	Their son
Maggie Dobbs	School caretaker
H. Craddock Fitch	Owner of Turnham House
Kate Fitch	Village school headteacher
Jimmy Glover	Taxi driver
Gilbert Johns	Church choirmaster
Louise Johns	His wife
Mrs Jones	A village gossip
Vince Jones	Her husband
Barry Jones	Her son and estate carpenter
Pat Jones	Barry's wife
Dean and Michelle	Barry and Pat's children
Revd Peter Harris MA (Oxon)	Rector of the parish
Dr Caroline Harris	His wife
Alex and Beth	Their children
Marcus March	Writer
Alice March	Musician

Jeremy Mayer	Manager at Turnham House
Venetia Mayer	His wife
Neville Neal	Accountant and church treasurer
Liz Neal	His wife
Tom Nicholls	Assistant in the Store
Evie Nicholls	His wife
Anne Parkin	Retired secretary
Sir Ralph Templeton	Retired from the diplomatic service
Lady Muriel Templeton	His wife
Dicky & Georgie Tutt	Licensees at the Royal Oak
Bel Tutt	Assistant in the Village Store
Don Wright	Maintenance engineer (now retired)
Vera Wright	Cleaner at the nursing home in Penny Fawcett
Rhett Wright	Their grandson

The Village Green Affair

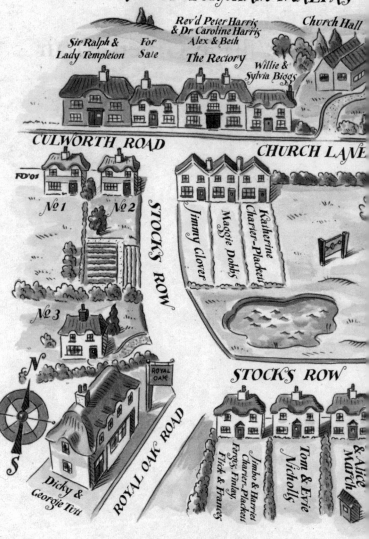

THE VILLAGE OF TURNHAM MALPAS

Rev'd Peter Harris
& Dr Caroline Harris
Alex & Beth

Church Hall

Sir Ralph &
Lady Templeton

For
Sale

The Rectory

Willie &
Sylvia Biggs

CULWORTH ROAD

CHURCH LANE

FD'01

No 1

No 2

STOCKS ROW

Jimmy Glover

Maggie Dobbs

Katherine Charter-Plackett

No 3

ROYAL OAK

STOCKS ROW

N

S

ROYAL OAK ROAD

Dicky &
Georgie Tutt

Jimbo & Harriet
Charter-Plackett
Fergus, Finlay,
Flick & Frances

Tom & Evie
Nicholls

& Alice
March

Chapter 1

The stranger was already sitting on the bench outside the Royal Oak when the first bright streaks of dawn appeared in the east. It was a typical early morning in that part of the country: a slight mist lying over the fields; cows already in their milking parlours; the cocks crowing; the early traffic booming along the bypass; and the birds singing their morning hymn. Malcolm the milkman, who didn't speak until he'd been delivering milk for at least two hours, gave him the briefest of nods as he left a full crate outside the pub door.

Beginning his schedule of opening up the Village Store, Tom propped the door wide open. Blinds up, lights on, newspapers heaved in from the doorstep, coffee machine started up for those who bought their breakfast in the Store before leaving for work in Culworth, and finally a general look around to make sure everything was in smart order for the day.

The stranger stretched his long legs out in front of him, locking his ankles together, and observed the ancient village waking up. He noted the geese by their pond beginning to take notice of the new day by flexing their wings. Yes, this *was* the place, he thought. The thatched roofs and the cottages crouching round the green would attract everyone, and the best part about it was there were no signs of the twenty-first century; not an aerial, not a lamppost, not a billboard, not a house number, nothing to mar the beautiful thirteenth-century ambience. Best of all there were the stocks. Believe it or believe it not, they were complete, top and bottom, and untouched by any modern repairs. In addition, the whole of Culworth was waiting just eight miles away to make it a success. The pub, not yet stirring, would provide the victuals. Very handy, that. The punters always needed food and drink.

In the man's inside pocket was information which would knock the villagers sideways if they tried to stop him. That was the advantage of being a lapsed historian. He knew exactly where to go to find old deeds and agreements; old, very old, information about the land. He slipped his hand into the inside pocket of his corduroy jacket and pulled out a copy of the fourteenth-century deed agreed by one of the first Templetons at the Big House. He smoothed his fingers over the old writing, relishing the antique spelling and the elaborate language, a smile curving his long mouth, illuminating his face.

A shadow flashed past him and a loud 'good morning' broke the peace. God! He was a big chap.

The stranger hailed him. 'Good morning to you. You're on the road early.'

The runner broke step, turned back and looked down at him.

The man on the bench was shaken by the runner's expression. It was ... he'd have liked to use the word 'heavenly' or even 'angelic' but that was ridiculous. Compassionate, perhaps, sounded more realistic. Whatever it was, it shook him.

'Good morning, sir. Nice village you have here, sir.'

2

'Indeed. Can't stop, though. Just starting my morning run.' The runner took in the beard, the dark brown corduroy trousers and jacket, the slightly frayed tweedy shirt, the ancient walking boots. 'I see you're not inclined to my way of greeting the day.' He smiled.

And again there was that strange feeling of otherworldliness. 'Not my scene.'

'A visitor, are you?'

The tall man got a nod for his answer. He smiled again. 'Well, must be on my way or I shan't be back in time for breakfast.' He nodded a goodbye and left, picking up his pace without effort.

The stranger watched him circle the green and continue on down ... now what was it? Ah! Yes, that was Shepherd's Hill.

But someone else took his eye. She was opening the gate into the school playground. A well-rounded woman, short and energetic, wearing trainers, bright red cropped trousers and a sleeveless matching top, just right for the promise the weather held for the rest of the day. Caretaker, no doubt. He'd wait a while longer though, see what the day still had to bring.

There was a continuous stream of people entering the Village Store. First a trickle of shoppers collecting their newspapers and bits and pieces, carrying their takeaway coffees and rolls to their cars, then the mothers, after dropping their children off at the school – that made quite a rush – then a steady stream, and quite a collection of people who stayed to gossip outside on the pavement where a seat had been placed and the postbox stood. The local bus stopped briefly right outside the Store, the driver clearly impatient to be off to the bright lights of Culworth. Now that was handy, a bus right where he needed it. And, yes, the Store was a big draw. He rubbed his hands in glee. Turnham Malpas was more active than he'd realized; all to the good, so far as he was concerned.

His long reverie was broken by the drawing back of the bolts on the pub door, allowing a short, thin chap to put out a sandwich board on the pavement announcing they were serving coffee. Like Tom in the Store, he propped open the door and, at the same time, took in the crate of milk. The man on the bench felt that was somehow symptomatic of the whole village, a certain openness. Coffee! Now that was an idea. Languidly he picked up the small haversack he'd dropped beside the bench and went in to the pub.

From the outside he could see that it was very old, and he almost dreaded going in because he feared being disillusioned by finding the pub had been modernized inside. To his relief it hadn't. The huge inglenook fireplace was genuine, and the horse brasses, the warming pan and the farm implements on the old brick walls looked as though they'd grown there. Genuine through and through. Wonderful. Because of all that, he liked the publican even before he spoke to him; evidently he had good taste. He found a settle, took off his cap, pushed his fingers through his hair and called across, 'A coffee, landlord, if you please.'

While he waited he ran his hand along the gleaming well-worn table in front of the settle, feeling, as much as seeing, the history which felt to ooze from every joint. It shone smooth with years and years of polishing. He ran his fingers along the curved arm of the settle several times and fingered the small bowl of flowers, which proved to be genuine. Miraculously, a tray appeared, tastefully laid

4

with a small silver coffee pot, silver cream jug and sugar basin, and a paper napkin.

Dicky discreetly left a bill with the tray, saying, 'Enjoy,' before he made to disappear.

'Landlord! I don't suppose you have a fresh croissant to go with this?'

'Name's Dicky, and yes we have. New round here?'

'I am.'

'Won't be two minutes.'

The coffee was gloriously welcome and the croissant, when it came, was so fresh it might have been served in a pavement café on the Champs-Elysées. Utterly wonderful.

The stranger picked up a menu from the table. It was a clear attempt to wheedle you from the bar into the small restaurant, signposted by an arrow and the name Georgie's Restaurant fastened to a low-hung beam above the bar. He began to smile. The licensed trade was obviously very much alert to modern day needs. No flyblown pork pies on a doily for them, nor yesterday's egg and cress sandwiches under a plastic dome. He thought he might try lunch there. Just a chance to meet people, see what made them tick before he launched this new project. His spirits rose.

Just then the outside door burst open and a woman entered backwards, staggering under the weight of a large cardboard box.

'It's me, Dicky,' she shouted. 'Brought you the flyers for the Scout jumble sale, Neville brought them home last night.'

Then she let the door slam shut after her, and, as she turned round, he saw her full face. He was stunned, staggered almost, by what appeared to him to be her startling good looks. She wasn't classically beautiful, but wholesome and, he sensed, spirited. This was the first time since... Marie ... he'd felt so enthralled by a woman. He gave no outward sign of his shock, though unexpectedly, his heart bounded, but she, on the other hand, didn't seem to notice he was there.

Dicky appeared through the door that led into the back. He took the box from her. 'Thanks, Liz. I was coming across for them later, once I'd set up. Thank Neville for me, greatly appreciated.'

'Not at all, it's a pleasure.' The Liz person waved cheerily. 'Au revoir! Must get back to the nursery. Be seeing you!' She left at speed.

The stranger, quietly eating his croissant and drinking his excellent coffee, was left alone to still his racing heart.

Liz Neal sprinted back to the church hall to begin storytime. She loved this part of the morning, when the children gathered round her and her assistant Angie Turner put out the mid-morning snacks for them all. Running the playgroup might not be the occupation thought appropriate for the smart wife of the premier chartered accountant in Culworth, but she'd given up worrying herself about that. She loved doing it, and it was the nearest she would ever get to being qualified at anything because the years had gone by and Liz hadn't bothered herself about a career when she was growing up. Her mother had said, 'An attractive girl like you will have a husband and a nice house and a family. You don't need to train for a career.' So she hadn't, and at nineteen she'd met Neville Neal, an ambitious, self-obsessed newly qualified accountant. Her parents had lent them the money for him to set up his own business and they'd never looked back. Well, at least Neville had never looked back, but occasionally Liz did and wished ... oh, how she wished.

She picked up the story of Goldilocks from the book corner because the children knew it and loved the lines they could repeat without her help, and adored the illustrations.

'"Who's sleeping in my bed?" said Baby Bear,' they all bawled.

By the time the story was finished the children were ready for their milk and fruit, and Liz and Angie for their coffee.

Angie slurped a good mouthful from her mug before she spoke. 'I know some of them can be naughty just like my twins were – are – full of energy from morning to night, but you can't help but love 'em, can yer?'

'No. Have you thought any more about that course I want you to go on?'

'Is that kind of thing for me? Really, I mean ... they'll all be so clever.'

Liz raised a disbelieving eyebrow. 'And you're not?'

Angie looked embarrassed. 'Well, you know I never did well at school, not ever. I'd make a fool of myself.'

'Angie Turner! You would not. You took to this job brilliantly. Within a week you were making constructive suggestions. Remember? Your finger right on the pulse. So I'm putting you forward.' She glanced round the children to check that they were happy just in time to see one of the girls pour all her milk over Toby.

'Sara! What are you thinking of? Toby has his own milk, he doesn't need yours.' Angie had already pulled a clean shirt from the 'spares box' and was stripping off Toby's soaking shirt.

'See what I mean?' said Liz. 'I'm definitely putting your name down. The very best thing of all is that you never lose your temper.'

Angie grinned at her. 'All right then, I'll give it a turn.' Secretly she was delighted by Liz's conviction that she would do well.

Liz smiled her delight at Angie's decision. 'Well, there we are. That's good. You see, I might change my mind and decide to leave the nursery, and then you could step into my shoes.'

'Me? In charge? I don't think so.'

'You've got to have some belief in yourself. Where were you when self-worth was given out? Right at the back of the queue, I guess. Well, forget it, now's the time to move forward. Children! Toilets and then out to play. Off you go. Come along.'

'I'll clear up.'

Liz shook her head. 'No, I'll clear up, you go and supervise them.'

While she rinsed the plates, threw the paper cups into the bin and wiped the tables, Liz remembered that Neville, unusually, would be home for lunch. Neville. If she could have seen her own face Liz would have been horrified. The mention of her husband's name had made her look to have sucked hard on a lemon. Her lovely brown eyes had gone hard, her sweet mouth painfully twisted and her nose wrinkled with disgust. In two weeks it would be their silver wedding anniversary, and the huge affair Neville had made of it was embarrassing. A quiet get-together at the George with close friends would have been enough for her, but no, seventy guests, many she didn't even know, a small band for dancing, a bar, gifts for every one, a table to display their own gifts. Liz shuddered

8

... And there was nothing at all to tempt Hugh and Guy to attend, for there were no invitations to a few of their twenty-something friends to make it more enjoyable for them.

'No, no, we don't want your friends there being noisy and ridiculous,' Neville had said.

Hugh had protested, 'But, Dad, our friends aren't like that. OK, they like a drink, but they wouldn't be so thoughtless as to get drunk at an occasion like a silver wedding anniversary. Well, I'm sorry, I shan't be there.' And he'd left the dining table in a hurry.

Guy had said exactly the same, and he too had left and they'd heard the front door slam as the two of them departed for the flat they shared in Culworth. So most of the pleasure of the party was gone for Liz. In fact, Neville would have baulked at the idea of Peter and Caroline being invited had it not been for the fact that Peter was the Rector and Neville felt the need to keep a foot in the door of heaven.

Wryly Liz decided that was because of his nefarious dealings with the town councillors, especially those on the planning committee. She knew for a fact that brown paper envelopes passed in a one-way stream from Neville to a weasel called Kevin who worked in the planning office and always had his ear close to the ground and not just about planning. No doubt Kevin would have ingratiated himself on to the guest list, a list Neville was in charge of and she had never seen.

Angie shouted from the church hall door, 'We're ready to come in. OK?'

'Yes. Everything's ready.'

Liz repeated exactly those words to Neville when she'd got the lunch ready later on.

'Everything's ready,' she'd said, as Neville roared in from some meeting or other and immediately disappeared, giving Liz a birdlike peck on her cheek as he rushed by.

'Just got this to finish, won't be long.'

But he was twenty minutes long. He then bolted down his sandwiches and salad, grabbed his briefcase, waved aside the fresh cheese scones she'd baked between leaving nursery and him coming home, and away he went without exchanging a pleasant word with her. It would be the same that evening; a draught of air from the front door as Neville sped into the house. Later, after working in his study all evening, he'd have a slow walk by floodlight round his meticulously kept garden making notes of things to remind the gardener about, a whiskey in the sitting room with Liz and then bed.

Their first early years, filled as they were by the arrival so close together of their two boys, had been happy enough, but gradually, as the boys grew, he'd killed by neglect any passion she might have had for him, for there wasn't room in his life for close contact of the sexual kind, not even at Christmas. Liz blamed herself; she'd grown bored with his passion by numbers. She'd once overheard someone in the village call him a 'cold fish', and they were absolutely right, he was.

She'd cleared up, opened the post that had come after she'd left for the nursery that morning and wondered what to do next.

The phone rang. 'Caroline here, Liz. I'm home early. Cup of tea?'

'Yes, please.'

'In the garden? Bring a cardy.'

'Lovely. I'll be two minutes.'

The Rectory door stood open so she pushed the door

10

wider and called out, 'It's me.' Then she walked down the hall into Caroline's kitchen and immediately felt warmed and caressed by it. It always had that effect on her, and heaven knows she'd come into this kitchen often enough over the last fourteen years. And there was Caroline the creator of this kitchen and its atmosphere, putting tea things on a tray. The back door was already open, beckoning her out into Caroline's beautiful garden. When they'd first moved in, the garden had been nothing more than hard, rock-like dry soil decorated with stones and a few parched bushes but now it was a triumphantly luxurious country garden, which, summer and winter, never failed to thrill her. At the back of her mind Liz compared it with their own garden at Glebe House, which was regimented, stark and stylish. No leaf was out of place, no bush was allowed to fling itself over the edge of a wall, whereas Caroline's garden seemed to wallow in freedom.

'Isn't it a lovely day for late April?'

'Liz! Hi! Bring the biscuits.' Caroline led the way into the garden, which, although she admitted it to no one, was her pride and joy.

'I know I ask this each time I see you, but how about the twins? How are they progressing? I saw Alex out the other day helping collect for the Scout jumble sale.'

'Truth to tell, they are both doing very well indeed. No problems, so far as we can tell. Beth hasn't had a nightmare for weeks and weeks, and as for Alex, he's fine. He reminds me from time to time how much Beth needs reassurance and what he calls "looking after".'

'You never say *why* she needs looking after. What does he mean?' Liz asked but didn't get an answer. She knew she wouldn't but still she asked. They told each other everything, and it was so unlike Caroline to evade the truth.

11

Caroline froze for a moment, then relaxed and asked Liz if she needed the sugar. When Liz shook her head Caroline grinned, 'You're still dieting then.'

Liz nodded and then asked, 'Well?'

'After that business with Andy Moorhouse, I mean.' Caroline hated lying but she had to; no one must know the real reason for their problems. What had happened out in Africa had almost been the end of the twins. She put Liz's cup of tea in front of her and asked, 'How's Neville? I haven't seen him for days.'

'As right as he ever is.'

'That doesn't sound any too happy.'

As Liz put down her cup it rattled slightly in the saucer, and Caroline raised an eyebrow.

'What's the matter?'

'Do I ever complain about Neville?'

'Not in my hearing you don't.'

'Well, I am now. I need to tell someone.'

'About how unhappy you are?'

'You get first prize for being so perceptive. Yes, about how unhappy I am. We married when I was only nineteen, all stars in my eyes and as naïve as it was possible to be. Hugh and Guy coming so close together definitely sharpened me up. I was on a high and Neville at least noticed I existed then. But there's no need for mothering now they're grown up, and I haven't got Neville any more, either. I've fallen into a great void.' Liz got out a tissue and blew her nose.

Caroline reached across the table and patted her hand in sympathy.

'You see, now the twins are so much better you've got doctoring to go back to, and you feel valued outside your home. I've nothing.' Tears welled in her eyes and she

12

gave a small apologetic smile. 'Sorry for being so feeble. I managed to squeeze in making some cheese scones between getting home from nursery and Neville coming in for lunch, but he just waved them aside, as if they were of no consequence, and rushed out of the door. I was so upset. How pathetic can you get?'

'I'd no idea ... you always seem so confident and full of verve ... so *happy*.'

'I'm going to confide in you now, not because you're the Rector's wife, but because we've been friends for so long ...' Liz looked up. 'We never sleep together, not any more.'

Caroline, as the Rector's wife, was the target for more intimate disclosures than you could shake a stick at, but this, from someone who appeared to her to be a sophisticated, up-to-the-minute woman, came as a shock. She was struck dumb, and Liz didn't know what to do or where to look.

Finally Caroline said, 'Well, maybe that's right for you. Nowadays, unless one is rampaging round the bedroom two or three times a night one gets the idea that one's marriage has failed miserably. But it's not like that, not really. Every night or twice a week suits some people, whereas twice a month is perfectly satisfactory for others.'

'It's not even once a year.'

'I see. That is a bit ... well ... miserable.'

Liz began to feel foolish. She should never have said a word about it. After all, Caroline had never suspected anything was wrong with her. Which there wasn't, not really. But he was so cold, and even more self-obsessed than when they married. How she'd admired that early ruthless ambition of his, but in truth it was that very ambition which had killed their marriage. If someone

13

didn't match up to his expectations, he dismissed them as worthless and of no use to him in his meteoric rise to … what? Wealth? Position? Adoration? Yes, he loved adoration, and she, his wife, no longer adored him. In fact, in some ways, she despised him.

'Ummm? Sorry, I didn't catch what you said.'

Caroline repeated her piece of advice. 'I said, a holiday, that's what you need, on your own. With space to think, to refresh mind and body. How about it?'

'But how would Neville manage on his own? He has difficulty finding the kettle.'

Caroline burst out laughing. 'Finding the kettle? You've been too thoughtful over the years, Liz. Much too kind.'

From their spot in the garden they could hear movement in the kitchen.

Alarmed someone might have overheard their conversation, Liz whispered, 'Is that Dottie? I thought we were on our own otherwise I wouldn't have—'

Peter appeared in the doorway. 'Hello, you two. Is there any more tea in the pot?'

'You're back! Sorry, darling, we've drunk it all. Shall I …?' Caroline made to get up.

'Stay where you are. I'll make a pot and drink it in my study. I've got notes to make.'

'OK. Good meeting?'

'If a quarter of an hour discussing the merits of horse manure for the Dean's recent venture into rhubarb growing and the best time of year to apply it, has anything at all to do with applying to the Lottery fund for money for the Abbey bells, then yes.' Peter stood quite still for a moment, smiling and admiring Liz and Caroline sitting there in the sun in their bright frocks.

Liz sat there admiring *him*. Being 6ft 5in he'd had to

step out of the doorway onto the garden path in order to stand upright and, with the sun catching his strawberry-blond hair and emphasizing the extraordinary blue of his eyes, she didn't think there was anyone more gorgeous than Peter Harris, Rector of this parish. Then she saw the loving expression on his face when he looked at Caroline, and almost choked; the glow of deep love between them seared her heart. It was all too much. Much too much, and she felt sick with dissatisfaction at her particular plight. If Neville looked at her like that *for one single moment* she'd be satisfied. Liz daren't look at Caroline because if she did she'd have to leap up, rush home and break down in tears. The Harrises' pleasure in each other, compared with the stark emptiness of her life at the moment, was unbearable.

Peter turned to go inside and for a while the only sound was of birds twittering in the beech hedge along the bottom of the garden. Eventually Caroline cleared her throat and said, 'We'll talk about this another time, eh?'

Liz said, 'Yes. Yes, of course. Sorry for burdening you with it all. Just nonsense really. Well, no, it isn't. It's very real. I've tried the candlelight supper and the wine and the sexy nightdress – but it makes no impact at all. I'm appalled, *appalled* I've sunk to such ridiculous levels. It's pathetic. I realize we've completely and absolutely lost contact. Just forget it.' Liz got to her feet. 'Must go. Remember how lucky you are, you know.' She nodded towards the house. And left.

Caroline heard Liz call out to Peter to say she was leaving and at the same time heard the kettle reach boiling point. That was clearly how Liz felt – close to boiling over, she thought, and that was a dangerous place for a wife to be.

Within a couple of hours of leaving the Rectory, Liz drove into Culworth to meet Neville for a drink. It was something she'd rarely done before but somehow she thought that doing the unexpected might revive something. Might shock him into looking at her properly, instead of just checking if she reached his standards of what was appropriate for a leading accountant's wife. Why he imagined he should be *considered* a leading accountant she couldn't imagine; after all, Culworth was a minor country town, not in any way the level of a leading accountant in the City of London. Sad really, she thought.

Having parked her car, she marched along the High Street and into the glossy offices of Neville G. H. Neal and Company, Chartered Accountants.

'Good evening, Penny,' she said to the girl on reception. 'Mr Neal available?'

'May I ask who's enquiring?'

Liz, in her present mood, was determined not to tolerate this rudeness. 'Well, Penny, it's his wife, Liz Neal. You and I have met on several occasions. We talked for quite some time at Christmas at the staff party, remember, and we met by chance in the Abbey coffee shop one Saturday morning not long ago, and we talked when I collected Mr Neal after he'd had that horrific time at the dentist and didn't feel able to drive himself home.'

'Oh! Yes, of course. Sorry.' She didn't bother to check the diary, however, just said offhandedly, 'He's busy.'

'With a client?'

'No, but he's too busy to see anyone.'

'He'll see me.'

Penny got to her feet in haste. 'It's more than my life's worth if I let ...' But Liz was already heading for Neville's office. She tapped lightly on his door and went in without waiting for a reply. He was leaning back in his chair, his feet propped up on the edge of his desk reading a sheaf of papers. 'I did say no ... Liz! What on earth ...?' He sat up straight, putting his feet on the floor at the same time. 'Is there something the matter?'

'Has it come to such a desperate state of affairs that my coming to the office creates waves?'

'No, no, it's just that you don't usually—'

'Time I did something surprising then, Neville.'

His ice-blue eyes widened, his narrow nose appeared more accusative than usual, and his voice was thin with a hint of a whine to it. 'You've chosen a difficult time. I've got these figures to run through for tomorrow. What have you come for?'

'To have a drink with you.'

'Oh! I see. Why?'

'I might even step right outside my box and suggest a meal out.'

'A meal out! Well, if you wait till I've finished—'

'No, Neville, I won't wait. I won't. This time you're putting me first. Put those papers in your briefcase now – you can read them when we get home.'

Neville hesitated. This really wasn't on. He checked the solid silver clock on his desk. It was ten minutes before the office would close and he was never seen leaving so early. Bad example, he always thought for the owner to be witnessed leaving before time. Begrudgingly he muttered, 'Let's wait till half past then. I never leave early.'

Liz flung her arms wide. 'Oh, my God! The world's come to an end!' She went round his desk, reached a hand out and snatched the papers he held, then stuffed them into the briefcase standing at the side of his chair.

17

'There we are, that wasn't difficult. Your spectacles, let's have them.' She pulled them from his face before he had a chance to do it for himself, forced open his case, put them in and snapped it shut, almost trapping her fingers. 'Now, off we go. I quite fancy that new bar and restaurant up the Headrow.'

Neville watched her set off for the door with his brief-case and didn't know what to do. No glasses, no figures – there was no point in staying on. Furious anger welled up inside him. He'd been press-ganged, commandeered, taken prisoner almost and, most importantly, he'd lost control of his life. He set great store by his strong control.

Liz called out, 'I've kidnapped your boss, Penny. Goodnight. Make sure everything's locked up when you go.'

Neville followed her, his face unfathomable, his eyes unwilling to meet Penny's. Instead they slid away from her and focused on Liz, whom at that moment he hated more than anything in the whole world for putting him in this intolerable position.

Once they were outside he said through gritted teeth, 'Give me my briefcase.'

'No.' Liz tucked her hand in the crook of his elbow and steered him up towards the Headrow.

This was the modern bit of the Culworth shopping area, a road unfamiliar to Neville because he still shopped where he'd always shopped – in the traditional old part. Not only was he furious he was also uncomfortable, because he didn't recognize where he was.

'I won't go another step. I'm not moving, Liz.'

'If you want to look a fool being dragged along by your wife then be my guest.'

Making an exhibition of himself didn't fit with being an important figure in the community, so he followed Liz. The area was full of bars and just busy enough to make it feel full of buzz. When they sat down at a table in a spanking new bar they were handed a vast menu with all the drinks listed plus the food for later.

'Now,' said Liz, smiling sweetly, 'isn't this pleasant?'

Neville, leaning towards her, snarled, 'Have you bloody taken leave of your senses? You're making me look a fool.'

She ignored him. 'A spritzer. What would you like? A whiskey as usual?'

'Do you listen to a thing I say?'

'All the time, Neville, all the time. It's a whiskey, then, is it?'

'Double.'

'Steady, now. Stepping out of your square like this could be dangerous. However, a double whiskey it is.'

Liz saw someone she knew and twinkled her fingers at them, a gesture she knew Neville hated.

'As if being in this place at this time in the evening isn't bad enough, do you also have to draw attention to yourself? I am so angry I can barely speak.'

Liz patted his knee and said gently, 'Neville, she's just someone I know. She runs a nursery the other side of Culworth. What's the harm in me acknowledging her? It's an exceptionally pleasant spring evening, your glamorous wife is beside you, and all you have to do is enjoy yourself.'

'I haven't time to enjoy myself.'

'I've made you time to enjoy yourself. Get your whiskey down you and, as Dicky would say, "Enjoy!" Life's too short.'

'Now I know you've gone raving mad. This is not me. I don't sit in bars, especially bright, shiny bars like this, with you quoting Dicky Tutt at me. He's a brainless fool who mistakenly imagines he's a stand-up comic. Dicky Tutt indeed.'

'Dicky does the human race more good in one week than most people do in a year.'

'With the Scouts, you mean?'

'Yes, I do.'

'And where's that going to get him in this world? I can tell you – absolutely nowhere. He'll never be rich.' Neville was at his most sneering.

Liz wondered how it had happened that he could be so bitter. 'It won't bring him wealth, that's for certain, but he's well loved and that counts for a lot. Do *you* feel well loved?'

Neville drank his whiskey right to the bottom of the glass. 'Of course I am,' he muttered. 'You love me, anyway. Don't talk about such things in public; it's embarrassing.'

As it sometimes can happen in a busy place, a sudden silence fell just as Liz said, 'Well, to be honest, I don't feel I love you *right now*.'

A woman spluttered with laughter, and Neville thought he heard another say, 'Not surprising!' He was so blinded by anger at the humiliation of it all that he banged his fist on the table with such force that Liz leapt from her chair. She knocked over her spritzer, which spilled across the table, and Neville narrowly missed a stream of it running off the table and down his trousers. He jumped up, muttered some expletive, which was completely out of character, and stormed out of the bar.

Liz paid their bill but, by the time she was outside on the pavement, Neville had disappeared.

Standing outside and wondering what she should do next, Liz remembered his briefcase. Had he taken it with him? She couldn't remember. Should she get it for him, or cause him even more aggravation by making him have to come to collect it tomorrow?

A waiter stood in front of her holding it aloft. 'Your ... husband's, madam?'

'Thank you, thank you very much.'

He was already home when she got there, but that was because she'd stopped at a fish and chip shop and sat eating in the car, feeling sorry for herself and wondering if she really wanted to be in the explosive situation that she'd deliberately created.

Chapter 2

The next morning Liz was in the Store early buying juice and fruit for the nursery. Now that Tom ran the Store it was unusual to find Jimbo serving his customers. He raised his boater in greeting and gave Liz a smacking kiss on her cheek.

'Good morning, my dear Liz. How's things?'

'Fine, thanks. And you? What are you doing serving me? I thought you'd given all that up.'

Jimbo smoothed a hand over his bald head and replaced his boater. 'Tom's day off. Truth to tell, I miss the cut and thrust of the day behind the counter, so one day a week is excellent therapy.' He paused to take someone's money for a newspaper. 'I'm asking everyone who comes in if they know anything about a strange chap who was seen in the village yesterday.'

'Yesterday?' The only thing she could remember about yesterday was the fearful row she and Neville had when she got home. 'I don't remember seeing anyone new.' It had been the row to end all rows. 'What did he want?'

'That's just it, no one knows. Apparently he sat outside the pub for hours, then went into the pub, wandered about, went into the church and chatted to Zack about the village as he polished the pews, caught Greta Jones just as she was leaving here after work, then got on the teatime bus into Culworth.'

Liz shook her head. 'I don't know anything about him.'

She wished she could have sat mum like the mystery man all the evening, then perhaps Neville wouldn't have thrown such a paddy. Well, it wasn't a paddy, more a bitter, ghastly verbal attack. His words came back to her: *bitch; cow; evil; inconsiderate; thoughtless; scheming ...*

'I need apple juice, have you got any?'

'In the back. Won't be a mo.' Jimbo disappeared.

While she waited, in her mind's eye she could see Neville's tortured face glaring at her, his mouth spitting out the words, till in the end she could see his mouth working but could no longer hear what he said. She'd eventually walked away from him but he'd rushed after her and grabbed her arm far, far too roughly for her liking.

Eventually Jimbo reappeared with a four-pack of apple juice. 'Sorry about the wait. Tom's moved the storeroom round and it doesn't make sense to me yet. That all?'

'Yes, thanks.'

As she piled her shopping into the glorious green carriers Jimbo provided she remembered saying to Neville last night, 'Leave go of my arm, or that leading Culworth accountant will be finding himself up for assault, and I mean it.'

Jimbo interrupted her thoughts. 'Be seeing you, Liz.'

'Thanks, Jimbo.'

'You all right?'

'Fine, must rush.'

Once Neville had let go of her arm, she'd run upstairs and gone to bed. But Neville didn't sleep in their bedroom

23

that night, for which she was grateful. She'd found out this morning that he'd slept in their guest bedroom. Somehow him doing that felt to be a milestone in their relationship, a step back in actual fact. It would be far harder to move back in than it was to move out in the heat of the moment. Still, what difference did it make? None.

'Hi, Angie, all set?' she called as she arrived at the nursery. 'I've got the juice and the fruit and a packet of biscuits for you, me and our work experience girl. What's her name? I never can remember.'

'Millie. You look a bit peaky this morning. Are you all right, Liz?'

'I'm fine.' Liz decided to pull herself together and not allow snatches of the row to fill her mind. Best not, she needed all her concentration because she could hear the first of their children arriving, and they needed and deserved the whole of her mind focusing on them, and not on her troubles.

Almost everyone who came in the Store that morning mentioned the silent chap who'd apparently gleaned all he could about the village but told nothing in return.

Someone said, 'Was it that Kevin from the council, that one what snoops about regler?'

Someone else, who knew Kevin's mother from Penny Fawcett, shook her head vehemently. 'No, absolutely not. I know 'im and it wasn't 'im. Kevin doesn't have no beard.'

'Maybe he stuck it on as a disguise.'

'No, that chap yesterday was tall and thin. Our Kev's round and fat due to all them free lunches people give 'im when they want to know the latest from the planning department. The things that go on in that department!

Every one of 'em deserves to be in jail.' The customer tapped the side of her nose with her forefinger and leaned her elbow on the counter. Jimbo drew close so as not to miss a word. 'They say that Mr Fitch is not above passing the odd brown envelope in our Kev's direction for services rendered.'

'No!' Jimbo leaned a little closer.

'Remember that time when Old Fitch wanted to build houses on Rector's Meadow and Sir Ralph stopped him? Well, our Kev, as his mother calls him, had to *hand back* the money Old Fitch had given him to engineer pulling down that ancient hedgerow to make room for them big diggers to get into the field. You know the hedge Lady Muriel got all worked up about. Remember?'

Jimbo nodded. The customer rested her forearms on the counter.

'Apparently he'd spent all of it on that classic BMW he drove about in after, but he nearly came unstuck there. 'Ad to sell it quick smart, 'cos of Old Fitch demanding his money back.' A wicked grin crossed the customer's face. 'What gets Old Fitch mad as hell's the fact that Sir Ralph gets his own way about things just by behaving like the gentleman he is, whereas Old Fitch always 'as to pay up front. But then, he's no gentleman.' The customer laughed like a drain. 'Two slices of your best ham, please. Cut thick.'

'Seeing as you know so much about our Kev, what do you know about that thin chap who was about yesterday?'

'Nothing. Drawn a blank there. Lovely chap, though, very pleasant to talk to.'

This lack of knowledge began to aggravate Jimbo. If the chap was a genuine visitor, why did he need to be so secretive about his reasons for spending most of the day in the village? Someone said he definitely wasn't a smelly old tramp, that was for certain. He appeared well educated and knowledgeable about things. Later that morning another customer claimed they'd seen him getting a lift down from the Big House in Barry Jones's van, and, surprise, surprise, the two of them had been spotted leaning on the gate of Rector's Meadow.

'No!' said Jimbo, egging the speaker on to further revelations by putting a lot of expression into his voice.

'So, if you want to know, I reckon Barry Jones might be able to help.'

Forthwith Jimbo summoned Harriet from the kitchens to take over at the counter, and departed for the Big House in such a hurry he forgot to remove his boater and apron.

As he was hastening up the drive of the Big House he spotted, out of the corner of his eye, Barry's old red van parked in front of the huge old barn, which had stood neglected and absolutely unused since before Jimbo had come to live in the village. Now, that could be interesting. He bumped across the approaches to the barn, parked beside Barry's van and leapt out.

Barry was sawing a huge oak beam. He was about half-way through it and sweating copiously when he caught the sound of Jimbo's voice. He laid down his saw and straightened his back, glad of an excuse to take a rest.

'Hello, there.' He studied Jimbo from head to foot, amused he was there and guessing why. 'I reckon you're on a fishing trip.' He grinned widely and waited for a reply.

'I'm not, you know. I was on my way to see Old Fitch and spotted your van.'

'Mr Fitch is in Sweden this week. You'll have to wait till Monday.'

Jimbo took a moment to look around the barn. It was huge, and so high it would be possible to put another floor in and make an upstairs. It didn't need much intelligence to realize it was being seriously renovated.

'Why don't you use an electric saw of some kind?'

'No power in here yet. The electric's coming next week if I can get this lot finished.'

'What's it being renovated for, then?'

'Mr Fitch has decided he's got to make money out of anything that stands still long enough. Reckons there's going to be a slump and he's getting prepared.'

'What's he going to do with it?'

'Doesn't know yet. I'm just doing the basics. Magnificent barn, don't you think? Fifteenth century. You've got to give them credit.' Barry prepared to begin sawing again.

Jimbo stood looking about him, admiring the skill of fifteenth-century builders. 'That chap everyone saw yesterday, is he thinking of renting it? Is that why he was here?'

Barry smiled secretly. 'No. He's not wanting the barn.'

'Oh! Right. A little bird tells me you were seen with him, leaning on the gate into Rector's Meadow.'

'Just passing the time of day. He said he was wanting to rent a field but I don't believe a word he said. There's word flying round the village that he's planning to start a market on the village green. They say that's why he's interested in the field, wants it for car parking. But I don't believe it. It's all nonsense thought up by those idle gossips in the bar who have nothing better to do. I mean, a market in this village when there's the big one in Culworth every week? Doesn't make sense.'

Jimbo agreed. They'd obviously got the wrong end of the stick. Barry was right, it would be a waste of time and money to set up a market in Turnham Malpas. 'The barn's still available for rent, then?'

'I don't know, ask Mr Fitch. Do you fancy it?'

'Oh! No, no. No good to me. Pat all right? She does a great job for me, you know. Best day's work I did setting her up in charge of the outside catering staff.'

Barry smiled again. 'Thanks for the big increase you gave her. She's thrilled to bits.'

'Good! She's worth it. I'll be off.'

He knew exactly who he would see next. If Mr Fitch was not here then the estate manager Jeremy Mayer would be a very good second best, mainly because Jimbo knew he put the fear of God into Jeremy owing to some exchanges of opinion he'd had with him over the years. He hadn't meant to; it had just happened that way.

You no longer found Jeremy by looking for a huge overweight man, or listening for loud panting sounds and groaning floorboards, because his heart attacks had frightened him and, with the able assistance of his wife Venetia, he now hit the scales at a mere eleven stone.

Jimbo put his head round the door of Jeremy's office and said, 'Are you free?'

'I am.' Jeremy enjoyed Mr Fitch being in Sweden or whichever godforsaken place in the world he decided to visit, because it meant he was entirely in charge of the estate and his word was law. Well, until Mr Fitch came back and went through everything that had happened in his absence with a fine-toothed comb. He leaned back in his chair, trying hard to subdue that feeling of inadequacy which invaded him when confronted by Jimbo; he had such style, had Jimbo.

'How are things, Jeremy? Going well? I came to see Old Fitch but Barry tells me he's not here, but you're a very excellent substitute.' He smiled benignly, hoping to put Jeremy Mayer in a mellow mood.

'I am? Sit down.'

Jimbo nodded. 'The barn. It's being renovated, substantially renovated. Why?'

'To rent out.'

'What for?'

'For a business of some kind.' Jeremy shrugged.

'Any idea for how much?'

'No. Are you interested?'

'I bet I'm not the first one who's interested. That man ...' Jimbo snapped his fingers as though endeavouring to remember the man's name.

'You mean Titus Bellamy?'

Jimbo pretended to think for a moment, 'Yes, that's right, that's the man.'

'He is waiting to see Mr Fitch, and no, he isn't interested in the barn.'

'What is he interested in?'

'He told me, but it was so roundabout I knew less when he'd finished than when he started. He played his cards very close to his chest. That all?'

Jimbo placed his thumb and forefinger very close together and suggested he must have let something slip even if it was only a tiny bit.

'Sorry. Can't help you.' Jeremy picked up a sheaf of closely typed papers and put his glasses on.

Jimbo took the hint. As he was leaving he asked, 'Not even a single word?'

'Something to do with the village green, I think, and

29

some project or other he has in mind. Good morning to you.'

As Jimbo drove helter-skelter down the mile-long drive, his eager mind was scanning every single idea he could think of for even a hint of why someone should be interested in the village green. Whatever for? Mr Fitch and the village green? And why leaning over that gate with Barry Jones? That field had nothing to do with the village green. Occasionally the cows were put in it, but it was very much a field no one displayed any permanent interest in.

His mind dwelt for a while on the barn. They were getting very cramped at the back of the Store, with the mail order having gone through the roof since he'd established his website. There'd certainly be no more expansion there, but the barn ...

He dashed in, heading straight for the kitchens. Harriet was back in there, as Bel had come to do her middle-of-the-day stint on the counter. 'Harriet!' He beckoned her with an eager finger. 'Come with me.'

'I'll get nothing done at this rate. What are you up to?'

He closed his office door behind them and sat her down on a stool. 'Listen!' His voice full of enthusiasm he placed his boater on the top of the boxes of dried fruit, smoothed his bald head and wondered briefly how on earth to phrase his idea in a very tempting way that would excite her interest and more so her support.

'Yes? Be sharp about it; I've a lot on today.'

'I've just been up to the Big House. Old Fitch is restoring that big old barn, the one you can see on the right through the trees when you're going up the drive.'

'Yes?'

'Well, he's going to rent it out for business purposes.'

'Yes?'

'Well, you know you were saying the other day how you'd no room to move in the back here ...'

Harriet's face lit up, but being a practical business-woman her first question was, 'Can we afford it?'

'Don't know yet. Old Fitch returns Monday, so I shall hasten up there on winged feet and ask. Then I'll do my figures and we can make up our minds after that. Expansion here we come, hopefully.'

Harriet, more cautious than Jimbo, sat thinking for a moment. 'There's one thing for certain: we simply cannot expand where we are, and I'd have more room for some state-of-the-art kitchen equipment I hanker after.'

'Exactly.'

'And maybe we could hire it out for events, too. Yes, it's a brilliant idea. If it looks right on paper then let's go for it. Not too far away for us to keep an eye on things, is it? Is that what that strange man was after?'

'I didn't find a thing out about that, except it's some-thing to do with the village green and holding an event on it. What exactly I don't know, but apparently everyone in the village is convinced they have inside knowledge.'

Harriet stood up ready to go. 'Well, whatever it is, it won't affect us, will it?'

But the rest of the village thought differently. Not affect them? Of course it would, and whatever it was had to be stopped. As of now. This week! This minute! So, after church on Sunday morning, there was a gathering in the churchyard which mushroomed into a crowd, and Willie Biggs, being in charge of the keys while Zack had a short break, thought they'd make more of a fist of it if they had chairs and a roof over their heads, so he opened up the

31

church hall for an impromptu meeting. It just materialized out of a combined urgency to put a stop to this invasion of Turnham Malpas by someone without even the slightest connection to the village.

Grandmama Charter-Plackett was the first to get to her feet. 'This very morning I've spoken to someone who knows someone, and they reckon this chap is after starting a market every week here in Turnham Malpas.'

The air was filled with gasps of complete astonishment and horror, and everyone jabbering at top decibels. Grandmama was enormously gratified by the reception her statement received, learned that very morning by a couple of judicious phone calls to a friend who'd happened to mention the market in her own village only twenty-five miles away.

'He's called Titus Bellamy and he's got four other markets going,' Grandmama continued. 'He's discovered a charter from the archives that gives him permission to hold a market on a Thursday morning in Turnham Malpas from eight till one. Apparently, it lapsed at the time of the Black Death and he's going to resurrect it. We're talking history here and no mistake. If it is true, *I* don't want it, not when my son pays rates and staff to keep the Store open week in week out for everyone's benefit. He can't keep going with that kind of opposition. This chap doesn't allow trash apparently, he's got very high standards, and my Jimbo is very uptight about it because that's in direct competition with him, believe you me. We'll kill it quite simply by none of us shopping in his pesky market. No trade, no market. Sound common sense. Who's on my side? Hands up!'

This colossal shock raised a myriad hands in the air but some were slow and others hovered well below shoulder level. Grandmama's eagle eyes noted the reluctant ones and vowed to target them with her persuasive tongue. She sat down in a flurry of indignation. How dare they not support her Jimbo wholeheartedly? How dare they? She'd show 'em!

There was a small number of those present who were fascinated by Grandmama's revelations, and sneakily thought that a bit of competition might bring down Jimbo's prices. But they kept their own counsel. After all there were times to stand up and be counted, and times to keep well below the parapet. Grandmama on a mission was not to be taken on lightly.

At the back of all their minds was the next piece of news: that their old adversary Craddock Fitch was encouraging the whole affair by renting out his field to be used as the car park, without which the entire idea would be stymied.

'But,' said Vince Jones from down Shepherd's Hill, 'the chances of us persuading Old Fitch to abandon his money-making scheme for the sake of the village are absolutely nil.' He emphasized his point by slicing the air with his hands.

They all had to agree. After all, money was Old Fitch's prime consideration, though he had softened a little since his unexpected marriage to Kate Pascoe.

'We'd do better if we called in the Health and Safety from the Council,' Willie Biggs called from the back row, having entered later than he'd intended because of standing in for Zack the new verger. 'They have a lot of clout, they do, more than ever. Anywhere people gather, whatever for, is of interest to them. And an event on the green means people gathering. They can put a stop to his plans.'

Someone was designated with the task of finding out this Titus Bellamy chap's address or phone number. Another vociferous opponent was charged with speaking to Health and Safety, another with confronting the leader of the council with the intention of getting the council to stop the whole thing, and yet another with formulating plans for a protest. Having explored as many avenues as they could think of they dispersed with a rallying cry of, 'If we fail then our motto must be don't shop in the market, no matter how tempted we are. That'll sort it in a matter of weeks.'

The idea that the market would simply collapse if they ignored it carried a lot of weight, and they all felt heartened by the meeting, thinking they'd got the better of Titus Bellamy, whoever he was, before he'd set up a single stall.

The silent, uncommunicative man faded from everyone's mind as the weeks sped by. Summer had just arrived and there were more interesting matters to discuss, such as the disastrously bad start to the season the Turnham Malpas cricket team was suffering and the fact that the school house was being altered to provide more classroom accommodation as the number of children at the school was escalating. Mainly due, they all decided, to the large families now occupying the newly built houses down the Culworth Road.

'Breeding like rabbits they are down there. All young and newly married – well, some of 'em are married – and babies popping out like shelled peas,' said Maggie Dobbs, who was suffering the most due to the disruption the builders were making to her daily life as school cleaner. 'Bringing dirt in to the school like there was no tomorrow, it simply isn't fair. Bet my wages won't go up with all the extra work. I'll have *two* buildings to clean. One's bad enough.'

Jimbo also had other things to concentrate his mind, like arguing with Mr Fitch about putting another floor in the barn, so they could have a first floor as well as the ground floor, and who was going to pay for it, and if he could sublet any part of it he didn't need for now. Everyone in the village knew about Jimbo's new idea to expand his website business, and the comments in the bar varied from 'How well he must be doing' to 'Still, that'll be more jobs for the village.'

On the surface it appeared that only Jimbo continued to have a nervous twitch about that silent Titus Bellamy. Everyone else thought it had died a natural death, before it ever got started. It nagged Jimbo now and again, but in the end, racking his brain to puzzle out the real significance of the man's visit became futile.

It wasn't that he came and then went – lots of people did that, tourists and the like – it was, as Dottie said, the fact that he asked questions, visited Jeremy at the Big House, leaned over the gate to Rector's Meadow with our Barry, talked to Zack in the church, and sat quietly listening in the bar. A genteel man he was, unusual to look at, but nevertheless acceptable and well spoken – when and if he did choose to speak.

'No, there was definitely something very mysterious about him,' said Greta to Sheila, as Sheila selected a tin of lentil soup for the new fad diet she'd imposed on her Ron. 'Very definitely.'

Willie, seated at his usual table in the bar, muttered into his homebrew, 'Lovely man, they all say, but what was he doing? That was the question. Was it really about starting a market?'

Jimmy the taxi said philosophically, 'It'll all come out in the wash.'

Willie found his acceptance of the situation irritating. 'Do you know something I don't? If so, out with it.'

Indignantly Jimmy said he knew nothing, that he'd better things to do than gossip. He got to his feet and departed from the bar, leaving Willie to his own thoughts.

The man certainly wasn't from the planning department, he wasn't that kind. Ordnance Survey? Drains? Street lighting? Street signs? No, they'd seen the lighting committee off before now; after the last episode they wouldn't be trying that on again. Willie downed the last of his home brew and wandered home, hoping his Sylvia's spate of spring-cleaning would have worn itself out and he'd be able to sit in his favourite chair in peace and nod off for an hour.

It was Tom who was the first to find out what Titus Bellamy really was up to, because he caught sight of the headline on the front page of the *Culworth Gazette* as he was hauling the bundles of newspapers into the shop first thing one Thursday morning. Bold as brass it was, in large capital letters.

Chapter 3

'Oh, my God!' shouted Tom. 'I don't believe this.' His disbelieving eyes scanned the headline and then he read out loud: 'THURSDAY MARKET FOR TURNHAM MALPAS.'

So here it was in black and white, cutting a swathe through all the speculation, all the planning, that had gone on ever since Titus Bellamy had first visited the village. He speed-read the piece beneath the heading and dwelt for a long minute on the effects it would have on the village, and on Jimbo and the Store in particular. He couldn't decide whether or not it was a plus or a minus. After all, it was only one morning a week, but it could cause sizeable damage to Thursday's trading. It might not be groceries, though it did say organic a couple of times, which was significant. So Grandmama was right, after all. It *was* a market. Having read it through twice, he decided to ring Jimbo, but, realizing it was not yet seven o'clock, he delayed his call until he'd set up the Store for the day's trading.

As he switched on the coffee machine something else hit him right out of the blue. Here was Jimbo facing lots of expense setting up the old barn as his major bakery and as a venue for events, and now this threat was hanging over him. No warning. No nothing. He could delay no longer and dialled his number immediately, dreading Jimbo's response.

There was silence on Jimbo's end of the phone as Tom read out snippets from the *Gazette*. Tom had expected a tirade, but Jimbo didn't explode. He simply said, 'Thank you for letting me know.'

His response made Tom realize that the news had devastated him far more than he had imagined it would.

Jimbo sat on the bed with the receiver in his hand, head bent, thinking.

Harriet came in from the bathroom. 'Who was that at this time in the morning? Some minor catastrophe that could well have waited until nine o'clock?'

Jimbo didn't appear to have heard her.

'Darling! What's the matter?' She touched his shoulder and lowered her head to see his face.

'Over my dead body.'

'What is?'

'A market on the green.'

Harriet, struggling to get into her too-tight jeans, thought she'd misheard him. 'What on earth are you talking about?'

'That snooping man, Titus Bellamy, claims he's holding a country market on our village green each Thursday morning, starting next week.'

'I see.'

'Believe it or believe it not, Rector's Meadow will be the car park. That was why he was leaning on the gate looking at it, and Old Fitch is charging car parking fees – with a man on the gate. And we've just pledged ourselves to vast and possibly damaging expense to expand our business, plus the capital it took to reopen the Store. Hell's bells! So while Old Fitch and I were negotiating about the barn he was also talking to this

Titus fellow. Talk about stabbing us in the back, and then some.'

'Darling, it's only one morning a week. Surely it can't hurt us that much? It'll be a load of old tat and it will die a natural death, believe me. It'll be like a car boot sale, most of it rubbish, apart from two matching Georgian wine glasses or something or other which someone has the luck to find. Honestly! Country market indeed. Huh!' But at heart Harriet felt sick.

'I shall ring the council. This minute.'

'Too early. Have your breakfast first, and ring them when your brain has cleared.'

'He can't have had permission, can he? Have you ever heard of a market on the green?'

Harriet shrugged her shoulders. 'No, but then we haven't lived here five ... six hundred years. There might have been at one point.'

'I don't believe it. I do *not* believe it. I *will* not believe it.' Jimbo stomped off into the bathroom, muttering to himself.

At breakfast, Fran, munching her muesli, said, not very helpfully, 'There could have been a charter for the market, but for some reason it fizzled out. That was how it used to be; the local landowner got a charter from the king for a market. In St Alban's, in Hertfordshire, they've had an outdoor market for over a thousand years in the same place and it's still going strong. Every Saturday, I think it is, or is it Wednesday? Or Wednesday *and* Saturday.'

Harriet, desperate for Jimbo not to get too worked up, gave Fran a slight shake of her head, hoping she'd shut up. But she didn't.

'It could bring business to the village, you know, Dad.

39

To the Royal Oak, the church, and why not our Store? Could be a godsend.'

Jimbo, trying hard to be rational about it, felt close to throttling her. He tightened his grip on the butter knife, pressed too hard, and the dish skittered across the breakfast table, before being brilliantly fielded by Harriet, who reminded Fran that the clock was ticking and the school coach would be leaving shortly. 'I've put the envelope with the permission for you to go to that French day at Lady Wortley's on top of your school bag.'

'Huh! French day! I think I'll throw a sickie.' She dashed away to clean her teeth.

'You won't, young lady,' Jimbo shouted after her. For a brief moment he dwelt on the talent Fran had developed for languages, and then returned immediately to the market problem. 'Once it gets established it will be all too late to protest. I'll ring our Kev straight up on nine, to find out about permission.'

The clock on his desk was old and decrepit, but well loved by him, and when it chimed nine, Jimbo was dialling. By some underhand means he'd ferreted out Kevin's direct line.

'Good morning, Kevin. Brilliant day, isn't it? Jimbo Charter-Plackett speaking, from Turnham Malpas. Have you time for a word?'

Kevin may not have risen very far in the echelons of the council hierarchy, but his knowledge of the goings-on in the council, legitimate or otherwise, was unparalleled.

'Just.'

'Right, I won't beat about the bush. This business of a market on the village green every Thursday. Just how legit is it?'

'Very. Titus Bellamy's found an old charter in the archives from the early fourteenth century signed by a Templeton, giving permission for it. There's nothing that can be done. Health and Safety's noses are considerably out of joint, but as yet they haven't come up with any concrete objections to it. Even the car parking's been solved by Mr Fitch; he's opening up a field for it.'

'So you're saying it's all signed and sealed?'

'Oh, yes. Could hit your Thursday trade, I expect?' Kevin sniggered.

'Exactly.' Jimbo could have knifed him straight through his heart for that snigger.

'Some of these old agreements in rural areas cause an awful lot of problems. Health and Safety are always gnashing their teeth about something or another, but often their hands are tied.'

'Keep me informed, mmm? I wonder, would you be able to make use of a couple of tickets for the British Grand Prix? Been stuck with a couple and I can't use them. How about it?'

'Certainly, I could. Thanks, much appreciated. Glad to take them off your hands. You know the chap who's running it has four other markets doing really well. The stalls are mostly organic – meat, dairy, bakery, fish ... Let me see,' Jimbo could hear a rustling of papers, then Kevin continued, 'Organic greengrocery, collectables, jewellery, an artist, a potter, you name it.'

So much for Harriet's 'load of old tat', thought Jimbo.

'Well, that just about covers everything I sell, but there you are. Nice to talk to you. I won't forget about the tickets.'

Jimbo banged down the receiver and cursed the world in general, and himself in particular, for lining the pocket of a slimy little sneak. Well, at least now he knew what he was up against, and it was no good anyone saying, 'It won't affect your trade.' *It would*!

Now he'd have to set to and bribe someone to get the Grand Prix tickets for our Kev. But he had an idea about that, and when Liz Neal came in that morning he beckoned her into his office, placed his boater on the top of a carton of Brazil nuts and, as he always did, gave her a huge welcoming kiss.

'Liz, have you lost weight?'

'Maybe. You want to tell me something? If it's about the market I'm sick of hearing about it. Everyone I meet has an opinion on it.'

'Are they keen?'

Liz smiled. 'Keen? I'm afraid they are. In fact, some of them are thinking of having stalls.'

Had Jimbo had hair in any quantities on his head it would have stood vertical with shock. '*Villagers*, you mean?'

'Oh, yes.'

Jimbo groped blindly for a seat. 'Traitors, the lot of 'em. Traitors!'

'They've a right—'

'What about my rights? Mmm? I, who serve them every single week, not some fly-by-night here one morning and then gone the next. I'm deeply grieved by their lack of loyalty to me.'

Liz studied his face and saw his wrath was genuine. 'I'm sorry, Jimbo, very sorry.'

'Change of subject. Neville goes to the Grand Prix, doesn't he? Could he get me two tickets, do you think? I don't expect them for free.'

'Oh! Are you going? That would be lovely. I'd be

delighted for some sympathetic company, instead of all those stuffed shirts Neville invites.'

'Er! They're not for Harriet and me; it's a sweetener for that Kevin in planning. He's given me the latest on the market so I had to reciprocate, though I hate myself for it. Apparently this chap, Titus Bellamy, has got four other markets in full swing. Wait till I see him; he'll wish he hadn't been born.'

Liz looked at Jimbo and felt she needed to bring some sanity into their conversation. 'He's a businessman like you, Jimbo, earning his crust, doing his best. You should cooperate with him, welcome him. See how you could use his market to your advantage as well as his.' Liz kissed his cheek and handed him back his boater.

'Thanks.' Jimbo absentmindedly smoothed his hand over his remaining hair and placed the boater on his head.

'Was that it?'

Jimbo didn't reply so Liz went back into the Store to get her shopping. She felt quite intrigued by this Titus Bellamy person. There were such exaggerated stories about him going round the village, the most ridiculous being that he was Richard Branson wearing his gardening clothes as a disguise — 'Well, he was tall and thin, and he did have a beard, didn't he? And that Richard's always looking for openings.'

Behind the tinned soups appeared to be the hot spot for the morning, but only if you hadn't tired of the market. Vince Jones, ostensibly there to pick up Greta's week-end shopping order, but in reality meeting his bowling club cronies over a freshly brewed coffee from Jimbo's machine, as they did regularly as a kind of midweek committee meeting during the bowling season, slunk behind the soup section, steaming coffee in hand. Club matters had been pushed aside by the immediate urgency of the threat of the market.

'Well, I don't agree. A market's going to bring nothing but trouble. There's going to be all the riff-raff from Culworth gathering, and guess who'll catch the fallout?'

'Us.'

The smallest member of them all, insignificant but with a permanent mission to be different from everyone else, piped up, 'You're all making a mountain out of a molehill. One morning a week, that's all. A bit of competition won't do Jimbo any harm. A chance to buy good food at reasonable prices, and it can't be said the goods in here are cheap.' He waved his paper cup of free coffee about to emphasize his point. 'I for one will patronize it. Well, I will if I like what I see.'

'You won't get no free coffee in the market, don't forget that,' someone reminded him.

Those opposed to the market nodded sagely in agreement, and the smallest member of the committee had to admit they were right about that.

'It'll all fall on us, will the clearing up,' said the treasurer.

'Exactly. Us. You and me. They'll leave mountains of rubbish when it's all over. Before we know where we are we'll be overrun with rats.'

There was silence while his cronies shuddered at the thought, and unintentionally Vince worsened the situation by telling them that he'd just seen the council vermin officer out the back of Hipkin Cottages with traps. 'It'll be Alan Crimble's compost heap encouraging 'em, I bet. He's obsessed, he is. Takes all the food waste from the pub home with him. He'll be selling compost soon he has that much. I wouldn't mind, but his garden's no bigger than my hen run.'

Vince muttered loudly, 'I bet the council won't send no one round to clear up, and if they do volunteer their help they'll put our rates up. No, the rubbish'll be our problem. And rubbish there'll be. Cardboard boxes of all sizes, bubble wrap, food waste, paper cups and plates from the food stalls, wrapping paper, you name it.'

Consternation took hold, just as Willie Biggs came round the corner of the soup section.

Vince, fired up with gloom, continued, 'We'll *all* have rats. To say nothing of the thieves and the fly-by-nights. The noise. The hullabaloo. The crowds. Place won't be our own, it won't. Good old Turnham Malpas will be gone for ever. We'll have street lighting and house numbers before we know where we are.'

Street lighting and house numbers were issues always bound to create a kind of strangulated fury amongst the villagers, not least in Willie Biggs.

'Well, I'm against the market for all those reasons and more. Here we have Jimbo running a store, which, let's face it, is a blessing, an absolute blessing, and he doesn't need that kind of competition. No, my word he doesn't, and I for one will oppose it in support of Jimbo. After all, he's here six days a week, open till seven now. My Sylvia won't spend a single penny there, no matter how good the food is. It's not on. And if I see anyone I know, which is everyone, buying stuff, I shall let them have the sharp edge of my tongue and not half.' He nodded his head briskly, whisked a can of tomato soup from the shelves for his and Sylvia's lunch, and hastened off, leaving Vince and his bowling cronies well satisfied that in Willie Biggs they had an earnest supporter of their protest. What form their protest should take was another question.

Liz told Neville about Jimbo's request for Grand Prix tickets that night when he came home.

'But, and I mean this, he's not to have tickets with us. Buy some as far away as possible. Please.' She fully expected Neville would be in agreement with her, but he said he owed Kevin himself so he'd get him seats next to them if he could.

'Feather in my cap,' he added, 'because I can make it look as though I'm treating him but it'll be at Jimbo's expense.'

'Didn't you hear what I said?'

Neville was still smiling at his crafty trick, that stiff smile of his which barely cracked his face. 'I've said I owe him, so I will get them. Leave it with me.' He picked up his glass of whiskey and found the remote control.

'Neville, I am not, I repeat not, sitting with Kevin even within earshot. It would ruin my afternoon. I find the Grand Prix unbearable at the best of times, but Kevin Smickersgill as well? Oh, no!'

Her protest was completely ignored so Liz picked up the remote control and switched the TV off.

'Do you hear me? I shan't go if I have to tolerate that man. Then you won't have a hostess and you'll have to cope on your own. Right?'

Neville wagged his finger at her. 'This is a storm in a teacup. There's nothing wrong with the man, and in the past he's been very, very useful to me. That property I bought in Old Fold Yard, you remember? Kevin told me the day before it came on the market and I snapped it up for a song. We made fifty thousand with that, and I did no improvements whatsoever, simply because Kevin knew exactly the right person to buy it, and the chap couldn't put his money down fast enough. So, Kevin is joining our party. My final word. Put Channel Four on, please.'

'I'm embarrassed that you have any dealings with him whatsoever. He's a sleazebag.'

'I wish you wouldn't talk about my business acquaintances in that tone. Put it on, then.'

Liz flung the remote control on to the carpet and got to her feet. 'Put it on yourself. All you do in this house is switch on the remote control.'

'I see. Making a cool fifty grand for us doesn't count.'

'Of course it does, but I'd rather you enjoyed my company and paid some attention to me as well. Or rather to *us*. It's over a year since you looked at me with desire. Let alone did something about it.'

Neville looked nonplussed. He tossed back the remains of his whiskey, picked up the decanter and refilled his glass. He opened his mouth to say something, changed his mind, and instead switched the TV back on as loud as he could bear it.

'Well? Have you nothing to say?' Liz shouted above the TV but knew he couldn't hear her. So she pulled out the plug and stood in front of him, hands on hips. 'Neville! Answer me!'

At his most scathing he declared, 'You sound and look like a fishwife.'

'No wonder. A fishwife is all you deserve. I see Peter look at Caroline and I *crave* for you to look at me like he does her. His face glows with love, and hers for him. I'm so envious of them, jealous even. That's a prize I would love to have, it's way above any fifty grand. Poor as a church mouse I'd be, gladly, *willingly*, if you and I had love like that.'

Somewhat triumphantly Neville roared back, 'Ha! But you'd miss your designer clothes and your fantastic holidays. Oh yes you would, and don't deny it. It's true.'

'I'd live in a hovel with you if we had love like theirs.' Liz flung herself down in her chair and wept angry, despairing tears.

Neville shouted over the noise of her abandonment, 'Liz, we'll soon have been married twenty-five years. My God, woman, you can't expect passion at our age. It's disgusting even to think about it.' The look of disgust came into his eyes and by the time it reached Neville's mouth his face was twisted with it.

Through her tears Liz saw his expression and knew whatever they'd had between them was surely over. She accepted her defeat almost with relief.

'It's half-term, next week,' she said. 'I'm going away for a few days, right? Don't know where, just going. I need time to think. I'll go tomorrow, after nursery.'

Neville leaped to his feet. 'Think? What do you need to think about? And what about me?'

'You? You'll die of starvation, I expect, but that's up to you.'

Neville didn't die of starvation. He had a couple of meals out, though it felt lonely sitting all by himself in restaurants which were well past their best, but he couldn't afford to go to established places like the George, not because of the cost, but because he didn't want to meet anyone he knew as they'd only ask about Liz, and what could one say? It wasn't normal for a wife to go away on her own. In fact, it was very, very unusual, though the married women in his office sometimes went away together for a 'girls' weekend' in Barcelona or somewhere, but that was different from going alone.

What the blazes was she going to *think* about? What was there to think about that she couldn't share with him? Not for one moment did Neville think he might be to blame. She was being completely unreasonable. He'd never been very enthusiastic about that side of marriage anyway, and had been very surprised to find himself the father of two sons in less than two years of marriage. He'd been quite glad to find a valid excuse of their twenty-fifth wedding anniversary coming up to forget all of that and concentrate wholly on making a fortune so they'd be able to leave money to the boys.

In his position as church treasurer he needed regular opportunities to confer with Peter, and he decided that he might just make it this week in the hope Caroline would ask him for a meal so that would be three evening meals taken care of, and the kitchen could remain immaculate, which he much preferred.

He spoke to Peter after morning service and they agreed he'd call at the Rectory on the Monday evening. 'About five-thirty?'

Peter had agreed, thinking it was an odd time for him to suggest, but there was none so ruthless as Neville when he had a project in mind that could be to his advantage.

'He's on his own this week,' Caroline replied when Peter told her Neville would be coming the next evening. 'I expect he's hoping for an invite to a meal.'

Peter looked up at her. 'Do you mind? Is it convenient?'

Caroline thought carefully about her reply. 'I wouldn't mind. It'll give me a chance to find out about him.'

'He's an excellent treasurer, I can't fault him on that, but I don't know if I want to dig any deeper.'

'We'll see, we'll see. Just to be difficult, I'll do enough food for him but we won't let on until the very last minute. I want to see him squirm when he thinks he isn't being asked.'

'Caroline! That is an aspect of your character I haven't come across before.'

She passed him the thick wad of the Sunday paper. 'Read this and ignore me.' She laughed. 'It's only Neville who brings it out in me. He is a ...'

'Yes, I know, a slimy toad.'

'Well! Really! And you the Rector.'

'Give me a kiss?'

'I certainly will.' Caroline wrapped her arms around his neck, sitting herself on his lap as she did so, and kissing his mouth with fervour. Peter held her down with his right arm across her thighs and enjoyed kissing her some more.

When they were finally breathless she stood up and laughed. 'Poor Neville.'

'Why poor Neville?'

'He's given it up.'

'Given what up?'

'Sex.'

'How do you know?'

'Liz told me.'

'Poor Liz.'

'Indeed. That's why she's gone away. She's very upset. He won't have anything at all to do with her, you see.'

Peter picked up the paper and shook it out. 'Now that is very sad, but he's always been what Sir Ralph calls a cold fish, and I don't expect he'll change now.'

'Liz is still attractive, though, don't you think?'

'Oh, yes, very. Someone would find her just right if she ever left Neville.'

'Perhaps he just needs a nudge in the right direction.' Caroline looked speculatively at him. 'You'd be just the right person to do it.'

'I would not.'

'You'd do it so beautifully he'd scarcely notice what you were driving at, but he'd take it to heart without realizing. You could be saving their marriage.'

'Hush! Someone's coming downstairs.'

It was Alex. 'I've finished my homework and Beth almost has. What shall we be doing this afternoon?'

Peter groaned, realizing he'd have to give up his Sunday paper before he'd even begun reading it. 'Swimming?'

'Excellent! You coming, Mum?'

'Yes, OK. I need some exercise. Does Beth want to come?'

'She won't want leaving behind.'

On the following day Neville arrived at the Rectory promptly at five-thirty. Peter let him in and the two of them settled in the study with the door closed.

The church business took all of half an hour and then Peter offered Neville a whiskey and mentioned the one subject that was on everyone's lips.

'The market? Do you have an opinion? Everyone I speak to has one so I expect you have, too.'

'Well,' answered Neville, sounding to have weighty opinions which he was eager to divulge, 'he's a great chap, is this Titus Bellamy. In fact, he's become a client of mine.' His smile was full of self-satisfaction. 'I can assure you that he will do nothing but good for the village.'

51

Peter laughed. 'I wouldn't say that in Jimbo's hearing. He's very upset about it, feels it'll take business away from him.'

'All's fair ... as the saying goes. He's had his own way in this village for far too long. Time he had some competition. I'm all in favour.'

'Well, we'll wait and see. I'm surprised Titus has got permission.'

Neville settled back in his armchair ready to impart news he'd gathered from our Kev. 'Well, you see, there's very little they can do about it. There was a market here way back in the fourteenth century, but when the Black Death decimated the area in thirteen forty-nine it lapsed and never got going again. After all, Derehams Magna was completely emptied of people, as it still is, so I suppose it didn't seem worth starting it up again. A document Titus found in the county archives gives him the right to hold the market.' Neville appeared to ruminate for a moment as though deciding to impart some information known only to him but then the expression on his face became shifty and he obviously changed his mind. 'The council are steaming mad because they can't find a single document to deny him that right. Health and Safety thought they could put a stop to it – in fact, they've been quite savage about it – but he's organized a car park, and has even got the St John Ambulance to have a tent. Believe me, there's no flies on Titus. Oh, no. I've given him bits of advice here and there to make life easier for him, and he's in the starting blocks awaiting the off.'

'I wouldn't tell Jimbo you're in league with him.'

'I've no fear of Master Jimbo. He's a marshmallow compared to me. But I think he'll find everyone is on Titus's side. All the people I've spoken to are.'

Peter didn't agree but said nothing and began to make it look as though the meeting was finished, so that Neville could go – without the invite Peter intuitively knew he was hoping for.

'Caroline keeping well, is she?'

'Oh, yes. Very well. She's delighted to be back in general practice at last.'

'Wonderful woman, is Caroline.'

'I know, I'm lucky, but then, so are you.'

Neville nodded his head, but said nothing. Then he stood up and admitted that Liz was away.

'Needing a holiday?'

Neville nodded sagely. 'That's right, yes, in need of a break, but I couldn't get away.'

Peter suddenly got an image of Neville pecking at Liz's cheek and thinking that should satisfy her. 'Wives need looking after, you know, Neville, not just the occasional peck on the cheek. Love demands to be expressed. They need nothing less than the whole works. Frankly, between you and me, that's what makes the world go round in a marriage, but of course you don't need me to tell you that, I'm sure.' He smiled encouragingly.

Neville flushed furiously, and, as he did so, Peter invited him to eat with them.

But Neville was so embarrassed at the thought that the Rector, of all people, had spoken so intimately to him about marriage and … well, such things … that he had to refuse.

Caroline, knowing nothing of their conversation, leapt out into the hall as she heard the study door open. 'Neville!' She opened wide her arms, took hold of his hands, kissed his cheek and exclaimed, 'Has Peter asked you to eat with us? I do hope he has. I've made masses of food because Alex is always hungry, so there'll be plenty for you. I've laid a place. Do say you'll stay.' She beamed at him, and although what Peter had said had embarrassed him to death, Neville found himself thanking Caroline and agreeing to stay, thinking at least he wouldn't need to cook when he got home.

That night Caroline had hysterics in bed when Peter told her what he'd said to Neville in the study.

'You didn't! Oh, help! Do you know, I don't think I have had a more awkward meal in all my life. It was ghastly. I even found it hard to swallow my food I felt so restricted by him. What is the matter with the man? I don't know how Liz puts up with him.'

Peter turned over and put his arm around Caroline's waist. 'Change of subject. I'm really concerned about this market. Neville thinks everyone's in agreement with it, but they're not. Some are very angry about their village being spoiled, really angry. Placards and such, you know. Some are secretly planning to break it up. We could have an almighty to-do. We might even need the police.'

'It's so difficult for you and me because we have to keep impartial. Trouble is, I can't make my own mind up about it.'

'Neither can I. We'll just have to wait and see. Goodnight, light of my life. God bless you.'

Chapter 4

At about nine o'clock on Wednesday evening a huge furniture van rumbled into the village and parked at the edge of the green opposite the lychgate. Three men got out and went round to the back of the van and opened it up. With a precision born of experience they began unloading the tables, stacking them along the edge of the green, systematically, two lots stacked four high. Then one man got in the cab, and drove the van round until it was opposite the Store. The other two men walked round and followed the same procedure, then the van went further round, parked outside Thelma and Valda Seniors' old house, and unloaded some more tables.

By this time net curtains were twitching and the entire episode was under scrutiny. Even the people drinking in the Royal Oak pulled the curtains aside to see what the noise was all about.

'Well, they're efficient if nothing else.'

'Just look at that lot. It's going to be bigger than I expected.'

'Good grief, there'll be no room for punters with all them stalls.'

'There must be about thirty tables. It's gonna be big, isn't it?'

'I didn't realize. Jimbo's going to explode.'

After the van had left, the bar burst into a hubbub of vigorous discussion at such volume it became difficult to hear what one's very own neighbour was saying.

Sylvia and Willie Biggs were adamant they would never buy a thing at the market.

Vera Wright raised a sceptical eyebrow. 'Don't be too hasty, you might find things so cheap you can't afford to ignore it. Jimbo isn't exactly cheap, is he? Lovely food but ...'

'If you've no car then you're stuck with the Culworth bus, when it decides to come, or you pay Jimbo's prices. I reckon this market could be a godsend.' Jimmy Glover picked up his ale and, taking a huge gulp, finished his pint.

Willie said, 'Sylvia and I shall make a point of shopping at the Store. It's only right, he's got the overheads of a lovely shop, *and* he's here every day, *and* we've known him a long time, *and* everything's very fresh, *and* he orders things special for yer.'

Irrelevantly, Don Wright piped up, 'Then again, he isn't open on Sundays.' He nodded sagely, and they all agreed so as not to upset him, because it was true what he'd said anyway. Such a pity about that fall he had; he'd never been the same since.

A row broke out on the table by the inglenook fireplace. What had begun as a mild chat about the pros and cons of the market turned nasty. Voices were raised, tempers were running high, two bangs on the table with someone's fist and in a trice a fight broke out. It involved Colin Turner and some other men from down Shepherds Hill. Colin was a big chap, star of the village cricket team and known for a temper that could explode in a split second.

'Dicky! Come quick!' Jimmy roared.

Sylvia shouted, 'It's Georgie we want!' She bellowed, 'Georgie!'

But chairs were knocked over – three customers sprang off theirs to avoid being thrown to the floor – beer glasses were smashed into smithereens and Vince Jones mistakenly landed a blow on Colin's nose, which incensed him and so he felled Vince to the floor, where he lay senseless.

Gasps of horror, shocked silence, and then Georgie was there, all five feet nothing of her, hands on hips, telling Colin what she thought of him. 'You're banned for a week for that. Vince is an old man compared to you. He's a pensioner. You should be ashamed of yourself. You're more than a head taller than him, and twice as heavy. Shame on you. Out.' She pointed dramatically at the door, glaring up into his eyes defiantly.

Colin opened his mouth to object but Georgie hadn't been a landlady for twenty-five years without learning how to quell a fight with gimlet eyes alone. Colin closed his mouth and went out, pretending to cuff a few of his friends as he passed to let everyone know he hadn't been utterly subdued.

Dicky arrived with a jug of water and a towel. He shouted, 'Mind out!' to those gathered about Vince.

Someone, horrified by Dicky's obvious intention, called out, 'Dicky! That's not right. Don't. Poor Vince.'

But Dicky did. He upended the whole jug, and Vince spluttered into life. Dicky handed him the towel and gave him a heave up onto his feet.

When Vince emerged from the towel Dicky declared, 'Vince Jones, you're banned for a week, too.'

'Me? He hit *me*!'

'You hit him first.'

'I only caught him a glancing blow.'

'Anyone who dares to give Colin even a glancing blow is an idiot. I certainly wouldn't.'

'Well, you're nothing but a shrimp, Dicky Tutt. Knee-high to a teaspoon, you.'

Angered by this derogatory reference to his lack of height, Dicky squared up to Vince. With his fists at the ready, he said fiercely, 'Now we've got a constable in the police house again, we won't have long to wait if I send for him. And I will. I'm not tolerating a disorderly house.'

This Vince didn't challenge, and the furore died down. The rest of the customers settled back to drinking, and watched Georgie clear the glass away and mop up the water. Vince trundled home on his bike to Greta, contemplating a week of the Jug and Bottle in Penny Fawcett and not liking the idea.

Georgie went round talking to her customers to re-establish confidence again, and within ten minutes the whole thing had blown over. But the discussions about the market lingered on until closing time.

The leaflet that had been pushed through every letterbox said the market opened at eight-thirty in the morning. What the village hadn't bargained for was the stallholders arriving just after six to set up their stalls. It was impossible for them to do this silently. The village filled with busy sounds: boxes being unloaded; trestle tables being snapped upright with loud bangs; van doors opening and then slammed; extra shelving erected on the tables; dogs barking; children shouting; engines revving and the vans rumbling off to park in the field. Some vans stayed *in situ* so their owners could refill their stock from them, which caused trouble when the mothers arrived bringing their children to school, and the sickly sweet smell of doughnuts cooking on the stall nearest to Jimbo's Store wafted across the cottages all morning and completely ruined Jimmy Glover's breakfast porridge.

It was fascinating to watch all the activity before the customers arrived but when they did come it became totally absorbing, and even those who'd vowed not to buy anything from the stalls felt drawn just to go have a look, only *look*, mind.

It was the fancy awnings over the stalls which added style, and gave the impression of a medieval fair so tempting that even Jimbo and Harriet felt the urge to go and check out the opposition.

'I'm *not* going.' Jimbo turned away from peeping between the show cards in his window display.

'*I* will, then. Only for research purposes, you know.'

'No! Absolutely not. We shall neither of us be seen even glancing across, never mind walking round.' Despairingly he added, 'I'd no idea it would be so *thriving*.'

'Please, darling, we've got to know.'

Jimbo firmly shook his head.

'Right, well, I'll ask someone to go instead of me. Bel, you'll go, won't you?'

'I'm sorry. No. I'm dead against it. My Trevor is, my Dicky is …'

Jimbo protested, 'Your Dicky is set to make a bomb today. They'll all be piling in there for food, for beer, for toilets … you name it. So don't tell me he's against the market because he can't be. Well, he'd be an idiot if he was. What's he going to do, shut his doors? I doubt it.' Jimbo stormed off into his office and closed the door with a bang.

He found his hidden bottle of whiskey and his special

glass, and drank a tot before he sat on his chair for a think. All that money he'd be throwing at the barn ... He knew he couldn't expand, without it and yet he wished he didn't need it. Trouble was, he couldn't think of a single serious reason for shutting the market down.

Suddenly he realized the bell was scarcely jingling this morning. He was right; they *were* all forsaking him. When it did jingle he restrained himself from rushing out in heartfelt gratitude to greet whoever it was.

Tom was at the door. 'Titus Bellamy would like to see you.'

'Would he indeed?'

Just in time Jimbo remembered to calm his inner turmoil. Being angry would do no good at all. He went out to meet the infamous Titus, feeling grim inside but smiling on the outside.

'Good morning, Mr Bellamy. Nice of you to call.' Jimbo's outstretched hand gripped Titus's firmly and shook it vigorously. There was an air of refinement about the man. He wasn't the usual bluff and hearty market trader, far from it. In fact, Jimbo warmed to him immediately, until he reminded himself that this man standing so quietly before him was most likely to prove a thorn in his flesh.

'Call me Titus. Everyone does.'

'Then you call me Jimbo.'

'Thought I'd better make myself known. No reason why we can't be friends, is there?'

Jimbo found himself agreeing with him. In his head he was thinking, 'Damn him!' But he heard himself say, 'No reason at all. We're all trying to earn a crust.'

'You've a wonderland of a shop here. An absolute wonderland.' Titus gazed round, seemingly dazzled by the displays. 'Have you had a chance to look round the market?' His grey eyes looked pointedly at Jimbo, as though pleading for approval.

'No.'

'Will you come and take a peek? I'll introduce you to the stallholders. They're all great friends of mine, and lovely people to know. They all do my other markets, too. OK? Will you come?'

It was hard for Jimbo to refuse despite his anger. The chap was so pleasant, the very kind of man he'd be glad to have as a friend. 'Very well, but I haven't much time.'

'That's fine, neither have I.' Titus turned to leave, but at that moment his way was barred by Liz Neal coming in to post some parcels. Her arms were laden and she was in danger of dropping the lot.

'Whoops! Sorry,' she said.

Titus caught one parcel and Jimbo another, and she managed to cling on to the rest. They carried them to the Post Office counter for her and when they'd handed them over Jimbo introduced them.

'Hope you had a good holiday, Liz. This is Titus Bellamy, who's organized the market. Titus this is Liz Neal who runs the village pre-school.'

Titus held out his hand for Liz to shake. 'I've an idea you must be Neville Neal's wife. Yes? I've just taken him on as my accountant. I'm pleased to meet you.'

So this was who she was, this person who'd somehow occupied his thoughts ever since he saw her that morning in the pub all those months ago. He liked her eyes; they were large, kind and the deepest velvet brown. Her face was sweet and natural, her figure slender. She attracted him, very much.

Liz, even though her head was filled with instructions

about the various parcels she was posting, took time to notice his gentle eyes, his full, generous mouth – nothing mean or picky about it – his thick hair, and that beard, which she found she rather liked. Normally she hated them. 'Nice to meet you, Mr Bellamy.' His hand was comforting and somehow it made her feel ... well, cherished.

He still held hers as he said, 'I'm Titus to everyone else.'

'Titus, then. See you again soon.' She quickly withdrew her hand, then turned away to sort out her parcels.

So Jimbo and Titus left to go round the market. After all he'd said that very morning about not going as he and Harriet had been peering between the show cards in the window display, and here he was going for a tour. Damn the man for being so pleasant. He was thankful Harriet had gone to collect produce from his league of farmers' wives who kept his preserves and chutney supplies up to scratch; at least she wasn't witnessing his change of heart. Though he knew he'd confess eventually, because someone would tell her if he didn't.

Jimbo had expected to sneer at what he saw, but he was agreeably surprised by the standard of the goods on the stalls. Everything was of the highest quality. In fact, he was rather jealous of the cheese stall and wished it had been on display in his store, but it was out here in the market and he quietly ground his teeth at the thought. The only stall he didn't like was the pottery. Lovely woman – pleasant, chatty and amusing – but her pottery offerings were chunky and, what was worse, dull. Who in their right mind would want to drink from one of those mugs? Not Jimbo.

They reached the last of the stalls where the chap was

selling fresh fish, and excellent it looked, too. He'd have been proud to have it in his store except he never had fresh fish because of the smell.

'I'm envious of this fresh fish, my word,' said Jimbo. 'I don't sell it because of my other stuff. The all-pervading smell, you see.'

'Your opinion would be appreciated,' Titus said. 'I won't have anyone selling shoddy goods – well, except for Cassandra with the pots. Four children to feed and clothe, things are hard for her. We've had a talk but it's had no effect. Well?' He looked at Jimbo and waited.

To be fair, he had to approve; he could do no other. 'Someone in the village said it would all be rubbish and you wouldn't last for long, but they're quite wrong. Everything is excellent, truly excellent. Good luck to you.' He held out his hand and so did Titus, and they shook hands vigorously.

Titus smiled. 'Thank you for your opinion. From a man who truly knows what he's talking about it's very encouraging. Perhaps some time we might have a drink in the pub together. I've taken a liking to it. I expected it would be all tarted up inside and the whole impression of the outside therefore ruined, but it isn't, and the home brew is excellent.'

Jimbo went back to the house and sat in his chair in the study ruminating on what he'd seen. This was competition on a grand scale. No point in trying to do Titus Bellamy down. He'd just have to concentrate on other aspects of his business to make up the shortfall, because shortfall there was definitely going to be.

Liz wandered home through the market, inspecting all the stalls and realizing that Titus Bellamy had a success on his hands. It was busy today but once the market became better known there would be hundreds of people coming to Turnham Malpas on a Thursday. She spotted Jimbo and Titus talking to Cassandra. That Titus ... she couldn't understand why she felt she knew him. *Had* she met him before? He definitely rang bells, somehow or other. She smiled when she thought about Jimbo being persuaded into looking round the market, after all he'd said, but she rather thought that perhaps Titus could charm a monkey out of a tree.

Back at Glebe House Liz put her key on the hall table and her purse in the cupboard in the kitchen where she always kept it, and looked at her right hand as she closed the door. She put it to her cheek and imagined it felt warmer than the other one. That, of course, was rubbish. Total rubbish, but she suddenly liked that right hand better than the left; it felt smoother and softer. She recollected Titus's face, then roughly dismissed her sentimentality. She was being foolish all because she lacked warmth and comfort in her own life.

These few days away had only served to emphasize her loneliness. Yes, she had her two boys and they were always willing to take her out for a drink or a meal when things got too bad – well, Hugh more than Guy – but relying on them for companionship was ludicrous. Somehow she'd have to shake up Neville and make their marriage work for both their sakes. A dead marriage was a prison sentence and she for one wasn't going to tolerate that, not at forty-five.

According to the flier, the market would finish at one o'clock. Sure enough, the stallholders began clearing away as the church clock struck one. Each of them had taken more money than they had anticipated, considering it was the first time they'd opened in Turnham Malpas, and they congratulated each other in anticipation of even better days yet to come.

But opponents of the whole idea waited to see the mess that would surely be left behind, anticipating concrete evidence that the market was a nuisance and not to be tolerated. But as the last of the trestle tables was loaded into the huge van, three useful-looking chaps appeared with an old truck well past its best, and began clearing the rubbish. Within half an hour the whole of the green was cleaned and tidied, including the pieces of paper that had blown onto the pond. The geese took charge of their green again and settled comfortably for an afternoon snooze beside their pond, having benefited greatly from being fed by the stallholders and the people buying from the stalls.

Truth to tell, the opponents to the market were left with no ammunition for their campaign, but they gathered just the same in the Royal Oak that evening to discuss the matter.

Willie returned from the bar carrying a tray loaded with drinks. They'd pulled two tables together and were seated round, anticipating a good natter comparing notes.

Distributing the drinks, Willie got them wrong and Don finished up with Sylvia's gin and orange. He loudly and agitatedly complained. 'I've got a wrong 'un. This isn't mine. This isn't mine, I didn't order this. Where's mine?'

'That's all right,' said Sylvia, 'you've got mine and I've got yours. Here we are.' She swapped their drinks and Don calmed down. Sylvia looked round the tables. 'Where's Jimbo? He said he'd be coming.'

Grandmama Charter-Plackett, who had allied herself to their cause because of Jimbo, looked surprised. 'He's obviously forgotten. I'll give him a buzz.' So she dug in her bag for her mobile and they all eavesdropped on her one-sided conversation.

'But you said—'

'So, you're not against it now?'

They all watched her eyebrows shoot up her forehead as she said, 'You *like* the chap? How can you like him? I'm astounded ... I know nothing went wrong, I watched from the bedroom window ... Well, of course I didn't walk round to see ... You what ... walked round it with this damned Titus? You traitor! I assume you won't be joining us, then?'

They thought she might explode she was so angry. So angry she couldn't speak. She threw her mobile into her bag and sat arms crossed, lips folded into a thin, straight line, breathing deeply.

They all had to admit that nothing had gone wrong. They'd expected the stalls would be filled with rubbish, lots of shouting of wares – 'apples ten for a pound', 'sausages, eight for a pound', 'early strawberries sweet as sweet, just right for his supper tonight with a splash of cream' – piped music, cars parked everywhere to avoid paying in the field, and, in particular, rubbish everywhere after they'd left. None of their anxieties had materialized and the reason for the meeting soon melted away.

'Look,' said Grandmama Charter-Plackett, having recovered herself when she'd downed her whiskey, 'this is the first time and they'll be on their best behaviour. We've to remain vigilant. Familiarity breeds contempt and within a few weeks things will deteriorate, believe me. Then we've got to strike.'

There were hearty shouts of agreement, in particular from Willie Biggs. 'It was the stallholders' vans that were the biggest nuisance. The mothers had a right problem 'cos the kids didn't know which way to go to find their mothers at lunchtime. That'll have to be sorted or we'll have an accident.'

There were cries of 'hear, hear' all round, and Willie volunteered to get the drinks in again, so they all put money in his cap to fund it. The conversation broke up, and anyone listening from the other tables would have heard Grandmama saying, 'I shall go over there as soon as we finish and find out what's going on.'

Greta Jones agreed. 'I've come for Jimbo's sake, I can't work for him *and* support the market. That wouldn't be right.'

Tom agreed. 'Same here. We were dead quiet this morning and not much better this afternoon. I feel real sorry for him, what with all the expense of the Old Barn, setting it up and that. It's not right.'

The genuineness of Tom's voice inspired them all to agree, and they decided to meet at the same time next week for a progress report. The Anti-Market Action Committee had been formed.

After the meeting Grandmama marched purposefully across to Jimbo's house, putting on her charming look as she went. After all, he had a right to do as he wished – well, so long as it agreed with what she thought was fitting. She'd never been given a key to Jimbo and Harriet's house, except when she lived there for a while, so she had to knock.

She presented her cheek for Harriet to kiss as she

stepped into the hall. 'Late, I know, but I shan't be long. Where is he?'

'In his study.'

Grandmama pulled a face. 'Like that, is it?'

Harriet nodded and opened Jimbo's study door, but made no move to follow her in.

Jimbo was at his computer, entering figures. He paused eventually and nodded at the armchair. 'Sit yourself down, Mother.'

'I am appalled that you didn't attend the post-mortem meeting.'

Jimbo looked at her soberly. 'I was so disarmed by his charm that I went. It was a market worthy of Turnham Malpas, and ultimately can do us nothing but good. OK?'

'OK? No, it isn't OK. It's a damned disaster for you. Just answer me one question. I see you're entering figures. What's this Thursday like compared with last Thursday, or any other Thursday come to that?'

Jimbo checked the screen. 'Thirty per cent down. My God! Thirty per cent? I must have got it wrong.'

He took a closer look at the screen and realized what he'd said. It was bloody awful; it *was* thirty per cent! 'Don't fret, Mother, I shall be at the next meeting of the "Against the Market Campaign", believe me.' He lay back in his chair and smote his forehead with his hand.

'Things may level out,' his mother consoled. 'After a few weeks, you know, these things do. Still, we will need to keep a close eye on it.'

With this gloomy prophecy Grandmama left, her mind churning round and round, thinking of ways to combat the market but coming up with absolutely no ideas. She walked home the long way past the school as part of her walking for health routine, and, glancing across at Glebe

House, she saw Neville's study light on. She suddenly wondered if *he* had anything to do with it, slimy toad that he was. He always seemed to have his fingers in lots of pies. Grandmama shuddered. She didn't like the man but in defence of her son's livelihood there wasn't much she wouldn't do, however repulsive.

Neville, in fact, was rubbing his hands together at that very moment. He'd just asked Liz about the market and she'd confirmed that it seemed to be a triumph. So, the money he'd invested in Titus Bellamy Markets Ltd appeared to be yet another of his successful investments.

Grandmama strode across the road up his garden path, stepped across a narrow flower bed and tapped sharply with her door key on his study window. That'd give him a surprise and a half, she thought.

Startled, he leaped up from his chair to find Grandmama with her nose almost touching the glass of the window to his private sanctum. Neville was greatly disturbed. Not even Liz's cleaner got as close.

He rushed to the window, undid the security locks and opened it, saying icily, 'This is a little unorthodox, Mrs Charter-Plackett. At this time of night, too.'

She ignored his indignation. 'Good evening, Neville. Been a gorgeous day, hasn't it?'

Puzzled by her apparently innocent question he stuttered, 'Y-y-yes, it has. Can I help you in any way?'

'Yes. I need a straight answer.' Privately she thought that would be impossible for Neville Neal. 'Are you *pro* or *anti* the market? Just answer me straight off the cuff, no prevaricating.'

Without the moon and with his back to the light it was difficult to judge his expression for herself, but eventually he said, 'Anti.'

'Excellent.' Grandmama patted the hand holding the window open. 'It's good to know we can rely on you. Love to Liz. Goodnight.'

Grandmama's father would have called Neville a lying hound. She was astute enough to guess he was not only 'pro' but actively involved. One day she'd get him. Oh, yes. Neville Neal wouldn't last much longer if she'd anything to do with it. Nor would the market, come to that.

Chapter 5

That same night Liz lay awake thinking about things in general and in particular about Titus Bellamy. He'd been brought to mind after she'd asked Neville who had knocked on his window. When he said that it had been Grandmama, and that he had told her he was anti-market just to pacify her, she turned on her heel and went immediately to bed, but not before she'd warned him that Grandmama was a formidable enemy.

'Why not speak the truth?'

'Because I don't want anyone to know that I've invested money in his enterprise to help him get started in Turnham Malpas.'

'*You have*? You never said.'

Neville smiled that smile that never reached his eyes. 'Can't tell you every little thing, now, can I?'

'Why have you?'

'Pleasant chap, a little gullible ... I can make a lot of money out of him and his market.'

'What you mean is he's a thoroughly decent man.'

Neville, leaning against the frame of the study door, nodded gravely. 'That's right.'

'You won't ruin him, will you?'

'What does it matter to you if I do? He means nothing to you.'

'He doesn't, but he seemed ...'

'Have you met him, then?'

'Yes. When I went to the Store to post the parcels he was in there.'

'Well, we'll wait and see. Must crack on.'

He made to close the study door but Liz prevented him. 'There are times, Neville, when I thoroughly dislike you. Sometimes you resemble a particularly nasty, very hairy spider spinning an evil web. But don't forget what I said: Grandmama is a formidable enemy.'

As Liz lay in bed, her thoughts moved on to the silver anniversary party on Saturday. She wasn't looking forward to it as she should have expected to. Fortunately Caroline and Peter would be there, as well as Jimbo and Harriet, Ralph and Muriel ... Liz paused for a moment to think about Muriel. It was all so sad that, to put it bluntly, she had lost her marbles. Ralph was covering up beautifully for her, but there were times when even his skill left her floundering and looking foolish. Such a pity. All that love and kindness gone, and nothing left but a shell of what she had been. Apart from those six people, there was no one else she particularly wanted to have there.

Liz had bought a gorgeous dress in the smart designer shop in Culworth that was too expensive for most people. She'd never wear it again, it was too outlandish, but she didn't care. She'd outshine everyone and why not? It was her party, after all. Her wedding dress had been simple, almost countrified. Neville's mother had worn an acid-yellow silk dress with exaggerated flounces and a fishtail sash at the back. God! She'd looked ghastly. All that money and still she couldn't dress well. An idea sneakily crept into Liz's mind. Had she done exactly the same thing with her designer dress? Damn it, she'd wear it no matter what. Come on, Saturday, she thought, let's get it over with.

The catering people had taken over the kitchen by four o'clock on the day, so apart from making a cup of tea for Neville and herself just before they arrived Liz was free to prepare herself for the evening. Neville was growing more anxious by the hour. He was snappy, abrupt, examining every inch of his garden, checking the floodlights, supervising the caterers, whom they'd used several times before and who had always turned up trumps, checking every inch of his dinner suit for fear of stains or creases, and generally behaving as though they were expecting the Queen at any moment.

'For heaven's sakes, Neville, calm down. Everything is under control. Finish your biscuit and go and hide in your study.'

'What will you be doing?'

'I shall be hanging about in case the caterers need me. Go on.'

There was the usual panic in the kitchen: things missing; too many meringues crushed and useless; the plum sauce too runny; the specialist coffee insisted upon by Neville hadn't arrived in time so they'd brought a substitute.

'Don't even mention it,' Liz suggested to the head caterer. 'There's nothing you can do about it now so serve what you've brought. He'll never notice.'

'Yes, but if he finds out—'

'I shan't tell him. Will you?'

'Er ... er ... no I will not, thank you very much. Mr Neal in a strop is not a pretty sight.'

'Exactly.' Liz glanced at the clock. Time she disappeared upstairs to get ready.

Hugh and Guy were loafing about in their old bed-rooms.

'Hi, Mum. OK?'

'Yes, thanks, Hugh darling. I do appreciate you both deciding to come after all. Your dad's delighted.'

Guy said quietly, 'We've come for you, not Dad.'

Hugh closed the bedroom door. 'Tomorrow we're telling him about our decision to leave the company.'

Liz knew this was coming but had hoped it wouldn't. 'I see. He's built the business for the two of you; he'll be devastated.'

'*We're* devastated at the way he runs the business. There's far too much ducking and diving, and we don't like it. It's not the way *we* want to run a business.'

Hugh put his arm around Liz's shoulders. 'The two of us can go into business together, we're capable of doing that, and he'll have to find new partners, ones who think like he does. It'll take months to sort out the partnership situation, by which time he might have got used to it. But we can't carry on as we are, knowing Dad's fiddling all the time. It's just not right.'

'I know, I know.' She reached up to kiss his cheek. 'I just wish you hadn't chosen this weekend. Could it wait another month or so?'

Guy, less sympathetic than Hugh, said emphatically, 'No. We want to be out of the way before the balloon goes up. Which it will. It's inevitable.'

Tears welled in Liz's eyes. 'I know what you mean. If the two of you get tainted with his fiddling you'll never be able to set up in business.'

'Exactly. It's his fault, you know. We tried talking to him about it but to no avail. He has been warned.'

Liz opened the bedroom door, raised her hand to

acknowledge she understood, and went into her bathroom to shower before the party. But everything went wrong. The bra she wanted to wear had lost a hook in the wash; she put her thumb through the new tights she'd bought specially for this evening, thought she'd wear them – after all, no one would see the big hole – decided *she* knew about it and that would spoil things for her, so took them off; smeared her lipstick because her hands were shaking; and finally, Liz lay on the bed and cried in exasperation.

Neville came in to hurry her up. 'They're arriving already. For God's sake, Liz, pull yourself together. Is that the dress you're wearing tonight? Gone a bit over the top, haven't you?'

Between gritted teeth she shouted, 'Get out! Just get out!'

'OK. OK. I'll go and hold the fort.'

Loathing the prospect of the evening, Liz at last left their bedroom. She paused by the banister and looked down into the hall. Hell's bells. Oh, no. Standing there talking to Jimbo was Titus Bellamy. She hadn't thought of Neville inviting him. *Now* what should she do? He wouldn't like her dress. He would find it monstrous given the event. Briefly she studied him talking to Jimbo and liked what she saw. He was wearing an impeccable dark suit, not a dinner jacket like Neville and Jimbo. He was no ordinary man. He had poise and confidence, talking to Jimbo without a trace of awkwardness. He appeared ... so relaxed, not an inch out of place. But for *him* this dress would be a no-no. He'd hate it. She was already dragging it off as she crossed the landing into the bedroom, then she stepped out of it and kicked it across the carpet.

From her wardrobe she chose a simple full-length turquoise gown she'd worn to a party in London, straightened her hair, found the necklace that matched the dress and clipped it on, checked her lipstick, engulfed herself in her newest perfume and walked down the stairs with a welcoming smile on her face.

Both Jimbo and Titus watched her coming down towards them. Jimbo was smiling and Titus was too, but his smile was more than a welcome, it was a recognition of something. Liz felt suddenly so confused she scarcely knew what she was saying. Her mind was spinning, her eyes drinking in Titus.

As an old friend, Jimbo drew her to him and kissed her cheek, whispering, 'Why, you look wonderful!'

Titus leant forward as though he too would kiss her, but changed his mind. She was grateful he did. He took her hand instead and held it tight. 'Good evening, Liz. May I call you Liz?'

'Yes, of course. Everyone else does.'

'You look charming, doesn't she, Jimbo?'

There was something going on here Jimbo couldn't quite understand, but he agreed she did, then quietly drifted off thinking they were best left alone. Maybe he'd imagined the bonding that felt to be between the two of them. He glanced back before he entered the sitting room and saw Titus still had a tight hold on Liz's hand. My God! What was he witnessing? Surely they hadn't had time to start an affair already? Had Neville seen the two of them? He searched for Neville and spotted him talking to Kevin by the temporary bar in the dining room.

That blasted Kevin. Was there anyone alive not beholden to him for past favours? Neville and he appeared to be in close cahoots about something. Kevin had that very white skin that sometimes goes with vivid red hair, his made more obvious by the fact that his hair was very frizzy and thick, his lashes long and red, encircling small and, well, let's face it, piggy eyes. He was fat, too. In fact, in Jimbo's eyes, he very much resembled a Tamworth pig.

Liz swam into view. Maybe she didn't know it but she was dazzling tonight, positively lit up. She went straight to Neville, who looked slightly surprised at her appearance, and even more surprised when she kissed his cheek, and then positively startled when Liz made a fuss of Kevin.

From where he stood, and above the babble of the guests, Jimbo could hear her. 'Good evening, Kevin, I'm delighted you were able to come. And your gift, we opened it last night when Neville brought it home. I adore crystal, and your glasses are absolutely beautiful, so elegant.'

Kevin positively simpered. 'Why, thank you, thank you very much. I'm delighted you approve. You have such good taste, it's an accolade for me to hear you say that.'

Jimbo, who knew how much Liz loathed the man, decided she must have been drinking before she came down. Were she sober she would never say any such thing.

The meal was to be in the marquee on the back lawn and was announced shortly afterwards.

The layout for dining was seven large round tables with ten place settings at each of them. Guests were carefully placed according to their standing in Neville's view. Therefore Jimbo and Harriet, Peter and Caroline, and Sir Ralph and Lady Muriel were on the next table to his. On his own table there was himself, Liz, Kevin, two councillors and their wives, the chairman of planning and his partner, and, to Neville's amazement, Titus Bellamy. In the confusion he couldn't remember whom he had placed in that seat, but it certainly wasn't Titus.

He squinted a look at the place card and, yes, it definitely said Titus Bellamy. Damn and blast, how had that come about? Then he guessed exactly how it had happened, because when the wine was served Titus raised his glass to him and smiled boldly right into his eyes. Then he toasted Liz.

Neville looked at Liz as she lifted her glass and saw someone very different from the wife he'd looked at earlier. She'd changed her dress, all because, he supposed, he'd made an adverse comment about it. So she did care what he said about things. Becoming aware of his scrutiny, she looked up at him and her face was glowing with life. Shaken to the core by the embarrassment he felt at Liz's blatant passion in full view of his guests, Neville was speechless.

Peter, waiting for Neville's signal to say Grace before the food was served, stood up and said it without his instruction.

Neville didn't hear a word of Peter's brief grace, not a single one. After all he'd said about being married twenty-five years, that naturally there was an end to passion, now he couldn't work out what had happened. Perhaps that look was because of her gratitude for the exquisite diamond necklace he'd bought her. Yes, that was it. The most expensive piece of jewellery he'd ever bought. Neville remembered her expression when he'd given it her. Liz had recognized it for what it was: an astoundingly eye-catching piece of jewellery, with diamonds so clear and sparkling, so magnificent. But no, it couldn't be that. She wasn't even wearing it. So …

Titus asked him a question but Neville was hardly listening. Instead he leant towards Liz and whispered abruptly, 'Where's the diamond necklace?'

'In the safe.'

'Why aren't you wearing it?'

'Because ...' Why wasn't she wearing it? Liz didn't know why she'd taken it off along with *that* dress. 'Because it shouts money and it's not right here. Ralph would think it vulgar.'

'Vulgar! Is it vulgar? Tell me.'

'In London circles I would wear it gladly, but not here.'

'*Is it vulgar?*'

'As I've said.' Liz turned to speak to the chairman of planning and, as there was no way Neville would be guilty of a social gaffe in front of *him*, the matter was dropped.

The band tuned up in the dining room, where the parquet flooring lent itself to dancing, and provided background music to the meal, so after the speeches, most people either went into the floodlit garden or to the temporary bar and dancing. The first one to claim Liz was Neville, with his strict adherence to matters of etiquette. He could have been forgiven, because of the occasion, for holding her close, but he held her almost at arm's length and it made dancing difficult. She tried getting close to him but he wouldn't have it.

'Hold me closer, please,' she said, 'we look ridiculous like this.' But he wouldn't. It was something to do with the panic he felt after catching Titus clearly gazing at Liz across the table with something rather more than common politeness. What was the matter with the man? But when he'd looked at Liz she was returning his gaze in spades.

As he and Liz broke apart at the end of the dance, Titus spoke close to his ear. 'May I have the next dance with you, Liz?'

She held out her hand to him, he took possession of it, and they moved away, allowing Neville no time to reply. He was left alone in the midst of the couples gathering for the next dance.

That was the moment when the gossip about Liz and Titus began.

They were scrutinized by scandalized eyes for the whole of the dance. He held her close and they talked animatedly the whole time, laughing, totally absorbed in each other and spinning about to the exaggerated rhythm of the samba till they were quite dizzy. When the music ended Titus bowed deeply, kissed the back of her hand, and they stood close together talking, the centre of everyone's attention until the next dance began.

Under pressure from Harriet, Jimbo claimed Liz for the next dance, manoeuvring her into the garden at the very first opportunity he could. Luckily he found Ralph and Muriel sitting on a bench and he plumped Liz beside them.

'I'm going to get Liz a drink. Can I get something for the two of you?'

Muriel looked up and vaguely remarked, 'It's time for my cocoa, Ronnie dear, please.'

Ralph smoothly asked Jimbo for a whiskey for himself and a juice for Muriel.

Ralph took Muriel's hand to prevent her wandering off, which she had a habit of doing. What he hadn't bargained for was Muriel asking Liz who it was she'd been dancing with.

'I was dancing with Jimbo.'

'No, dear, not Jimbo, I know Jimbo. I meant the one before that. Who is he?'

A little shaken by how lucid Muriel had momentarily

become, Liz answered, 'Titus Bellamy. He's the one who's started the market.'

Muriel didn't reply so Ralph and Liz filled in the time waiting for Jimbo and the drinks by discussing the market.

Sir Ralph approved. 'I can't see but it will do anything but good. Muriel and I walked round and thought the produce was excellent.'

Liz replied, 'That's very true. I'd thought they'd be selling rubbish but they're not. Jimbo isn't exactly pleased, though, as you can imagine.'

Ralph gave her a slow wink to warn her Jimbo was on his way back.

Muriel, having lost all sense of the need for tact, said loudly, 'That Titus Bellamy, my dear, do be careful. He's very taken with you, I can see, and you've got Neville to think of. These things begin with the smallest happening, and before you know it you're swept off your feet.' She patted Liz's knee and then took her hand. 'You know I'm right. He's a very attractive man, and tonight so are you, very attractive.'

Jimbo, setting the drinks down on the small garden table in front of the bench, must have heard most of what Muriel had said. Liz blushed and longed to crawl away, but Jimbo was handing her a G&T.

'Thank you, Jimbo,' she said. 'When I've drunk this I must get back to my guests.'

None of them had caught sight of Neville standing perfectly still behind one of his ornamental spiralled evergreens listening attentively to their conversation. He'd seen Jimbo and Liz disappear and thought they'd be together in the garden talking about him, but instead he'd overheard that daft old bat Muriel telling Liz to be wary of Titus Bellamy. He hoped Muriel didn't think she was right in this ridiculous assumption, because she wasn't, Liz would never ... A cold chill ran down his spine and made him shudder. He remembered that look Titus gave Liz when he toasted her ... Hang his investment! He'd strangle the man for his boldness. Liz was his wife! He'd damn well teach him a lesson.

Neville crept away before anyone on the bench spotted him, only to find himself hiding behind yet another of his ornamental bushes when he saw Titus outlined by the lights of the open French windows, stepping out onto the terrace with a look of pleasurable anticipation on his face. It was Liz he was greeting. By the looks of it there was nothing other than long-standing friendship in their attitude, thank goodness. But, he reminded himself, they'd only really met once before tonight, so how could that be? Neville felt his insides shrivel and he became helplessly rooted to his expensive paving. That dance ... a stranger would have assumed by the closeness of their bodies that *they* were the anniversary couple. What had he done? He'd danced as though he were her brother or her father.

That would have to be rectified. Keeping tight control of his voice, Neville called out, 'Liz! Liz! Have the next dance with me!'

There was a pause and then Liz called out, 'Go in then, I'm just coming.'

But Neville felt defeated when he got inside because he realized that the band had moved on from the tunes where dancing close was the norm and were now playing a tune he didn't know. That wasn't what he wanted. He wanted to be able to hold her close and show his guests he wasn't altogether a cold fish.

Liz went inside to dance with Neville. Their guests had to see with their own eyes that she and Neville were as one. So she went through the procedure of dancing the rock and roll number, glancing at him and smiling as often as she could bear. She convinced herself that the strange emotions she was experiencing for Titus Bellamy were a dream and that tomorrow she would wake up and things would be as they were. Normality was what she wanted: real, sensible, everyday, twenty-five-year ordinariness.

Liz made sure she wasn't anywhere near Titus when the party broke up. She hid amongst the usual Turnham Malpas people, even tolerating Sheila Bissett and her Ron.

Sheila gushed her thanks. 'Wonderful party, Liz, just wonderful. Thank you so much for asking us. We do appreciate being on the guest list. Goodnight.'

Liz got a kiss on both cheeks from Sheila and, over Sheila's shoulder, she saw Titus saying goodnight to Neville. As though he had personal radar Titus found her and gave a long, slow wink. Her insides simply melted.

'It's been a pleasure, Sheila, a real pleasure.'

Liz couldn't avoid saying goodnight to Titus any longer, but she manoeuvred it so she was outside the front door when he caught up with her. She knew she wanted him to kiss her right there and then, but still she was caught unawares when he bent his head and kissed her lips, so gently they barely touched hers. *This*, then, was how it felt, this electric feeling, this bursting with joy.

'Be seeing you,' he said softly before he left.

Be seeing you. Oh, yes, he would, definitely.

She walked back inside, blinded by the intensity of her response.

★

Hugh and Guy were staying over and had disappeared up-stairs leaving Neville and Liz alone amidst the after-party clutter. Neville had offered the waitresses extra money to clear up for them, so all they had to do was stack up the presents in a corner of the dining room – though they'd asked not to have them people couldn't resist – and discuss the success of the evening.

'It went well, don't you think?' Neville slipped an arm round her waist and kissed her temple.

Liz wriggled free. 'It did. And so it should considering how much it cost us. We almost topped Old Fitch, didn't we?'

'No, we didn't. He's lavish with his social events. We got it just right. Yes, it was highly successful. Glad we had a fine evening, so that people could spread out into the garden. I thought Muriel was on good form.'

He waited for her reply.

'Was she? I didn't see much of her.' She knew she sounded false.

'I went into the garden for some fresh air and thought I heard your voices. The two of you talking, you know.'

Alarm bells rang in Liz's head. 'Well, you were mis-taken.'

Neville leapt from his chair and grabbed her arm as she added another present to the pile under the window. 'No, Liz, I'm right.' With his face only inches from hers he glared right into her eyes. 'She warned you about Titus Bellamy, I heard her.'

'If you have reached the level of believing what an old lady, suffering from dementia or whatever it is, says then—'

'I've seen his eyes when he looks at you. I've seen *your* eyes, full of messages.' His grip on her arm tightened.

'Neville! You're hurting me.'

'I'll hurt you even more if you're not careful. How many times have you seen him?'

'I won't be questioned like this. You're being ridiculous. I met him in the Store and then tonight. You're deluded if you think there's something going on.'

Neville snarled at her. 'You're my wife, not a tart, and I won't tolerate anything untoward.'

Liz mocked him, she couldn't help herself. 'Untoward indeed! You're archaic. You're also paranoid. What can possibly be going on between us? We've only just met.'

A present placed awkwardly fell off the pile onto the carpet at Neville's feet. He let go of her to pick it up, and Liz made her escape up the stairs and into the bedroom at the speed of light. As an afterthought she locked the bedroom door.

Within moments Neville was at the door, rattling the knob and saying through gritted teeth, 'Open this door. I demand you open it.' Then he hammered on it with his fist. 'Open it right now! I haven't finished.'

Hugh and Guy appeared on the landing. 'Dad?'

But Neville was so incensed he didn't hear them.

'Liz! Open this door. At once! I have my rights.'

'Dad!'

Neville swung round, his face glistening with sweat. 'Ah! Boys.' He wiped his top lip with the silk handkerchief from his top pocket. 'Lovers' tiff. I expect you boys know what it's like.' He laughed, a strange, cracked laugh which seemed more like a cry for help.

'Is Mum all right?'

'Of course she is. Storm in a teacup, as they say. Goodnight, boys.'

He turned away to go downstairs, patting Hugh's

shoulder as he went as though apologizing. But his insides heaved and tossed, threatening to make him sick. Such terrible lack of control. How could he have behaved like that? How could he have accused her of something that wasn't? How could it be? As Liz said, they'd only met twice. He'd got it completely wrong. But as he sat in his study sipping his whiskey he was haunted by the look in Titus's eyes and that look Liz had when she looked up at him, so full of *life*. He knew he was right. The way they'd danced. Why couldn't he dance with her like that? Close and intimate. Warm and pleasurable. Comfortable with each other.

Worst of all, he'd given Titus the money to come to the village every week with his market. In one sense he'd actually *paid* him to see his wife. Neville tipped another double whiskey down his throat and fell into a drunken sleep.

That was Saturday night. Early on Monday afternoon, just as Liz was finishing her lunch, the phone rang. It was Caroline.

'I'm home. Tea? I've put the kettle on.'

Liz thought she sounded slightly abrupt. 'Lovely. I'll be there in ten minutes. Got a phone call to make.'

'Fine. See you then. Too cold for the garden, don't you think?'

'I agree.'

The teapot was at the ready on the coffee table in Caroline's sitting room when Liz arrived. The pretty china cups were laid out and a plate of Liz's favourite biscuits was waiting for her.

'Caroline! Thank you. You're just what I needed.'

'Am I?'

'Yes, I'm in need of a large dose of common sense.'

'I don't know about common sense, but I am in a state of surprise.'

'No more so than I.'

Liz took one of the biscuits before Caroline had a chance to offer them. 'I love these.'

'I know. So-o-o?' Liz knew from her look that Caroline was talking about the party.

'You noticed? I don't know what happened. It feels like he has known me for years. He hasn't but that's how it is.'

'The way you danced. What came over you?'

'If you lived the barren emotional life I do it might have happened to you. He's so ...'

'Yes?'

'Heart-stopping.'

Caroline paused to put more hot water in the teapot while she thought what to say. 'Liz, be careful. You're treading on dangerous ground. Does Neville realize?'

'Oh, yes. He does. He's very angry.'

'Hardly surprising.'

'We're not speaking. I got swept off my feet. But I shan't be seeing him again, shall I.'

'That's what you suppose, but he looked captivated by you.'

Liz studied her own feelings for a moment and then admitted so was she by him.

'You should never have invited Sheila Bissett. She's spread the news. They're all talking about it.'

'They're not. Oh, God! Well, nothing can come of it, so that's that.'

'Are you sure?'

'Absolutely. I don't believe in divorce.' But the tone of

her voice gave her away, it being barely convincing.

They chatted for a while more, about the success of the party, about the latest news in the village, in fact, until almost the time for the twins to be home, not mentioning Titus again. But he never left Liz's mind. In fact, he hadn't left her mind since Saturday night, and she didn't give a hang that Neville was so angry with her. And in her heart of hearts, no matter what she'd said to Caroline about being against divorce, Liz knew the dance they'd had at the silver wedding anniversary party was only the beginning of something important … to her and to him.

Chapter 6

The following Thursday morning there was no resistance to the market whatsoever. The more militant had hoped for an organized demonstration but after the pleasant events of the first week there was no enthusiasm for one.

However, at the civilized hour of 9 a.m., Grandmama Charter-Plackett appeared out of her back gate with a placard. Not for her the scrappy, badly written messages of most protest placards. Hers was beautifully printed, colourful and to the point:

NO MARKET
IN TURNHAM MALPAS
LEAVE US IN PEACE

She marched firmly, ringing a handbell she'd borrowed from the school, weaving her way between the stalls, not even sneaking a glance at what was on display, and taking up her position outside the Store.

Jimbo was at the Old Barn supervising the delivery of some kitchen equipment when he heard the bell. Having no idea it was his mother ringing it, he continued supervising the delivery until Barry came charging on site shouting from the van window, 'Jimbo, it's your mother making that racket. She's got a placard.' Frankly, Barry thought it hilarious but Jimbo was appalled.

His immediate reaction was to abandon ship, but his business mind told him to stay and keep checking the delivery, otherwise he might find that stunning cooker he could see on the van had 'not been delivered'. It took another quarter of an hour before he was free to go. He raced down the drive out into the road, down Church Lane, left into Stocks Row and screeched to a halt in front of the Store. His mother was still ringing the bell, and at such close quarters the sound was deafening.

Jimbo jumped out and went to speak to her. She stopped the bell, put it down on the seat, stood her placard up against the back of it and, with her hands free, removed her earplugs.

'There you are. Aren't you pleased with your mother? Do you see anyone else protesting? No, not a soul, but I'm here in defence of my son's business. Aren't you proud?'

She beamed at him, and was horrified to see the look of disapproval on his face.

'Don't you want me to protest?'

'I don't see the point. The market went supremely well last week, and apparently the same is happening today.' Jimbo shrugged. 'I don't see how we can stop it.'

'There's more people here this week. Word's getting around, and there'll be even more next week. I've seen three women I know from my exercise class in Culworth, two married couples from Little Derehams and a whole host from Penny Fawcett in that old minibus they all career about in. I tell you, that damned Titus Bellamy has struck gold. We've got to do something, and I'm doing it.'

Grandmama put her earplugs back in, picked up the

bell and her placard, and began ringing the bell again. Jimbo went inside the Store and firmly closed the door.

Several people came to have a word with her so she graciously refrained from swinging the bell while they chatted to her. But then Jimbo and Tom heard the sounds of an altercation and, looking out, saw Kate Fitch from the school apparently telling her in no uncertain terms that she wanted the school bell back, as they couldn't tolerate the noise and teach at the same time.

'But you promised me. Just for the morning, you said.'

'I know I did, Katherine, but I never thought of you ringing it continuously. It's got to stop and the only way I can do that is to repossess the bell.' She held out her hand.

Grandmama saw she was being unreasonable by refusing to return it, but her jaw jutted out and she held on to it. 'I'm sorry but ...'

'It's still only ten o'clock. We can't take another two hours of it. I won't have my children's learning interrupted by this racket.'

'Racket? Racket? This is a cry from the heart. My son's business is being *strangled* by this market, can't you see that?'

'Well, I'm sorry but—'

Grandmama answered her with another ear-splitting peal of the bell. Then she felt a firm hand on her shoulder. Indignantly, she swung round to see who'd dared do such a thing, only to find herself facing the much-moustachioed six-foot-tall new police sergeant, John MacArthur, already known to everyone as Mac.

'Good morning, madam.' It was said in village circles that his moustache had been seen to bristle when he was really angry, but he hadn't reached that stage yet. 'May I ask what you are doing?'

'It's very obvious, Sergeant.' She pointed with an authoritative finger to her placard. 'My son is losing business because of this market and I want to put a stop to it.'

'A one-woman campaign.'

Kate Fitch interrupted. 'I lent her the school bell but she's making so much noise with it I've come to get it back. The children can't concentrate because of it.'

'Breach of the peace, then.' He got out his black notebook, his police-issue ballpoint, flicked open a page and began to write. Grandmama, with her arrest in Culworth the Saturday they collected for Peter's Africa mission still very fresh in her mind, felt her determination begin to waver at the edges. When he got out his digital camera and asked her to turn her placard the other way so he could photograph it more easily she finally crumbled.

'If I stand here without ringing the bell, is that all right?'

'A silent protest is perfectly acceptable, Mrs Charter-Plackett.'

'You know my name?'

'Indeed I do. I know virtually everyone's name now.' He tapped his head. 'Stored away in here. A lot more strangers here today, I notice.'

Kate Fitch took her chance and politely removed her bell from Grandmama's grasp, then marched off back to school holding it by the clapper.

Grandmama agreed with Mac. 'There are. That's going to be the problem. Mark my words, it will get worse, and you'll have it to deal with.'

'Exactly. Now, no more noise, madam, please.' He

stalked away for a general inspection of the market stalls, thinking he might take the chance to buy some of that stinky French cheese he bought last week and so enjoyed.

Tom came out with a coffee for her, so she propped up her placard so everyone could see it and sat down on the seat for a rest. She was just finishing her coffee when she caught sight of Vera Wright amongst the stalls, stuffing a parcel into her shopping bag, the wrapping of which looked suspiciously like that from the organic meat stall.

Grandmama never shouted when she was out in the street, and patiently waited until Vera was within easy hailing distance.

Thinking she hadn't been spotted, Vera said innocently, 'Good morning, Mrs Charter-Plackett. Doing your bit? With the placard, I mean.'

'Exactly. It's plain you're not doing *your* bit. I am very grieved to see that you have bought some meat from the market. Don't deny it. I recognized the bag when you stuffed it in your shopper.'

Vera, appalled she had been caught, denied that was what she had done.

Grandmama got to her feet. 'I am not senile, Vera. I saw what you did. You are a traitor. You said you were on my side and Jimbo's side. How can we succeed if you do that?'

Vera sensed she'd lost the battle. 'The steak looked good and it was very reasonable. I never expected it to be so cheap. It certainly isn't cheap in your Jimbo's Store.'

'The least I can hope for is that the steak is so tough you won't be able to cook it through if you cooked it for a month of Sundays, and that will serve you right.'

Grandmama got a more tart reply than she ever

expected. 'Well, my Don likes it running red so that's all right.'

'That is insolent to me. Disrespectful, indeed. You've let yourself down, gravely let yourself down. I'm appalled. You'll be lucky if I speak to you again.'

'Well, that won't bother me.' Vera stalked into the Store, defiant to the last.

She complained to Bel about her altercation with Grandmama.

Bel, ever mindful that Vera had Don to cope with, said, 'Look, you know what it's like in this village: tempers flare, protests erupt, lifelong friends fall out, and then, before we know where we are, it's all blown over and we're all friends again. Am I not right? Things will settle down.'

Grandmama made a point of completely ignoring Vera when she emerged from the Store to wait for the lunch-time bus into Little Derehams.

Jimbo came out to sit on the seat. 'You know, Mother, there's no need to do this for me. While I appreciate your support I've reconciled myself to the market. I wish it would go away, but it won't, so there we are.' He tucked her hand in the crook of his arm. 'But I'll come to the committee meeting tonight, if you like. Now, go home when you're ready. I love the placard, by the way.'

'So do I. Leave us in peace. I thought that most appropriate. We're not used to all this hubbub, in Turnham Malpas, are we?'

'No, we're not, but maybe we need stirring up a bit.' He got up. 'Going home to work in the office. So glad I've got Tom, he relieves me of the daily grind.'

'Quite right.' She stayed for another half an hour and then walked the long way round to her cottage. She propped the placard alongside the front door, and found, to her surprise, that the front door was unlocked. Puzzled she checked the door again. Yes, it was unlocked, yet the key ... yes, the key was in her pocket. Of course! She'd gone out through her back door and forgotten to check if the front door was locked. She got sillier as she got older. That was a stupid thing to have done.

Thinking how very welcome a bite of lunch would be, she went into the kitchen, put the kettle on and began making a sandwich. It did, however, occur to her that maybe a glance round her sitting room might be a good idea, seeing as she'd left the front door unlocked.

Sure enough, she'd been burgled. All her Georgian snuffboxes were gone.

An unbearable, ghastly pain surged through her chest at the thought. The money they'd cost! But it was the love she bore them that hurt the most. That was a searing pain, running from her head right down to her toes. Who on earth in Turnham Malpas would dare do such a thing to her?

Paddy Cleary? But he was a reformed character now. He wouldn't dare, would he?

One of those boys who lived in the sheltered housing for teenage runaways down the Culworth Road? No, they'd all be at school in Culworth.

Could be anyone. Jimbo, she'd ring Jimbo. No, better still, the police sergeant, they'd all been given his mobile number. As luck would have it, Mac was still in the market; she could see his helmet towering above everyone right by the cheese stall.

'Sergeant! Sergeant! Mrs Charter-Plackett. I've just got home and I've been burgled. Can you come?'

He came in by the back door and she showed him where the snuffboxes had always stood.

'Eight of them. Eight of them, and one I'm convinced belonged to George the Third. I had them all photographed; you can have the prints for identification. They're valuable, very valuable to me.'

'Mrs Charter-Plackett, sit yourself down and explain your movements this morning. Have a think while I put the kettle on.' Sergeant MacArthur was renowned for drinking vast quantities of tea and eating equally vast quantities of biscuits and cake. He found the biscuit tin on the shelf with the tea and coffee, put everything on a tray and marched into the sitting room with it.

Grandmama was fanning herself with her handkerchief and leaning back in her most comfortable chair.

'I left the house through the back door, at nine o'clock prompt carrying my placard and the school bell. I crossed the green and took up my station outside the Store. Well near the front so everyone could see me and hear me, as you know. I didn't get home until just now. Who on earth could it be?'

Mac poured the tea and placed her cup on a small table by the side of her chair, then offered her the biscuit tin.

Grandmama shook her head. 'I'd choke right now if I took a biscuit. What are you going to do?'

'As the snuffboxes are very old and valuable, the antiques division will deal with the problem. We'll take fingerprints, yours included, and attack the question on a broad spectrum.'

Grandmama felt reassured by his approach. He did appear to have his head screwed on the right way round, she thought. Mac asked if anything else had gone.

'Nothing I can spot at this moment. I should tell Jimbo ...'

Just then Mac's mobile rang again.

'Sergeant MacArthur speaking.'

She watched his face, listened to the questions he asked and realized that she was not the only one to have been burgled.

'I'll be round within ten minutes. Certainly, madam. Yes. Yes, I'm actually in Turnham Malpas right now.'

The moment he switched off his mobile she asked, 'Who else, then?'

'Looks like the pub's been burgled upstairs, as they were busy in the bar with the market.'

Grandmama was scandalized. 'The pub? Well, I never. The pub. That's a first.'

'I'll be on my way. Someone will be along later this afternoon. Don't go round polishing, or there'll be nothing for the fingerprint experts to find.'

After he'd gone she noticed that in the short time he was there he'd drunk two cups of tea – well, one and a half – and eaten three biscuits. By the looks of it she'd better lay in extra supplies in case the fingerprint lot were as bad. Then she began shaking all over. It must be the reaction to the shock, she thought. She went to the cabinet where she kept her small supply of alcoholic liquor. A brandy was essential. The bottle shook as she poured, and a few drops escaped which had to be wiped up. The brandy went down a treat but her head spun and she almost missed sitting in her chair, having to grab the arm to stop herself falling on the floor. She'd ring for Harriet.

Harriet came immediately, recognizing the panic in her mother-in-law's voice.

The brandy was still out on top of the cabinet when she arrived. 'Katherine, how many of those have you had?'

'Just the one.'

'Are you sure?'

'Absolutely. Oh, Harriet, I've been burgled.' The whole story poured out and as Harriet sympathized with her the trembling stopped. 'You remember I'd earmarked those snuffboxes for the children when I die.' Out came the handkerchief and three or four sobs to accompany it.

Her mother-in-law never talked about dying, and Harriet felt alarmed.

'How about you have a lie-down on the bed for an hour?'

'Can't. Got the fingerprint people coming anytime.'

'Right. Well, sit there and have a nod. I must go back to the kitchens, I'm in the middle of something. I'll come back when I've finished and stay with you till they come. Right? I shan't be long.'

'Thank you, dear. Thank you very much. I knew we shouldn't have the market. Look what it's caused and it's not only me – the pub's been burgled, too.'

Georgie was deeply upset. It was the thought of her belongings coming under the scrutiny of total strangers. The thought that unknown fingers had sorted through her jewellery, pawed it over like some greedy Fagin. Georgie shuddered. She wouldn't have known except Dicky had told her she'd forgotten to put a necklace on that morning and she looked very bare around her neck. So she'd gone upstairs straight away to remedy the situation, and it was then she'd found about the theft. The crafty beggars had taken only the most precious items.

How had they managed to do all that with none of them downstairs hearing a thing?

Dicky tried to comfort her. 'We were all so busy. It was frantic, still is, and we've to get back in there and pretend nothing's the matter. Come on, love. Alan and

Myra can't cope, and Chef is going berserk trying to keep up. Put it to the back of your mind till we get over the rush, mmm?'

Georgie sniffed into her handkerchief, asked Dicky if her mascara was running. When told that it wasn't, she braced herself and marched downstairs saying the show must go on. 'If the market's bringing in the kind of people who steal, Dicky, is it worth us being so busy because of it?'

Dicky nodded. 'I'm afraid so. What we've got to do is make sure the back door is locked every time we've been into the yard with rubbish or an empty crate or whatever.'

Just before they went through into the bar proper, Georgie reminded him they'd never had to lock it before.

'It's the price we have to pay for increased business.'

Every single table was filled with customers. They were even standing wherever there was space, and the dining room had the beginnings of a queue. Dicky rubbed his hands with delight. This was the life. This was how to make money. He'd have to get more staff for Thursdays. Anti-Market Action Committee indeed. I should cocoa. He waded in saying, 'What can I get you, sir? Certainly, sir. With ice?'

Welcome quiet slowly took over Turnham Malpas. The rubbish was waiting to be cleared, the tables were stacked waiting for the lorry to come and take them away, and Titus Bellamy was still around somewhere because his car was parked outside the Rectory. Be surprising if that was where he was, as several people knew Peter and Caroline had gone to a special afternoon at Alex's school more than an hour ago.

So where was he? Lunching in the pub? That would be it. Of course.

But they were very wrong.

At that moment Titus was lunching with Liz.

When he'd seen her letting herself into Glebe House after finishing at the nursery he'd knocked on her door, hiding a bouquet of roses behind his back.

They looked unblinkingly at each other and, without a word spoken, Liz opened the door wider, thus inviting him in.

She shut the door firmly behind him and stood, arms folded so she wouldn't put them around him and hug him close, which she longed to do. 'Titus. What are we doing?'

'Falling in love?'

'Is that what it is? It's something I've never done before.'

'Never?'

'Never. And you?'

'I have ... with Marie.'

The way he said 'Marie' made it sound as though Marie was very dear to him. Her face drained of colour, her eyes widened.

He saw the shock she was registering. 'She died five years ago. But I was very much in love with her, so, yes, I've been in love before, and now I have the same kind of feelings again. Not because she looked like you, because she didn't, but when we met in the Store that morning I just knew. There's no ghost, Liz. I don't come with shadows to be faced. She died ... having ... during childbirth.' He reached out to give her the flowers.

'Thank you so very much.' Liz held the roses close to her face and breathed in their scent. It was exquisite.

She went to the utility room, filled the sink with water and placed the bouquet in it for a long drink. Then she thought of Neville.

She didn't want to think about him. At this precious moment Neville would have to wait. 'I need lunch. Have you eaten?'

'No.'

'Then eat with me.'

She prepared salad and paninis, and they sat in the kitchen at the little table she and Neville used at breakfast time. Tentatively she asked if the baby had survived.

Titus said, 'No. Marie should never have conceived. She was altogether too frail, and the baby too, but it was what she wanted.'

'I see. So she was an incredibly brave person.'

'She was determined. She was thirty-two and I was forty-five.'

'So you're fifty. I see. But you're very young at heart.'

'I feel it.'

'Titus, at the party we shouldn't have danced as we did. It's all round the village.'

He looked startled. 'Ah!'

They were silent for a few minutes, finishing their paninis, picking more salad out of the bowl, smiling at each other.

Titus laid down his fork carefully. 'You've truly never been in love before?' They could ask any question they wanted without fear.

'I *thought* I was, but I was only nineteen, I hadn't enough depth of soul then for that to be the case.'

'And later ... did it turn to real love?'

Liz studied this loaded question knowing only the truth would suffice. Had it ever turned to real love? When just the sound of his voice or the sight of him could set her heart thudding and she'd have given her life for him? If Neville had needed a kidney donating, would she have said to take both?

'No.' Liz got up to clear the table.

'And how about him? Has he loved *you*?'

'I don't think so. Perhaps at first, but not … no, not truly loved.' Liz gulped back her distress at what she'd said. The realization that all these years she'd been unloved hurt her beyond endurance. Suddenly she needed to be alone. 'Perhaps it's time for you to go. I think I heard that old lorry come for the rubbish.'

Titus sensed her distress and wished he'd never asked, but he had to know. 'Yes, you're right, time to go.'

'OK then.'

'Might I ring? We could meet but not here, not in this house.'

She nodded. Titus left.

Liz wept for all the empty, useless years.

Chapter 7

The Anti-Market Action Committee met that same night in the bar. But when Jimbo arrived they were discussing something that had nothing whatsoever to do with the market, well, it had, vaguely.

'Look! I know I'm right. His car was parked outside the Rectory, but he was coming out of Glebe House and it wouldn't be Neville he'd gone to see in the middle of the day, would it? I saw him go in when I set off, with a bunch of roses behind his back, and they were *red*.' Sylvia looked round them all with a significant expression on her face. 'And he come out when I was going back home. *Minus* the roses.' Sylvia picked up her gin and orange, and waited for their response to this juicy piece of gossip.

Jimbo said, 'Good evening, everyone. Who's that you're talking about? Not me, I hope.'

Grandmama patted his knee. 'Of course not, my dear. Just some village gossip.'

Jimbo looked round each face in turn but no one enlightened him. 'Well?'

Sylvia looked embarrassed but she did tell him. 'I was saying I saw Titus Bellamy going in and coming out of Glebe House.'

'And ...?' Jimbo raised his eyebrows and waited.

Sylvia almost squirmed with embarrassment 'We just wondered ...'

'Judging by the way they danced at the party ...' Sheila Bissett sniffed her disgust.

Jimbo was angry. But he didn't know why. Was he angry they were gossiping? Or angry with Liz and Titus? Possibly both. 'Well, that's nothing to do with the market, so can we press on? I'm short of time.'

Grandmama plunged in. 'You'll all have heard that the pub and myself were burgled during the market today. If that isn't proof we need to get rid of it I don't know what is. Apparently Georgie's very upset. All the jewellery that went was of sentimental value. She's very upset. We've never had to lock our doors, have we?'

Willie asked Grandmama what she'd lost.

'Well I *had* a set of eight silver snuff boxes, one of which I am convinced belonged to George the Third, and the whole lot has gone. Very valuable, they are. Fortunately I had photos taken of them so the police have got those. I'll never get them back, I'm quite sure, so the insurance will have to cough up, but that's not the same, is it? They didn't burgle yesterday or on Monday or Tuesday. Oh, no. It was on market day when we were all occupied and the village was humming with new people. Mac was on to it straight away.'

Willie, full of curiosity, asked, 'What did he do?'

'Got the fingerprint people in and they went through my cottage with a fine-toothed comb. Up and down, dusting this and dusting that.'

Dusting for fingerprints indeed! Would you believe it! Everyone leaned a little closer. They didn't want to miss a single word.

Willie asked if they'd found any fingerprints.

'Three full sets. They were obviously amateurs. Opportunists, the fingerprint people said.'

Vera, keeping somewhat of a low profile in view of her purchase from the organic meat stall, offered, 'Well, I never saw anyone who looked like a burglar.'

Scathingly, Grandmama said, 'They don't walk about with "burglar" printed on their foreheads, you know. How did the meat taste, by the way?'

Don answered her. 'Beautiful! Absolutely beautiful. Fried onions with it, and deep-fried chips and fried tomatoes. Delicious.'

Vera kicked his ankle, twice, but it had no effect. She blushed a deep red and all but disappeared into the cushions on the settle.

Sylvia was appalled. 'You haven't bought some meat from the market, have you?' But she knew from Vera's face that she had.

Don, temporarily as sharp as a butcher's knife, replied, 'And she's promised me some more next week. Two pounds a pound, that's all. You should try it.' Mercifully for Vera, he sank back into his usual stupor after this outburst, but the damage was done.

Greta Jones was scandalized. 'This is an Anti-Market Action Committee, Vera. How could you? Such disloyalty.'

Vince found it amusing. 'Vera! You shouldn't have done that. Watch yer backs, everyone! Two-faced Vera might strike again, and it could be you.'

Willie, who was enjoying the exchange, suggested, 'It was probably horsemeat, it being so cheap.'

Vera went dreadfully pale, and put her handkerchief to her mouth.

Jimbo asked, 'Did it have a strongish taste?'

Vera nodded.

'There you are, then. It probably was.' Jimbo felt wicked, but he didn't care.

Vera whispered, 'But it's organic meat ... they said.'

Bel, who was managing the dining room, had come to have a quick word during a lull and, having heard the entire conversation, commented, 'That's why it's safer to shop at Jimbo's, he never sells horsemeat.'

There was a lot of solemn nodding round the table. What Bel had said was proof if anything was that Jimbo's was best and the sooner the market disappeared the better.

Willie suggested delivering a leaflet to every house in Turnham Malpas, Penny Fawcett and Little Derehams, telling them about the burglaries and about the need for extra vigilance with doors and windows on market days.

'Excellent. I'll deliver some.' Grandmama toasted Willie for his foresight.

So Willie couldn't do anything other than volunteer, too. Then Sylvia, Greta and Vince also agreed to help. Jimbo offered to ask Fran and Harriet if they could lend a hand, and he'd undertake to get the leaflet printed.

The meeting ended with everyone feeling that good progress had been made, except for Vera, who decided, stuff them all, if that steak could get Don excited then he'd get steak next week; it couldn't be horsemeat, and he hadn't many pleasures in this life.

After Grandmama and Jimbo had left, the rest of them returned to the gossip of the week, all of them wishing they knew exactly what was going on. There was certainly something. And did that stuffed shirt Neville Neal know? Time would tell.

★

Jimbo told Harriet the moment he got home that he'd volunteered her for the leaflet drop.

'Oh! Right, that's fine. Did the meeting go well?' She was working on her tapestry, having been inspired by Evie Nicholls to give it a go, and was concentrating hard. So when Jimbo told her the current gossip she didn't quite take it in.

'It was the typical village meeting then. A hotbed of gossip as always.'

Jimbo realized she mustn't have heard a word he'd said. 'You didn't hear me. You see, I saw them at the silver wedding anniversary party, not just that embarrassing dance they did, but greeting each other in the hall. It was obvious they were bonding, not just saying good evening. And I caught them looking at each other two or three times and they weren't just looking, they were *telegraphing messages*.'

The tapestry was laid down and Harriet suggested it would be a good idea if he told her who he was talking about.

'As I said. Liz and Titus.'

Harriet was incredulous. 'What? Don't be ridiculous. No-o-o, you've got it wrong.'

'I'm not yet blind and deaf, I *saw* them.'

'Liz and Titus? Liz must have gone off her head.' But when she'd thought about it for a while longer she added, 'We did chat for a while, Titus and me, and I found him very charming indeed. Yes, I did. Rather intriguing, actually.'

'Intriguing or not, don't begin having lunch with him.'

'Excuse me?'

'It appears Liz and Titus may have had lunch together today, and everyone's talking about it.'

Harriet was scornful. 'In the pub? Well, that's nothing.'

'No, at Glebe House. I'm told he had a bouquet of red roses with him.'

'Oops.'

Jimbo wagged a finger at her. 'Keep right out of it, Harriet. Not a word. You mustn't jump to the wrong conclusion. I'm sure both Liz and Titus are very honourable people.'

'Liz is a desperate woman, I don't know about honourable. If I tell you something it must not leave this room.'

'Scout's honour.'

'This is not funny, Jimbo. Promise. It's important.'

'Sorry. I promise.'

'She told me a few weeks ago that she and Neville didn't have sex any more.'

Jimbo went to pour the two of them a whiskey each. 'Here, drink this. Don't tell me whose fault it is; I can guess. It's Neville, isn't it? That's plain to see when you think about it. He isn't exactly touchy-feely, is he?'

'The complete opposite. It's enough to drive her into someone else's arms, especially nice arms like Titus Bellamy's, isn't it? She was heartbroken when she told me. I mean, I know we're friends but we're not bosom friends like Caroline and me. I was amazed when she told me everything.'

'Hell!'

'What's more, her boys are intending to tell Neville that they both want out of the company because they don't like the way Neville handles the business.'

Jimbo tossed back the last of his whiskey and said. 'If he comes to me for counselling, I'll send him round to you.'

'No, thank you. What other advice can I give him but "go to it"!'

Jimbo roared with laughter. 'That's why I married you! I thought Caroline had all the common sense but I do believe it's you.'

'One wonders what he's doing to cause those two boys of theirs to quit.'

'Am I glad not to have set him on as my accountant. I wouldn't want him dickering about with our money.'

'How could he? An accountant never actually handles the money.'

'Advising investments in this and that which would benefit that and this, and, in a roundabout way, fill his pockets?'

'Ah! Right. Well, hush now, I'm sewing again.'

The doorbell rang and Jimbo went to answer it.

Neville Neal was standing on the doorstep and walked in before Jimbo had a chance to invite him. He was strutting about the hall breathing heavily but saying nothing.

'Neville, how can I help?'

His nostrils were pinched tight, which made breathing difficult.

'Harriet in?'

'She is, but you'd better calm down before you speak with her.'

'Yes. Yes.' Drawing in a deep breath, Neville said, 'Just come from the church finance meeting.'

'Right.' Jimbo watched him still pacing about and decided he'd never seen him so agitated before. Dear God! Had someone been gossiping at the meeting? Did he *know*?

Neville took three long breaths in an effort to calm himself. 'There, I'm in control again. Let me see her.'

Jimbo showed him into their sitting room but he wouldn't sit, so Jimbo sat down and he and Harriet waited for him to speak.

'I've just been ... come from the finance meeting at the church. They'd been gossiping about me, I could tell. It was in the air.' Neville's hands were twisting together all the time, and this a man who made no unnecessary movements. 'I got it out of Sir Ralph eventually when everyone had left. He knew, they all knew, but I didn't.'

He paced about some more so Harriet prompted him. 'Knew what?' She guessed but daredn't say, in case there'd been further developments she knew nothing about.

He snapped, '*You* know, I suppose, Harriet?' Neville placed a hand on the arm of the sofa and bent over her. 'About Titus Bellamy and my wife?'

'Only gossip, Neville, and I don't believe gossip without some facts to back it up.'

Jimbo felt Neville was becoming threatening so he offered him a drink, hoping it might well avert the almost inevitable crisis.

'Double whiskey, neat,' Neville muttered.

'Wouldn't it be better if you asked Liz?' The moment she'd said it she knew she shouldn't have. 'Well, maybe not. Sit beside me and tell me all about it.' Harriet patted the sofa cushion and at last he sat down.

'I'm told he's been to our house. Our house. How dare he? He sat in *my* home. I'll kill him.'

Jimbo handed him his whiskey then wondered whether he should have done.

Harriet murmured, 'If that's all he's been up to ... I sit in loads of houses but it doesn't mean I'm doing something wrong. Don't get it out of proportion.'

'With red roses? Possibly having lunch together, maybe

'... possibly ...' He made a fidgety movement with his hand.

'Well, no. But if that's what you think, you need to talk to Liz.'

Neville drank the whiskey and asked for another, but Jimbo dallied about and eventually sat down without handing him a second glass.

'Twenty-five years. After twenty-five years. What does it mean?'

Harriet took his hand. It needed saying and she was going to say it. 'Perhaps she's looking for love?'

'Love? Love? After all these years? Whatever for?'

How could he not understand? Harriet decided to illustrate her point with Peter and Caroline. 'I know Peter and Caroline have not been married as long as you have, but have you ever noticed the love in their faces when they look at each other, observed how they stay in physical contact when they're together? I don't mean silly hand-holding like a president or a prime minister does, but just being in touch? They're not embarrassing, it's just lovely and acceptable, and you *know* what they mean to each other by their body language. Perhaps that's what she needs. Loving contact. Consideration. Being put first.'

Neville didn't reply.

Harriet asked if she'd helped at all.

The two of them saw that Neville was on the brink of breaking down. His shoulders shuddered, his head shook in denial, his face flushed and his teeth began to chatter as though he were feeling indescribably cold.

Eventually he ground out, 'You mean bed?'

Harriet saw she'd got herself into deep water. 'Well, that too, of course. Goes without saying.'

She gazed across at Jimbo for help, but he looked away.

Harriet ploughed on. 'But most of all, Neville, you must talk to Liz about it. She's the one in pain.'

'Oh! And I'm not? You think I'm not? It's come as a terrible shock to me. I saw them at our party and knew something was going on, but for neighbours to see him at the door! That I had not expected. What would you say, Jimbo, if you'd heard this about Harriet?'

'First thought – immediate annihilation of the guilty party. Then, after I'd seen sense, I'd do what Harriet suggests: talk to her about it. Ask her where I'd gone *so* wrong she needed to go outside our marriage for comfort, and just hope ... I wasn't far too late.'

Neville heaved himself off the sofa like a creaking old man, but walked about like a man in a rage. '*Am* I far too late? That's the question.'

Harriet suspected he was but daredn't say so.

Jimbo stood up. 'Neville, if you'll excuse us, it's getting late and Harriet has an early start in the morning.'

'Yes, of course. I'll go.' Neville stalked out of the sitting room into the hall and was opening the front door by the time Jimbo caught up with him.

'Man to man, talk to her immediately you get back. Right?'

But Neville was walking so swiftly he was already level with the village pond and out of hearing.

Neville opened his front door, put the key back in his pocket and called out, 'Liz!'

She answered from the kitchen. She was sitting at their breakfast table with a small teapot, her favourite cup and saucer, and the biscuit tin.

'Meeting took a long time.'

'Yes.' Neville bent over her and kissed her cheek. He shouldn't have done that, he thought immediately. He never did kiss her with enthusiasm when he came home. In addition, she would smell Jimbo's whiskey on his breath. 'Is there enough tea for me?' he asked.

'Of course there is. I'll get you—'

'Stay where you are. I'll get it.'

He never offered to get his own cup. Liz knew immediately that he'd found out. She wished he hadn't. If it meant he was going to break the habit of a lifetime and be considerate she didn't think she could tolerate the hypocrisy of it.

He sat down at the table and poured himself, *himself*, a cup of tea. But where had he been after the meeting? Jimbo's? Not the Rectory, surely?

'Liz. Where did those roses come from? I can see them through there in the utility room on the draining board.' He nodded towards the open door. 'Don't they deserve to be where we can see them?'

Liz looked hard at him. 'Drop the deviousness. Try being honest and open for once. Ask me where I got them. Go on.'

'I naturally assumed you bought them.'

'No, you didn't. You knew I didn't.'

Forced into the open by Liz's direct approach he couldn't continue to pretend. So instead of saying how could I possibly know where they've come from he said, 'The entire village appears to know they were from Titus.'

'That's correct, they are. A thank you for the party on Saturday. Then, as I'd just started lunch, I suggested he might like to share it with me.'

'I see.'

113

'Good manners, you know. He arrived just before one o'clock and left at exactly five minutes to two. We had a panini each, shared a hearty salad with cold chicken left over from last night's evening meal, with coffee from the cafetière, and he likes his with cream and sugar. But then he doesn't need to watch his weight, does he, just as you don't. Oh! And we finished with one of those huge Jaffa oranges I got from the supermarket in Culworth the other day. Anything else you'd like to know? He has a good appetite.'

Liz looked him straight in the eye. And waited. If she'd been furtive he would have guessed. But she'd been open and honest. Well, not entirely honest but almost.

That still wasn't enough for Neville. 'What did you talk about?'

'Not much. He isn't a very talkative person, goes in for long silences.'

'Nice chap, though.' Neville smiled the smile that never reached his eyes.

'Yes, he is. Interesting, too.'

'Ready for bed?'

Liz felt a chill descend upon her. 'Yes. I'll clear up.'

'No, you go upstairs. I'll do this.' He rather imagined that was something Peter would say and congratulated himself, then added 'loving contact' by patting her shoulder before collecting their cups together.

Liz raced up the stairs, thrown off course by his behaviour. She hoped to God that was as far as he wanted to go tonight.

And mercifully it was. In their supersize bed they could lie without touching and always did, except tonight he got into bed and cuddled close to her, putting his arm around her waist.

'Goodnight, Liz. Sweet dreams.' He kissed the back of her neck and sighed contentedly. Neville thought for a moment how Peter would say goodnight to Caroline and added, 'God bless,' then made as though to go to sleep.

But Liz couldn't go to sleep with his arm around her and, while she waited for him to fall asleep, she lay puzzling as to why he was behaving so oddly. It was almost as though he'd been having lessons from ... not *Peter*. Please, surely not, but it sounded like the kind of thing he would say before he slept. She groaned in horror. She was so angry with Neville that she gave a sharp backward kick with her heel on his shin, and he jerked into consciousness.

'What's the matter? Are you all right?'

'I am, but you're not. Have you been to see a marriage counsellor or something? You're not behaving right. God bless indeed.'

Neville was at a loss as to how to reply. He'd no ammunition for dealing with this kind of emotional talk, he'd always avoided it at all costs. 'Er ... er.'

Liz sat up in bed and turned on the light. 'Well, it's disconcerting for me. I'm not used to you behaving like this. They're not your own words.'

He hadn't moved at all, either to deny it, or to repair the damage. He simply lay there flummoxed.

'You suspect me of double-dealing with Titus, don't you? You imagine we're having an affair, don't you? Well, you *deserve* it, let me tell you. I could almost say I have a *right* to have an affair, due to your neglect of me, your lack of interest in me and my life ...'

'I bought you that necklace and, believe me, it cost thousands. Doesn't that demonstrate how much I care?'

'Frankly, no.'

115

'What does then?' Neville recollected Harriet's advice, and wished he'd never asked.

'If things have got so bad that you think a necklace will make years of being ignored all right then it's all far too late. It dawned on me today that I have never been truly loved by anyone all my adult life, and that's heartbreaking. I thought you loved me when we got married but looking back on it I think it was a complete sham, that love of yours, and I was too young and inexperienced to know. Mother asked me once if I was happy, just after Guy was born, and I said yes. I absolutely meant it. But I'm not happy now.' She switched off the light and lay down again on the very edge of the bed, turned away from him, just not caring any more about his feelings or their marriage. 'Another thing – you've never discussed what Hugh and Guy said last weekend, which is typical of you not talking openly about vital matters.'

Neville wanted to crawl away. He pretended ignorance. 'Vital matters? What vital matters?'

'You know what I mean, that the boys told you they want to get out of the business for good because they don't wish to be involved with your underhand antics.'

Neville cringed. He hadn't discussed it with her because he couldn't cope with it. The public humiliation was more than he could bear. His own two sons wanting out from the business he'd built up for them. Everyone would know, and he was having to wait until he'd framed a plausible reason for it.

'Who told you?'

'They did, of course. I'm sorry it's happened, but it's your own fault, Neville.'

For Neville this was worse than thinking about Titus with Liz. Much worse. Where had he gone wrong? Where had everything gone wrong? His whole life was askew.

He got up and padded slipperless into the en suite, so full of pain and anxiety he didn't even feel the chill of the tiled floor. What was the matter with him? He didn't *do* emotional pain. No one but a woman or a soft idiot of a man felt emotional pain. Now, physical pain he understood. Like when he shut his fingers in the car door and had to go to A&E because he'd broken two of them and his hand had swollen to twice its size, or the time he fell down some steps and grazed his knee, leaving it without any skin on at all. With the door shut he sat down on the bathroom stool and wept small, tight tears, which trickled thinly down his cheeks.

Liz waited for his return, half-intending to get up to see if he was all right, because she had felt cruel the way she'd told him she knew about the boys, but by mistake she fell asleep after about an hour.

Neville eventually crept back to bed, but he didn't sleep all night.

Chapter 8

First thing on Monday morning, Sergeant John MacArthur took himself off to Culworth intent on visiting a couple of the more dodgy members of society who might have heard about Grandmama's snuffboxes. He felt motivated on her behalf because he admired elderly ladies who were brisk and up with it and didn't care what people thought about them.

On the surface it seemed unlikely that he would be successful. Culworth was a pleasant country town, dominated by the Abbey and its genteel occupations, and the thought that there might be an undercurrent of criminal activity was furthest from the residents' minds. But Mac knew different. They'd a thriving drug culture, for a start, and, just as active, a thieving element which kept Culworth police busy. Not international crime but definitely crime.

His first call was to a shady jewellery shop down by the river where the old docks used to be. The dock basin was now occupied by narrowboats and wedding-cake cabin cruisers.

'Morning!' Mac shouted as soon as he opened the door. He got no reply so he went round the counter and into the back. On the floor by the back door was Jackie Worsley, crouched in an odd foetal position, still in his pyjamas.

'Jackie! Jackie! Come on, son. Come on, then.' He

rolled him gently onto his back and saw the huge patch of bruising and severe swelling down the side of his face and his head. His breathing was shallow. Testing the pulse in his neck, the Sergeant, to his relief, found him to be still alive.

Mac dialled 999 and called for an ambulance. Then he rang for forensics and a team to investigate. By the time they'd arrived and he'd left them in charge it was ten o'clock and time for his morning coffee, but he decided first to call to see Mervyn at the old pawn shop next door just in case he'd seen something, or even received the same treatment.

But Mervyn was putting new items in his window display when Mac arrived. He was all right, then.

'Good morning, Mervyn. How's things?'

Mervyn's long nose required blowing before he answered. 'What you here for?'

'To see if you're all right.'

'Me? All right? Since when have you been concerned about my health?' He turned to look at Mac.

Mac smiled. Mervyn wasn't such a bad old chap, more sinned against than sinning, and he was a knowledgeable man to have on side. 'Since I found Jackie Worsley two hours ago, unconscious in the back of his shop.'

Mervyn kept a perfectly straight face and said sympathetically, 'Poor old Jackie. I thought he didn't seem so good last time I saw him. Hospital job?'

'Oh, yes. He's been attacked. Unconscious, he is. Cracked skull, I shouldn't wonder.'

Mervyn shuddered. 'Serious, then.'

'Yes, Mervyn, serious. Any bits of news for me?'

'How can I have news for you when I never leave the shop?'

Mac tapped the side of his nose with his forefinger. 'You do. I've seen you. Still, I'm here to warn you to take care. Someone's being a naughty boy.'

Mervyn moved from the back of the window, pulled the curtain across and returned to behind the counter. Attempting to sound disinterested, he asked, 'Been some nicking going on?'

Mac nodded. Then he delved inside his jacket and pulled out Grandmama's photographs.

Mervyn almost salivated when he saw the snuffboxes. He studied the photos with greedy eyes, then studied them again and licked his lips. 'These are wonderful. Never had stuff this quality in my shop. They're not from the Rectory at Turnham Malpas, are they? If they are ... she's a lovely lady, is the Rector's wife.'

'No. They belong to an old lady who doesn't deserve being robbed. A feisty old lady I've lots of time for. If you don't watch out she'll be in here doing her own detective work, she's that kind of person. If she does come in, watch your step. She's just as likely to fetch you one with her handbag as she is to buy the best gold necklace you've ever had in your shop.'

'Like that, is she?' Mervyn smiled, and it made his eyes sparkle. 'I like old ladies like that. These snuffboxes, how long have they been missing?'

'Since Thursday last week.'

'That job at that new market in Turnham Malpas?'

'That's right.' Seeing as there hadn't been time for it to be in the local paper, best not to ask how he knew, thought Mac. 'There's jewellery from the pub, too. They were so busy downstairs they never heard the burglars upstairs riffling through their belongings. Look, there's a couple of pictures, but not very clear.' He gave Mervyn one photograph of Georgie wearing a bracelet and another of her wearing a ring, which showed up fairly well on her hand.

Mervyn handed Georgie's photos back to Mac. 'Might be able to help with these silver boxes. No promises, mind. The other stuff, can't help at all. Leave it with me for a day or two. I don't do it to help the police, you know, and don't you think I do. I just can't bear for beautiful stuff like this to be bandied about all over the place and end up going for a song to someone who doesn't appreciate 'em. Not right.'

Then he swished wide the curtain which separated the shop from his living quarters, went behind it and dragged the curtain across the gap.

Mac quickly stepped back, knowing from experience that a cloud of dust would fly round as the curtain swirled shut. He picked up the photos, placed them carefully in their envelope and put them back inside his jacket, remembering to leave his mobile number on a piece of card on the counter.

As a courtesy to the two legitimate jewellers in Culworth, Mac called on each of them on his way back to his car in the station car park, warned them about Jackie Worsley and collected two coffees for his trouble.

Before he got into his car Mac went inside the police station to look up some regular 'customers' whose fingerprints and records he could examine on their computer. He discovered that two possible suspects were in jail, and a third had left the district. So maybe the burglaries were just opportunists, as he had first suspected. Regulars wouldn't leave three sets of fingerprints around Mrs Charter-Plackett's house, now, would they?

★

The feisty old lady so admired by Mac was at that moment stepping from a taxi in Culworth market square.

'Thank you, my man. There's a tip, too.'

She'd have coffee first to revive her and then on with her crusade.

She chose the Abbey coffee shop, as it was just about the most elegant place for coffee apart from the George, which Grandmama resented because of the prices they charged. She refused to patronize the George, unless Jimbo was paying.

Grandmama decided to sit in an armchair in front of a large coffee table. On the other side was a long, rich red sofa occupied by two peroxided women who ought to have known to dress better than they did. Grandmama tested her caffe latte, and approved.

She had to admit she loved people-watching when she was on her own, and the two women on the sofa opposite her were absolutely right for it. Their conversation was ripe with coarse language. Grandmama quite relished their colourful choice of words, but then the conversation became much more interesting.

'... He promised me one, blast him, and, as he promised, he came home with it Friday. Beautiful, such good taste. He does have an eye.'

'Let's hope it's just for the silver and not the women!' They both cackled with laughter and nudged each other. In view of her present predicament, the use of the word silver intrigued Grandmama, and she cursed the woman with the crying baby behind her as it partially masked Old Peroxide's voice.

'It's the most beautiful I've ever seen, decorated lovely it is, with, like, a castle on it. I've decided I'm going to collect them. He says there's more where that came from.

One hundred and fifty pounds, he gave. An absolute snip, he says.'

'A lot for a little box you can't use, even if it is silver.'

Old Peroxide bridled. 'You, my girl, haven't seen it.'

'No, but I'd like to,' said Young Peroxide, hinting furiously.

'Finished your coffee?' Old Peroxide twice struggled to get out of the sofa and managed it at the third attempt.

'You going?'

'Yes, home to show you my box. That's if you want?'

Grandmama hoped they didn't notice that she was already struggling to release herself from her armchair.

'Give me time to collect my shopping,' said Young Peroxide, carefully shuffling together three expensive carriers.

They both headed straight for the taxi rank outside Culworth station, and so did Grandmama. Never in her life had she used the phrase 'Follow that taxi!' But today she did. The Peroxides' taxi departed smoothly, with Grandmama's cab at a discreet distance behind.

'Don't get too close, I don't want them to know they're being followed.'

'You sound like a detective.'

In order to engage the taxi driver's enthusiasm she indulged herself in a piece of fantasy. 'That's because I am.'

'You look a bit ... well, old for a detective.'

'That's why I am one. No one imagines I could possibly be a detective at my age. But I'm the best in the business.' The taxi in front was now hurtling along at quite a lick, and Grandmama had to cling on for fear of being thrown off the seat. 'Watch! Watch! He's signalling.' But they were only turning into a driveway.

Grandmama shrieked, 'Don't drive in!'

So her driver slid quietly along the street and parked.

'Give them a chance to get into the house and then back up. I need the house number. Gently, gently. No screaming tyres.'

Obediently, the driver did as she requested.

Number fifty-seven, she noted. 'Right, pull further along and park again.'

As he parked she opened her bag, took out Mac's card with his number on it and dialled him on her mobile.

'Detective Sergeant? That you? Good. I'm parked in The Avenue in Culworth outside number fifty-seven. Got that? Fifty-seven, The Avenue. Two women have just gone inside, and the one who lives there is going to show the other one what her husband bought her yesterday, *a silver box*. Significant, eh? And she says there's more where that came from. Come quickly. You'll catch them with … hello?'

Blimey! thought the taxi driver. She really *is* a detective.

Grandmama shook her phone vigorously. 'Damn the blasted thing. It's died. Well, can't be my phone. Must be Mac's. Blast it. Right, come on, we're going in.' She reached out to open the rear door.

'You're not and I'm not,' said the taxi driver, alarmed. 'No way. You know the address. They'll keep.'

He revved up and drove away to find a wider stretch of road to turn round in. Over Grandmama's protests from the back he shouted, 'They could have guns and you're not going in and I definitely am not.' He spun round in the road and, driving past number fifty-seven again, headed back to the station taxi rank.

Grandmama howled but the driver refused to stop.

How could he? How could he? She ranted and raved in the back, scheming to leap out the moment he stopped, but the lights were with him and he didn't need to stop till he arrived at the taxi rank.

'Five pounds, madam, please. Thanks. You know, at your age you should take life a little steadier and give up this detective lark. It could get dangerous.'

The moment she grabbed her change Grandmama headed off to the police station, which, fortunately for her, was right by the railway station.

The taxi driver watched her and slowly shook his head. He wondered if she'd ever heard of the word retirement. But he guessed she hadn't because she raced through the door of the police station moving faster than that three-year-old filly he'd backed yesterday.

Not a single police officer on duty recognized her. Nor were they inclined to listen to this crazy, breathless old girl determined to have them racing out in hot pursuit of someone or other right in the middle of their morning break.

'Sorry, love,' one said. 'You sit down and catch your breath for a bit and then you can get on with your shopping. Here, have my coffee, I haven't started it yet. Do you good. Sugar?'

One taste of the coffee and she had to assume he was trying to poison her. 'Thank you very much, but no. If you drink this stuff every day, it's enough to give you a death wish.'

Feeling slightly insulted, the officer on the counter asked if she had a relative he could ring.

'You could ring your deputy commissioner and tell him my name. He knows my son.'

Too old a bird to fall for that kind of ploy, the constable

indicated with his pen that she should drink her coffee instead.

'But he does!'

Finally she came to realize that it was not the morning for catching thieves and so, quite overcome by her efforts, in particular that rapid march into the police station, she asked the constable to order her a taxi, as though she were staying in a hotel.

He stood at the door, put two fingers to his mouth and gave a piercing whistle, signalling to the first taxi in the rank to pull forward. Unfortunately for the driver, it was the taxi she'd originally hailed. But business being thin this morning he could do nothing but agree to take her. 'But let it be understood, I am not chasing criminals. I only do that on Fridays.'

Ruefully Grandmama agreed.

She was so full to bursting with her morning's adventure she couldn't just go home so she went to Jimbo's. Seated in his thinking chair, she complained loudly about the police force. She smacked her right fist into the palm of her left hand and shouted, 'I had them in the house, you see, with the silver box, and still the police wouldn't help me.'

'I'm glad you didn't go in,' Jimbo said.

'I should have done.' She clenched her fist again and thumped the chair arm. 'I should have done. Mac's damned phone packed up. I might have had a chance with him, but no, everything was against me. Even the taxi driver said he only chased criminals on Fridays.'

Jimbo left her drinking the coffee he'd made her and went to phone Mac. 'Your phone's working now then? My mother said she tried to phone you.'

'Sorry about that. Got in a tunnel and the dratted thing packed up.'

His reply appeared a little too glib to Jimbo, but he couldn't refute it.

'Your mother ...'

'Yes?'

'Try to discourage her from going out investigating by herself.'

'You try! Anyway, perhaps if the officers at Culworth had gone like she asked, they could have caught the thieves red-handed.'

'Get a bit obsessive about their routine, you know, don't like too much disruption.'

'You can say that again. However, I shall be seeing the deputy commissioner later this week. His daughter's getting married and he wants the best caterer he can find – and that's me. I might just have a word. Let that idle lot in Culworth know, will you?'

All he heard on the other end of the phone was chuckling and then it went dead.

Mac knew he needed rather more information than he had before approaching number fifty-seven. Such as who paid the rates for that house. A quick peep at the electoral roll would suffice. He might even take Grandmama with him when he did go so she could identify them. That would be an interesting experience! He was into that kind of thing for the book he was going to write in his retirement. But he just hoped she didn't intend to ask why his phone had packed up at the crucial moment. Phones 'packing up' was the most brilliant pretence and avoided no end of hassle. He smiled slyly at this thought, and there was a kind of secretive charm about his smile which he wouldn't have liked his wife to see. It didn't do for wives

127

to know what their husbands were up to every minute of every day. He planned to ask Grandmama to try again next week. Those two women might just make a habit of going into Culworth on Mondays.

Chapter 9

No one in the village saw Titus Bellamy from one Thursday to the next, and this week was the same, except for Liz, who saw him on Tuesday evening.

She was already seated in the reception area of the Wise Man restaurant in Culworth when Titus walked in. They were both filled to the brim with anticipation, and their eagerness spilled over into beaming smiles, clasped hands and their first real kiss. The tenderness of that first kiss silenced them both.

Then Titus bent over her and kissed her again just as sweetly as before. 'Liz. I've missed you.'

'And I you.'

'Let's go in.' He gently ushered her into the restaurant proper and made sure they were seated in a quiet corner and not by the entrance to the kitchens. 'No, not there, too noisy,' he said to the waiter. 'I prefer that corner by the bay window.'

'I'm sorry, sir, that table is ...'

'That's the one I want.' He smiled at the waiter, and led Liz across to it.

The waiter acquiesced and, having seated them, handed each of them a menu and discreetly disappeared.

Liz thought that Neville would have made such a fuss

about changing tables and here Titus had achieved his objective without so much as a raised voice.

'You do like your own way.'

'I hate sitting by the kitchen with everyone else's dinners wafting past me, as well as all the shouting in the kitchen each time the door opens. It quite spoils my appetite. How have you been since I saw you last?'

'Telling lies.'

'It's difficult not to. About tonight?'

'No, about lunch on Thursday. The roses were a give-away. I turned them into a thank you for the party.'

Titus smiled wryly. 'How did he find out I'd been?'

Liz had to laugh. 'If you have to ask that you don't know villages. You were spotted, flowers and all, at my door, both arriving and leaving, and someone told Neville. So he knew to the minute how long you'd been in the house.'

'Liz. Is he terribly upset?'

No point in not being truthful. This relationship – or whatever it was – had to be open and honest, she couldn't cope if it wasn't. 'Yes, he is.'

'Are you ready to order, sir?' the waiter asked.

'Not yet. I'll catch your eye when we are.' Said so gently the waiter couldn't possibly have taken offence.

Liz liked that. In fact, his every word, his every gesture, endeared him to her by the second. She looked into his eyes, fixedly, as though there was no looking away. 'You see, another thing that's happened is our boys, Guy and Hugh, have told Neville they want out of the business. They're both directors but they don't approve of the way he does business.'

'A double whammy then. That must be a terrible blow. Has he talked to you about it?'

'No. It's too difficult for him to talk about. That's his problem, not being able to talk about things that hurt.'

'I feel deeply sorry for him. He'll feel it so very much. His own boys.'

'He does.'

'Does he know who you're with right now?'

'No, I've told him I'm at an evening class for nursery leaders. A six-week course.'

'I see.' He seemed a little disapproving of her fib.

'I don't lie as a habit, I just couldn't upset him any more than he already is.' Liz wound her fingers around his and noticed a pale circle at the base of the third finger of his left hand. 'Your wedding ring?'

'I've removed it for greater truthfulness.'

She kissed the space where it had been. 'I think that's a beautiful gesture.' Liz had never felt moved to do that kind of thing before and wondered what was happening to her. 'I can't remove mine, not yet.'

Titus swirled her wedding ring around her finger. 'I hope you will for me one day soon.' His grey eyes studied her face and his grip tightened on her hand, 'My word, Liz, I can't explain how I feel about you. I can't find the words. Let's eat. Might do better on a full stomach.'

Titus picked up his menu and began to read it, glad of a reason for looking away from her. The words on the menu swam before his eyes so he ordered steak and all the trimmings because he couldn't distinguish between the words.

In a very small voice Liz agreed she would have the same. 'Did you know we had two burglaries in the village last Thursday while the market was on? You see, the village hasn't bothered to lock doors and windows literally for centuries. I think perhaps we'll need to learn, though.'

Titus looked shocked. 'Serious burglaries?'

'In the case of Grandmama Charter-Plackett, yes. She had some valuable silver snuffboxes taken. But I understand our village sergeant is on the case.' Liz smiled, inferring that the case would be solved any moment now. 'And the pub landlady is missing some trinkets of sentimental value.'

'That is dreadful.'

'It's not your fault, you're not to blame.'

'I didn't meet the landlady, only Dicky.'

'She's tiny, about five feet nothing, but she's formidable.'

The food arrived and Liz was outfaced the moment she saw her plate piled so high. How could this be? The excitement of knowing she would be eating with him that night had prevented her from eating much during the day so she was starving, but here she was, unable to eat.

Titus grinned. 'I like a woman with a good appetite. Get started. Go on.'

Seeing him picking up his knife and fork and tucking in gave her the impetus to attack her plateful. The rich sauce poured liberally over the steak, the organic vegetables, the tender new potatoes, the tomatoes grilled to a turn, it was all so delicious.

Titus, apparently, didn't drink alcohol, but he'd ordered a half-bottle for her.

As she took her first sip she asked, 'You don't drink?'

He shook his head but explained when he'd finished his mouthful. 'It doesn't agree with me.'

'Not beer or lager?'

132

'Not anything.'

Liz found him a very pleasant person to eat with. Neville always made her feel greedy. He was such a delicate, picky eater, and ate as though he enjoyed nothing. It put her off her own food. Whereas Titus ... Suddenly he put down his knife and fork and reached across for her hand. Tenderly, so tenderly, he kissed the palm. 'Are you happy in my company, Liz?'

'I am. Oh! I am.' She smoothed her fingers over his rather artistic-looking hands and taking each of his fingers in turn she put her lips to them. It dawned on her how little she knew about him, but how much it mattered that she did. 'Are you a musician, Titus?'

'I do play the piano. Yes.'

'Your hands are the giveaway. They're beautiful. I haven't a single ounce of talent in me. Not a single ounce. I don't paint or draw or play or sing. Maybe I am the right sort of person for Neville; he laughs at such talents. Mocks them, you know.' Liz's eyes filled with tears.

He handed her a tissue sympathetically. 'That's sad, I'm sorry because he misses so much of the quality in life.'

Liz began to laugh. A small polite laugh at first, which exploded into a loud guffaw. She hugged her sides, and still she roared with laughter. The other diners turned to look. Finally she got control and dried her eyes to stop herself from bursting into more tears for Neville's sad life. 'Titus! In your position you're supposed to rant and rave about the man, not feel sorry for him!'

'But I do. I can't help it. I'm enjoying his wife's company while ... should we be keeping an eye on the clock?'

'Oh! I didn't think. No, no, it's eight-thirty. We're all right for another hour.'

'Eat up. Then we'll go for a walk by the river for a while before you have to go.'

As they left the Wise Man Titus asked, 'Liz, forgive me. I never asked if you wanted a pudding. That's disgraceful of me. Shall we go back?'

'No, thank you, I'm absolutely full.'

Titus tucked her forearm into the crook of his arm and they set off at a good pace towards the river. It was growing dark but a bright moon lit the shimmering water of the broad river and lent a wonderful magical air to their evening. A group of swans, settling for the night, idled by the river's edge like ghosts. The lights strung along both sides of the embankment reflected in the water, and Liz was fascinated by the wriggling patterns of the lights. Here and there a boat bobbed in the water, adding a touch of life to the whole scene.

Titus stopped by a lamppost, so he could see her face clearly. 'Do you think we should be completely honest with Neville?'

Liz said, 'Are you mad? No. Not yet.'

'I'll go home with you now and talk to him about it. How we can't help ourselves.'

'What would we say to him? What are you asking of him?'

'Just that it's inevitable.'

'Well, no, Titus. Please don't spoil a wonderful evening. Leave it be.'

'I'd rather he knew.'

'I wouldn't want him to know, not until we're sure, the two of us ...'

'But that's just it, we *are* sure.'

'But of what?'

'That we want to spend the rest of our lives together.'

Liz, choked with emotion by his certainty, whispered, 'But it's too soon, much too soon. We'd be mad to say that after what ... four meetings, and two of those in public? Completely mad.'

'But that's how we feel.'

'I know it is but ... we're not in our teens. We're grown adults with responsibilities, we've got to be certain. I've got my boys to think about. I'm going home. Lunch on Thursday? My house?'

Then it was that he kissed her in a way she'd never before experienced, with a passion and an urgency that shook her to her roots.

Then he escorted her to her car and stood holding her, urgency all gone, cherishing her instead with such gentleness. That was another thing she'd never experienced before. Finally Liz opened her car door, kissed her forefinger, placed it on his lips and got in. Titus walked away to find his car, and drove out of the multi-storey, jubilantly tooting the horn till out of her hearing.

She sat in the car for a good five minutes, with a smile on her face, before she dared to start it up, thrilled that at last she'd found out something of what loving must be all about. But as for telling Neville ... It was much too soon. She couldn't quite believe it would last, you see. Not yet. It was too magical to be real.

Liz came back to earth the minute she walked into the house. She listened for Neville and heard him tapping away on his computer in the study; nothing new there then. But he must have heard her come in, because the front door had slipped from her grasp and slammed in the wind which had got up.

She imagined it being Titus sitting there hearing the

135

door bang and knowing she'd come home. Scarcely taking time to save what he'd done, he'd have rushed into the hall and embraced her. She could almost feel his arms around her, his lips on hers, his delight at her return. She wouldn't be lying to him about where she'd been. She shouldn't be lying to Neville but she was about to.

Liz was expected to knock at the study door and wait for him to call out, 'Come!' but tonight she didn't. She went straight in saying. 'Hi! I'm back.'

Neville didn't even look up. 'Good evening?'

'Yes, excellent.' That bit at least was true.

'Good tutor?'

'Excellent. Yes, he's very good.'

'Making a cup of tea?' He still hadn't looked at her and she was glad, because she knew remnants of Titus were still there in her face.

'How about hot chocolate for a change?'

The suggestion of change alerted him. He looked up, fortunately too full of his spreadsheet to notice anything unusual in her. 'We always have tea.'

'Well, I fancy a change. Chocolate it is then.'

Neville, uneasy at the alteration in his routine, said, 'All right. I'll be there in a moment. Did Angie go with you?'

'No, she's going on a course next term to qualify. This one's for the qualified.'

They always sat in the kitchen at their little breakfast table at night, to 'save the sitting room carpet', as Neville would say.

He came in rubbing his eyes, and sat down.

'Have you been working on that thing all the time I've been out?'

'Yes. We've had a brilliant year, you know. The best ever. I shall need more staff if we go on like this.'

'Have you thought any more yet about other partners to replace Hugh and Guy?'

Neville flushed a deep red, the colour flooding up his pale face like a wave. He leapt to his feet shouting, 'They're not leaving. I've told them. They're not leaving. I won't have it. I simply won't have it. It's their business and they've to buckle down and get on with it.'

Liz steadied the table to prevent her chocolate spilling. 'In that case you'll have to change your ways.'

'Change my ways? There's nothing to change. I don't do anything actually illegal, nothing anyone's going to find out about, anyway.'

'No, Neville, but you sail too close to the wind, and they do know what they're talking about. Don't deny it.'

He paced up and down the kitchen, slapping his hand on the worktop as he strode about. 'I won't have it. Nothing I do is illegal, just a bit ...' He rocked his outspread hand back and forth. 'They've nothing to fear.'

'One day perhaps, our Kev might spill the beans, and then where will you be?'

'Not Kevin. I pay him too well for him to spill anything at all.'

'You don't know who else hands him brown envelopes. One day they might pay him to tell all.' Liz pushed his mug of chocolate across to him. 'I'll warm it up if it's gone cold.'

Neville lunged across to the table, grabbed the mug and drank it down all at once. He was certainly upset. He shuddered momentarily, and wiped the sweat from his top lip.

'All that searching about in the archives that he does for people,' Liz continued. 'Heaven alone knows what he might find and hide or deliberately leave out for someone else to find. People like Kevin live on a knife edge all the time. Too many fingers in too many pies. Take my advice and forget him.'

Neville stood by the window, fists clenched, looking out at the darkened village. 'He's invaluable to me.'

'If you didn't use him maybe the boys would stay with you. It's the underhand goings-on they object to.' Liz got up to put the mugs in the dishwasher, thankful that his spate of being considerate to her had stopped as quickly as it began. But he took them from her, saying, 'I'll do that. You go to bed, I'll lock up.'

She went into the utility room to take a loaf out of the freezer thinking of Titus and how much he would like homemade bread for breakfast, forgetting that when she thought about him her face softened and her eyes shone.

Neville looked at her when she came back into the kitchen and recognized the expression from the night of their party. That was the look that belonged to Titus. He didn't need to ask. She'd seen him! He knew she had. He grabbed her arm and, staring right into her face, he could smell her breath. She'd been drinking wine and there was another smell – of another person who'd been close to her.

'You've lied to me. You've been with Titus Bellamy.' Both his hands were gripping her upper arms now, his thumbs pressing into her biceps. 'Answer me! Answer me!'

Titus's passion for truthfulness invaded her and she couldn't stop the words coming out. 'Yes, for a meal.'

Neville almost flung her away from him. 'Have you slept with him?'

Horrified that he imagined she would have slept with him on such a short acquaintance Liz shouted, 'No! Absolutely not. We have not. Most definitely not. Just a meal.'

'Are you being honest with me?' His pale eyes glared into hers from only five centimetres away, and she could see dark flecks in them and the mark on the bridge of his nose where his glasses had been. They stared into each other's eyes speechless, their two bodies painfully controlled.

Liz relaxed first. She could see he couldn't bear the idea of her leaving him. The shame of it would be intolerable to him. 'It was just a meal, Neville, that's all.' Liz pushed his hands from her arms. 'I'm going to bed now.'

'He rings you, does he?' Neville spat. 'How could you meet otherwise? There is no course, is there? It's all lies, isn't it? You've lied to me. *He's* made you lie, you who has always, always been so truthful with me.'

She thought of the half-truths he must have told her about his business deals over the years, but forbore to remind him. Each of them had to escape from this confrontation with as much of their integrity intact as possible. How else could they share the same house with any degree of peace? Civilized, that was how they had to be.

She spoke as calmly as she could. 'Neville, we haven't exchanged a single phone call. We arranged to have a meal tonight when he was here last Thursday. A meal is all it was.'

'Text, then?'

Scornfully she answered, 'We're not children.'

She could tell Neville's mind was springing about all

over the place, and she almost saw the worst possible idea leap into his mind.

With frightening venom he said, 'I *forbid* the two of you to meet *ever* again. Do you hear me? You are *not* to meet again. *I won't have it.*'

Liz stared at him, contemplating her reply.

'Did you hear me?' he bellowed with a passion she never knew he possessed.

She replied softly. 'I did hear you. Whether I shall do as you say is another matter. I'm weary of what I am expected to do according to your rules. From this day forward I shall behave as I wish. No more dictates from on high.'

Never before in the last twenty-five years had she so openly defied his wishes, and he couldn't believe it. His pale eyes went wide with shock, his lips trembled, his chin juddered, his fists came up to his chest and, for one terrifying second, she thought he was going to punch her. But somehow, that self-control, that shut-in, closed-in attitude of his held him back, and stopped him taking a step from which they would never have recovered.

'I shall sleep in the guest bedroom tonight to give us both time to calm down, and most especially time for you to consider your position. This business of a ...' he paused to find the best word for the situation, 'friendship with Titus Bellamy is quite simply not on.' He spun round and marched upstairs, his shoes making scarcely a sound as he made his way carefully up to the landing.

Liz heard the guest bedroom door shut with an unaccustomed bang. Then the sound of footsteps into the en suite and the tap running, as Neville kept to his nightly pattern, even opening the bedroom window as he always did. Then silence.

She wasn't giving in to him. She wasn't saying she wouldn't see Titus any more because if she didn't see him she'd wither away. What fascinated her about him? His warmth. That was it. Cuddly, loving warmth, and not just in his body but his character, too. Neville, by comparison, was ... reptilian. Disgusted at herself for making such a comparison, Liz checked the doors and went to bed, spending the night luxuriously spreadeagled across the bed with no one to hinder her, leaving her to dream of whom she liked.

Chapter 10

When the villagers heard the first rumbles of the vans and lorries entering the village the next Thursday in the early hours, they braced themselves for another adventurous day. There'd been a lot of speculation during the intervening week about the possibility of more thieving, and they'd all determined, after reading Jimbo's flyer – and not one of the houses in the three villages of Turnham Malpas, Little Derehams and Penny Fawcett had escaped having one put through their letterbox – that every single door and window would be locked, and, if possible, double-locked. They didn't want *their* treasures to end up in that second-hand shop down by the old docks in Culworth.

Poor Jackie Worsley had been in intensive care all week, with not much sign of improvement, by all accounts. Still if he would run a dodgy shop what else could he expect? Even so, not right, was it?

According to Titus Bellamy's rules, the stalls had to be up and running by eight-thirty. If not, the stallholder would lose his chance to have a stall the following week. But, by the looks of it, they were all present and correct by the time the first customers dashed in to get the best choice of the goods.

Vera Wright, determined not to miss out on the steak for

Don's tea, was there at 8.29 a.m. queuing by the organic meat stall. The huge joints of beef, the legs of lamb, the pork chops and the rolled, stuffed pork, all stacked up and fringed with clumps of fresh parsley, were almighty tempting. Vera thought she might get two pork chops as well, and if that dratted Grandmama Charter-Plackett spotted her, well, hard cheese. Oh! That reminded her, she'd visit that tempting cheese stall and dazzle her eyes with choosing some cheese, too.

She kept thinking she heard a familiar voice, and that it sounded like Jimbo's, but of course she was wrong, wasn't she? It couldn't be. Finally it was her turn to be served, and she carefully popped the chops and the steak right down at the bottom of her canvas bag, before turning away to check the other stalls.

She couldn't believe it.

She was seeing things.

She must be.

But it *was* him, as plain as day.

Wearing his boater with the emerald–green ribbon and his matching striped apron was … *Jimbo*! 'Well, I never,' she said out loud. His stall had an awning just like the others, and the table itself was covered with a splendidly embroidered afternoon tea cloth she'd have given her eye teeth for, laid out with the very best of Harriet's Country Cousin gateaux. Lemon, coffee, chocolate, orange … complete gateaux with twelve portions, and separate slices for individual portions. She could swear the slices were cheaper than the ones in the store, with dinky little boxes to take them away and bigger boxes for a whole gateau. Vera was speechless, fixed to the grass, unable to move. You had to admire him. He was a real marketing man, was Jimbo, because although there was a bakery stall they sold nothing so gorgeous as those gateaux. He'd found his niche and not half.

As for Jimbo, he was loving it. Having made up his mind that he might as well join the market, because it was obvious to his astute business mind that it was going to be a success, he'd rung Titus during the week and asked for a stall.

'I may have a spare stall,' Titus had said. 'Cassandra – you know, the ceramics person – can't afford to pay for her stall any longer. Just not doing enough trade to make it worthwhile. I did offer her three weeks free if it would help but no she wouldn't take charity, so-o-o if you want it that's fine. For what, may I ask?'

'Top-class gateaux. I admit not organic, but the very best quality ingredients, with fresh cream, butter and no artificial colouring. Can I pay for four Thursdays at once and get it cheaper?'

Titus had laughed. 'OK. OK. Ten per cent off to start you on your way, money to be paid in full before eight-thirty on Thursday, and there's not many I'd do that for. Right. Look forward to seeing you.'

So here he was, and the life suited him wonderfully well. He had missed the cut and thrust of the front of the Store. They were coming in droves this morning, from Penny Fawcett and Little Derehams as well as Turnham Malpas and Culworth. Especially Culworth. Loads of new faces. Drat! He'd forgotten his little notices advertising the Store, and he couldn't ring Harriet as he'd gone out in such a rush he'd forgotten his mobile.

So here he was wrapping slices of gateaux as fast as his fingers could manage, though the boxes were a delight to pack up. To one side he had placed cheerful coloured plastic spoons and paper napkins so you could eat on the spot if you couldn't wait till you got home. This was so much better than being angry about the market. Then he saw Vera gazing at him in amazement.

'Jimbo! Does your mother know about this?'

'No. I haven't told her.'

'I think I'll stick around in case she comes by.'

There was an evil grin on Vera's face. Jimbo laughed, and they were still laughing when Grandmama, carrying her placard, came bustling past at 9 a.m. on the dot, intending to stand outside the Store as she had done last week.

Determined to do her bit, she roared past Jimbo's stall, giving very little time to Vera. Then she stopped, thought for a moment, reversed, and found herself standing in front of Jimbo's stall. *Jimbo's stall.*

She was genuinely unable to speak. Horror, betrayal, disappointment and disbelief were all emotions that crossed her face. She tried twice to remonstrate with him but couldn't. She fingered her placard, changed her grip, and lunged forward. She walloped Jimbo twice, three times. He ducked and dived, attempting to avoid her blows, but she was so outraged she went round the back of the stall to get better access to him, and he had to escape between the other stalls. She had energy beyond her years and scored more hits than she ever supposed she would.

'Mother! Mother! Stop it! Please,' Jimbo shouted out in protest, which brought the crowds, but it continued until Grandmama had no more strength left.

Vera laughed so much she was almost ill. Finally Grandmama managed to speak. 'You're a rotten lowlife. You toad. You unspeakable rotten traitor, you. After all you've said and all the support I've given you. You're no son of mine. I disown you.' She stood the end of the placard on the ground and jumped on it till it snapped, then left it all lying there. Storming off to the Store, muttering loudly as she went, she was a spectacle all of her own, and Jimbo began laughing at himself for the exhibition they'd made in front of everyone. And it was still only five minutes past nine.

In the Store they'd heard none of the hullabaloo. The first they knew was Grandmama bursting in through the door, looking thoroughly dishevelled and gasping for dear life.

'Where's Harriet?'

'In the kitchen. Shall I get her?' Bel asked.

'No.' Gathering what was left of her dignity, she stalked through to the kitchen and collapsed on the very first chair.

'Water!' she croaked, like a woman coming home after a week wandering alone in the desert. 'Water, please!'

Harriet brought a glass over quickly.

Grandmama threw down the whole of it, wiped her mouth rather inelegantly on the back of her hand, and proclaimed, 'I've hit that *traitor* a dozen times with my placard. Next time he needs my help you know where he can go. To hell!'

Harriet, deeply concerned that she might be making a habit of being arrested, asked in horrified tones, 'Mother-in-law! Who have you hit?'

'That snake in the grass. He who was my son, namely James Charter-Plackett. A stall. He's got a stall. Did you know he's got a stall? Bold as brass. A damned stall!' She weakly held out the glass, indicating she needed more water. When she'd drunk half of that she checked Harriet's reaction and gave a hint of a smile, which became more than a hint, and finally turned into a full-blown gale of laughter. Then Harriet started laughing, and soon the three staff working in the kitchen caught it too, and before long they were all rolling round, screeching helplessly.

Just in time one of the girls heard Jimbo's voice in the front of the Store and flapped her hands to hush everyone. Jimbo marched in and surveyed the scene. Apart from his mother, who was calmly finishing the last drop of her second glass of water, everyone in the kitchen was applying themselves to their work. Jimbo looked at each one in turn and eventually Harriet could not hold on to her laughter any longer.

'I did warn you,' she said, 'but you wouldn't listen. Who's out there on the stall? You haven't left it with no one guarding it, have you?'

With immense dignity Jimbo declared, 'I've lent Vera my boater and apron, and she's holding the fort.'

Further laughter erupted at the prospect of Vera Wright in Jimbo's boater and apron.

'Jimbo, darling! You need a plaster on your forehead. Look at the blood! I'll get my first aid box and clean it up for you. At last I've found a use for one of my largest plasters. Here we are.'

Grandmama rose to her feet, checked her appearance in her hand mirror – tucking her hair in, tidying her scarf, running a finger over her lipstick – and then marched out saying, 'Harriet, my dear, inform your husband I shall not be speaking to him ever again.' She nodded towards the gash on Jimbo's forehead. 'He may need a stitch in that.' Jimbo piped up, 'Child abuse, that's what that is, there's such a lot of it about.'

As there was no reason now for her to avoid the market for Jimbo's sake she decided to have a meander between the stalls and see what she could see. She was agreeably surprised both by the quality of the food and the size of the crowd, and she spotted more than one person wandering along with a slice of Jimbo's gateau in their hands, greedily eating it up with one of his plastic spoons. She had to smile ... he'd done the right thing. Of course he had, but she ... Grandmama dodged behind a particularly tall man to avoid being seen. There, bold as brass, was Old Peroxide from the Abbey coffee shop accompanied by Young Peroxide, their heads together examining the very tasteful handmade silver jewellery on the stall straight in front of her. The tall man, taking exception to her hiding behind him, patted his pockets to check his wallet and walked away, casting a nasty glance at her as he went and leaving her completely exposed.

This could be her moment.

She approached them, her hand outstretched in greeting. 'Hello! How lovely seeing you again. Isn't it a marvellous market? Everything you need and more.' Seeing they didn't quite recognize her she reminded them where they'd seen her before.

'Oh! of course. It's your son who's in jewellery, isn't it?'

Grandmama pulled her brains together. 'It certainly is. Are you thinking of buying something? May I see?'

Young Peroxide, holding a pair of beautifully worked peridot earrings in the palm of her hand, said, 'Well, yes I am. These, look, for my daughter. What do you think?'

Grandmama laid on the charm with a trowel. 'Your daughter! Did you say *your daughter*. You're not old enough to have a daughter, I'm sure. You're teasing me!'

Young Peroxide fell for her ruse and blushed with delight.

Grandmama turned to Old Peroxide. 'You must be a grandmother, then? Surely not?'

'Well, I am!'

'Wonderful! Look, let me introduce myself. I'm Katherine and you are …?'

'I'm Flower and my daughter's Petal. My dad always called me his Flower right from the day I was born, so it kind of stuck.'

Grandmama wanted to puke but said graciously, 'What absolutely delightful names – they quite bring a tear to my eye. Now look, let's get these earrings bought and then we'll go to the Royal Oak and I'll stand us each a drink. My treat. How about it? I'd love you to accept.' She beamed so enthusiastically at them they simply couldn't refuse.

Flower and Petal looked at each other and decided that yes, they would, and thank you.

With the earrings safely wrapped and in her handbag, Petal followed her mother and their new friend to the Royal Oak. It was busy but somehow Grandmama man-aged to secure a table. Admittedly it was one of the ones they'd started to bring out on Thursdays to cope with the crowds and it was squeezed into a very tight corner, but it did make things feel very friendly.

The drinks ordered and paid for by Grandmama, the Peroxides clinked glasses and said, '*Bonne chance.*'

'Oh, my word! You've obviously travelled abroad.'

'We have indeed …'

Unwittingly they were cleverly trailed along by their new friend and, enjoying her charm and her offer of a second drink, they relaxed more and more. It was when she offered, and they'd accepted, a third drink, that Grandmama went in for the kill and eventually informed

Grandmama that Grandad was in jewellery, quality stuff, not rubbish.

'Drinking this early in the morning – we are naughty! But that's what life's about, isn't it? Having fun? My son, you know, is a jeweller, he ... well, he finds the jewellery trade very ... shall we say ... quiet at the moment. Confidentially, just between us, does your husband find it so?'

Flower and Petal flicked a glance at each other.

'Well,' said Flower, 'he's doing rather well at the moment. Isn't he, Petal?'

'Yes, Dad's doing very well.'

Triumphantly Grandmama said, 'There you are, you see, I knew my son wasn't getting it quite right. I wish you'd give me a few tips to pass on to him. I think he's using the wrong ... shall we say ... wholesalers. They're so expensive and then he can't get a good margin because it makes his goods too dear for the general punter.' Grandmama loathed the word 'punter' but it seemed appropriate for the present company.

'I could ask him if he ...'

'Could I give you my phone number? He could phone me with some names, couldn't he? I've got to be very circumspect with my son, he hates me interfering, but sometimes we women know we must.'

Flower hesitated and then agreed it would be a good idea. She was sure he wouldn't mind. 'I don't promise anything, mind.'

'Of course not, and on my part I wouldn't breathe a word. It would be totally confidential. Here we are, that's my number. I shall have pen and paper by the phone in preparation for his call. Just a thought, your husband's called ...?'

'He's Leonard, well, Lennie. Lennie Holt.'

Grandmama gushed. She thanked them so profusely she almost offered them a fourth drink but decided that frankly three were more than enough.

Preparing to leave, she said she hoped they'd meet another time. She'd so enjoyed their company. 'I must go. I'm supposed to be having lunch at the Rectory and I need to call home first.'

'We don't know your name, for when Lenny rings you up?'

Alarm bells began to ring. She dropped her gloves to give herself time to think. 'It's Katherine Plackett, with a double "t". See you again. Don't forget to give Lennie my number! And tell him that I do appreciate his help. My son is one of those who needs a good kick up the ...' Backside seemed appropriate for present company but she baulked at using such a common word and remembered to say 'posterior.' She twinkled her fingers at the two of them and departed, praying no one would call out, 'Bye-bye, Mrs Charter-Plackett' as she was leaving.

When she got home she took off her coat, phoned Mac with the name Leonard Holt, and then wrote herself a reminder that from now on when she answered the phone she had to say the number and not her name as she usually did. She propped the note on the phone and felt she'd done a good morning's work.

Vera had to be back on duty at the nursing home by one o'clock, so she was glad to see Jimbo returning to the stall. She'd been so busy and had so enjoyed herself that she was on a high when he arrived. She unbuckled the leather money belt and handed it to him.

'Jimbo! I've sold two of the big ones, *two*, and I've lost

count of how many slices. You've hit on a good idea and not half. Don't you think you need more stock?'

Jimbo slipped her a five-pound note. 'Thanks ever so much, Vera.'

'Thank *you*! I didn't expect anything. Your mother, how's she?'

Jimbo grinned. 'She's never speaking to me again.'

'Never mind. She'll come round. She's a feisty old bird, isn't she? You have to admire her.'

'Call at the Store while you wait for the bus and ask Harriet for some more stock. A couple of whole ones? Chocolate and lemon. Or whatever's to hand. Here, look, take this slice for Don for his tea, with my thanks to him for lending me his wife.'

When Vera entered the Store she got a round of applause. Everyone seemed to know what she'd been up to, and she felt enormously elated. The boater had kept falling down her forehead, and the apron was at least three sizes too big, but she'd loved it. It was kind of like performing on the world's stage for a while. She went in the back with her message for Harriet and emboldened herself to say, 'If ever Jimbo can't manage the stall one day, Thursday's my morning off. I'd be delighted to give a hand. I enjoyed myself that much.'

Harriet saw the pleasure in her face and said, 'Of course, yes, I'll tell him. I'm sure he'd be glad for you to do it one day. Thanks, Vera.'

Vera heard the bus pulling up and fled.

Had she stayed ten minutes longer she would have been devastated. Everyone at the market was so busy doing what they were doing that the motorbikes were upon them before they knew it. Five huge motorbikes,

1000cc's at least, roared into the village with horns blowing, loud music pouring out, and going at a speed that was asking for disaster.

First they charged round and round the green, scattering everyone, children coming out of nursery and adults still enjoying the market. The hullabaloo was tremendous and very upsetting, but it was when they decided to spin around between the stalls that the trouble really began. Stealing, they were, anything and everything from the stalls and, as the produce was all top quality, the cost to the stallholders was considerable. They revved and braked, braked and revved, stealing as they went, or throwing around what they couldn't carry away.

Grandmama, about to make an early lunch, couldn't help but hear and see what was happening, and was instantly on the phone to Mac.

He was in Culworth, which wasn't much help, but he alerted the police cars in the area. In the meantime the bikers roared on to the pub, where they demanded a round of strong lagers. What had been a cheerful, pleasurable morning in the Royal Oak was damaged beyond repair. Georgie had her hand on the phone, ready to dial 999 at the first hint of trouble, and Dicky opened the doors wide so his customers could escape if things got dangerous. Which they did when Alan Crimble, feeling daring for once in his life, refused to serve them.

Georgie whispered, '*Serve* them, and get them out at the front where there're some chairs. Do as I say.'

Dicky called out, 'Plenty of chairs out the front, gentlemen. Take your drinks out there, if you please.'

But they didn't offer to pay, and when Alan told them how much their bill was they simply laughed, and, weaving their way outside, pushed other customers to one side, angering the mildest of them by picking up their glasses and taking a drink as they squeezed by.

Georgie couldn't remember a time when things had been so appalling in the bar. She simply did not know how to get it back under control. They were such rough, brash men, so enjoying the mayhem they were causing, and there appeared to be no way of getting rid of them and restoring harmony. Alan and Dicky were completely helpless. What was worse, it appeared they were doing it just for fun. Fun? Yes, that was it, just for fun. They'd heard about the market and thought it would be a real lark.

The bikers sat outside lounging about, laughing coarsely and mocking anyone who walked by. The market itself was in turmoil, and Titus, who'd been sitting in his car in the car park by Rector's Meadow, counting money and keeping his books in order, was numb with shock. He hadn't experienced anything like this at his other markets.

He got out of the car and marched across to the Royal Oak, painfully witnessing his stallholders trying to create organization out of chaos. He stood looking at the men throwing down their lagers in great gulps. They were contemplating going back inside to order more drinks, and that was when Titus asserted himself.

'Gentlemen!' His voice was soft and controlled. 'Would you be so kind as to leave the village?'

A roar of amusement went up. But then something of his quietness got through. He had their attention.

'We're not accustomed to this turmoil,' Titus went on, 'and we'd be grateful if you could leave and allow us to clear up. In fact, you could help to clear up, couldn't you?'

They found that idea even more amusing.

'You're not children or even teenagers,' Titus continued calmly. 'Come on, chaps, do us a favour and go if you don't feel inclined to help. The police will be here soon. You don't want to get arrested, now, do you?' He cocked his ear as though he heard them coming.

First one got to his feet and then another, and eventually all of them mounted their bikes, revved up and, making rude gestures and shouting even ruder remarks to him, they turned into Stocks Row and then left down the Culworth Road.

But they soon wished they'd gone the long way round down Royal Oak Road, for, just round the first big bend, they came upon two police cars parked across the road. Before they could turn round and escape, another appeared out of a side turning and blocked their retreat. They were rapidly arrested, each and every one. Three of them were known to the police – they were the raggle-taggle of a group of bikers living in and around Culworth on travellers' sites – and the other two were from outside the area but whose acquaintance the police were glad to make.

Back in the village Titus was the hero of the hour. He tried to shake off his new status but couldn't. Georgie and Dicky were so grateful, and restored peace by giving everyone free wine with their meals in the dining room or a free drink in the bar. The stallholders' nerves were calmed by Titus's offer of half-price rent for their stalls next week. It wouldn't do his finances much good but it would perhaps ensure they'd all be there next Thursday.

It took much longer than usual to clear up from the market, and it was quarter past two before Titus sank gratefully into a chair in Liz's kitchen and began his lunch.

They ate in companionable silence until they were halfway through, when Titus asked, 'Was everything OK when you got back on Tuesday night?'

'He guessed.'

'Ah!'

'We had a terrible time, and Neville slept in the guest room.'

'It's time he and I had a talk.'

Liz almost leaped from her chair. 'No! No! It isn't, not yet. I need time.'

'For what, Liz?'

'What do you mean?'

'We both know our getting together is inevitable. It's written in the stars that the two of us should be together. You know that. I know that. So why can't I speak to him? I'm not going to attack him nor am I ...' He stopped, listened carefully, then put his finger to his lips and sat quite still.

Liz frowned at him. She drew a large question mark with her finger. Titus put his forefinger to his lips again. Then he pointed to the ceiling.

Liz listened, and then heard a floorboard creak above her head. Oh! God. Who was it? She hadn't heard anything when she'd first come in. She was tempted to go to the foot of the stairs and call up, but Titus shook his head. Liz knew, just knew, it was Neville. The stealthy steps were all him. One stair creaked as he came down, just one, but it was enough. Titus gripped her hand. They both sat there completely still, waiting.

Chapter 11

Then they heard more footsteps crossing the parquet flooring in the hall, and suddenly there was Neville, standing in the kitchen doorway.

Titus turned his head and asked quietly, without any sign of surprise, 'Have you had lunch, Neville?'

'No.'

'Do come and join us, there's plenty here. Where do you keep the plates, Liz?'

He knew but felt it wouldn't be right for Neville to imagine he, Titus, the stealer of wives, was familiar with Neville's own house.

Neville stood quite still looking at Liz. She got up and found a plate, cutlery, cup and saucer, a napkin, too, then laid them out and sat down again. It wasn't real, she knew it wasn't real. This wasn't actually happening, of course it wasn't. She hadn't instantly fallen in love with the most attractive man in the world, of course she hadn't. She was married to Neville.

Titus pushed the basket of rolls towards Neville, and the cold salmon, the dressing, the salad and the tureen of new potatoes. 'A feast fit for a king, isn't it?' he said.

Neville's hands were stiff, paralysed almost, and his actions clumsy, but he did take good portions of each, though he didn't begin to eat.

The whole situation was more than Liz could cope with. Here they were sitting together in Neville's kitchen eating food Neville had paid for, with Neville creeping about his own house making sure she and Titus weren't in bed together before eventually confronting them downstairs. Not a word was spoken between husband and wife. Only Titus, the hopeful lover, was able to find his tongue.

Titus laid down his knife and fork and began to speak. The kitchen was big, and its tiled walls and floor didn't cushion his voice at all. It sounded harsh, so unlike his normal voice. 'Do you normally come home for lunch?'

Neville's body jerked at his question because it put him on the spot. He didn't answer.

'Were you spying on Liz and me?'

'No, not really.'

In a voice as soft and gentle as he could make it, Titus suggested, 'I think so.'

'No, I came back for some papers from my study.'

'You were upstairs, and your study is downstairs.'

'I did *not* come home to spy on you.' Neville clenched his fist and banged it on the table.

'No good searching for us upstairs. I am a man of honour. I would not dream of sleeping with another man's wife in his own house. That would not be honourable. Believe me.'

'But you *can* meet my wife in secret. Make her deceive me by saying she's going to an evening class. You can bring her flowers *again* – I've seen them on the hall table just out there – bring them into my house ...'

'*Our* house, Neville.' As soon as she said it Liz knew it was a petty remark, but it annoyed her so when he called it his house, as she'd put in all the money for the deposit, and more, given to them by her father. This was how a parting of the ways became vicious, and she regretted what she'd said.

Neville took a deep breath. 'Have lunch with my wife in *my* house, *twice*, take my wife out for dinner, make my wife lie to me. Is that honourable? Mmm?'

'In our defence, all I can say is we met, and knew instantly, without any doubt, that we should have met twenty and more years ago. But we didn't. We've met now, and we can't help ourselves. We've quite simply fallen in love, it's as though we've been in love twenty-five years but we've only just met, and there seems to be nothing we can do about it.'

Neville appeared carved of stone. Titus poured him coffee and pushed the cream and the sugar his way. For an instant, Liz felt sorry for him. He couldn't and never had been able to cope with emotions at this level. He'd no vocabulary for it.

'What do you propose I do about it?' Neville said eventually. 'Give you my blessing, shake your hand and watch you walk away with *my wife*?'

'To be honest, yes. Eventually.'

'Would you like me to play the guilty party in the divorce to make life even easier for you?' There was a snarl in Neville's voice as he said this, and it cut Liz to the quick. She broke down in tears.

Titus immediately went to hug her and share his hand-kerchief with her.

Neville almost burst with rage. He leaped to his feet and threatened to punch Titus. The fury within him was more than he could bear. But he knew the situation was beyond him to control, and finally he raised his hands and crumpled back down onto his chair, broken by this situation he'd engineered. Liz and Titus could just about

159

catch what he said. 'You … ask … too much … of … me. I want my wife.'

'*Do* you?' The question was loaded with meaning plus a hint of mockery. Titus left a pause then continued, 'Or simply a housekeeper? Or a decorative, socially adept person to take with you to parties?'

Liz looked at him as he sat back in his chair, and thought: He will be so lovely to come home to. So lovely. But should he have said that?

Startled, Neville realized that Titus knew too much about his private life. He *knew* they weren't making love any more. He *knew*. As if that overrated pastime mattered: well, apparently it did. He felt the explosion in his brain must be visible to the other two. He stood up again and his chair crashed backwards onto the shiny tiles, his heart bursting with pain. She'd told him. Who else had she told?

Liz was appalled by the unaccustomed emotion in Neville's eyes as he looked at her, his eyes clouded by despair.

He strode out of the house without a backward glance. He'd parked his car behind the Rectory in Pipe and Nook Lane, so he walked all the way past Sir Ralph's and round the corner into the Lane with his legs in severe cramp, his heart thumping, his gait stilted and awkward. The humiliation he bore was too much. Finally he bent his body sufficiently to get into his car, put the key in the ignition … and couldn't turn it. Tears, which in his adult life had never done more than trickle down his cheeks once or twice – the last time only two days ago – now ran in floods down his face, as his shoulders shook and his legs trembled.

The sun, shining in through the car windows, went

unnoticed. The birds, chirruping around the hedgerows and busy about their nesting activities, were ignored. He sat there, howling, heeding nothing until he heard the back door of the Rectory open and Peter come striding down the garden path. Not him! Not him! Not that great lover of a husband. The car engine finally fired just as Peter tapped on the side window. Neville drove off, narrowly missing running over Peter's feet.

All the talk that night at the weekly Anti-Market Action Committee in the Royal Oak was about the horror of the motorbike invasion.

Their small group had swollen in size, as many more people saw the wisdom of stopping the market.

'It was terrible. Absolutely frightening. I've never seen anything like it. We don't want that happening in Turnham Malpas no more. Police got 'em, though, thank goodness.' Sheila Bissett looked grimly round the circle waiting for a response.

'Well, I agree, but if in them ancient papers it says a market can be held, how can we stop him?' This from Sylvia, who was torn between the market being stopped and, on the other hand, wanting to wander round and have a look at everything, because those who'd been had told her how good it was. Loyalty to Jimbo had stopped her going.

Greta Jones had to say something. 'Seeing as my employer has decided to break ranks and have a stall—'

Sylvia's eyes almost popped out of her head. 'Did I hear you aright?'

Vera, having been a participant in the event, piped up, 'You did. That's why Mrs Charter-Plackett ain't here; she hit him and almost split his head open.'

'Split his head open?' Curiosity got the better of her. 'What was he selling, Vera?'

'Gateaux like he sells in the Store. I know 'cos I had to put his boater and apron on when he went back to the Store for ten minutes to get a plaster for his head.'

Uproar ensued at the image this created in everyone's minds. A further round of drinks was called for. Decisions needed to be taken!

'I reckon,' said Willie, 'that we need to make a protest. Why don't we barricade the Culworth Road at six o'clock to stop the vans? Then there's no point, is there? No one in a month of Sundays will manage to go the other way down Royal Oak Road. You can barely get bikes down it, never mind vans and lorries. Same goes for Church Lane and Shepherds Hill. Too narrow and twisting. They'd never make it that way, and it's too far round anyway. This is serious. No burglaries this time, but there might be more bikers racing round once word gets about. We need a discussion with the police about more officers being on duty on Thursdays.'

'For the sake of the village we've got to stop it. Shame, though, 'cos the market's bloomin' good,' added Vera.

Lots of nodding took place, and Don added, 'That Sergeant's no good on his own; he needs backup, he does.'

Vera patted his hand. 'Quite right.'

Finally Ron Bissett was charged with going to see the police. Willie, Greta and Vince took responsibility for making placards, and Sheila, now hailed as good at organization after the glory of her fundraising for Africa, would gather people prepared to lie down in the Culworth Road by 6 a.m next Thursday. She already had plans for bringing her clipboard out of retirement, and six names of volunteers were written down on a piece of paper. She'd show 'em.

The man whose business was on the brink of ruin if they succeeded in all their projects, was sitting in the Wise Man dining room comforting his sweetheart.

'... I know it's hard for him, of course it is, but there's no point in not being honest.'

'Gently honest. He's all figures and columns of figures and everything adding up right, and love isn't like that. He doesn't know what to do. I've never seen him so upset. To be at home creeping about. I can't believe he'd do such a thing.'

'He knows, anyway, how we feel and what we're hoping to do. Here, have some more sauce, you might as well.'

'And what about the motorbikes? I didn't see any of it, being in the church hall, or hear it, for that matter – the double glazing is very effective – but it is very serious, isn't it? For you?'

'I'll try it for another two or three weeks, and if things don't improve ...'

'But I thought you said Turnham Malpas was the icing on the cake?'

'It is. Five markets makes the whole lot viable. It's what I've been wanting, but I can't expect these dear people to put up with what happened today just to make money for me, now can I?'

'Bit of excitement never did anyone any harm.'

'It could be the best market yet. It's even started well, which is a good omen. Liz ... come home with me?' He carefully turned the fingers of her right hand in his, examining each one carefully. 'Mmm?' Caring not a toss for

163

any other customer in the restaurant, he reached over the table and touched her lips with his own, lingering awhile, begging for satisfaction. 'Will you? Come home with me? If we leave now you will still be home by eleven. Will you come? I'll drive, and you can pick your car up from here when I bring you back. Will you?'

'Why?'

'I have an urgency about me, to hold you, to make you swoon with my kisses.' He burst into laughter. 'Sorry, that sounded very Shakespearean! Sorry about that. Will you, though?'

Liz knew there wasn't a chance of it stopping at kisses; their need for each other was so obvious. She traced the shape of his lips with her finger, allowing it to linger and then retrace itself, and she felt him tremble at her touch. If she went with Titus now, she and Neville would be finished.

Liz drew back. 'I can't, not yet. Absolutely not yet. I've finished eating. I'm going home. Thank you, my darling. Thank you for wanting me.'

Titus stood up, bitterly disappointed. He escorted Liz to her car.

'Goodnight, my darling, and thank you.' Liz briefly kissed his cheek and stepped away from him.

But he gently restrained her. 'Please?'

Liz put her hand on the arm that held her close, intending to say, 'No,' very firmly. Instead, to her amazement, she heard herself say, 'Yes. Yes, I will.' She can't have said it! She was going home to her husband as any dutiful wife should. But then, clear as day, she saw she was no longer a wife, only a woman living with a man she didn't love.

They each drove their own car to Titus's flat. It was on the ground floor and there was room for both of them to park in the driveway. He stabbed his key into the Yale lock, flung the door wide, drew her inside, kicked the door shut with the sole of his shoe, pulling her into his arms at the same time, and, almost miraculously, kissing her with an abandonment they had never known before. Certainly, an abandonment Liz had never known; every single inch of her body throbbed to his passionate embraces. He gradually drew her into the bedroom, stripped her clothes off, laid her on the bed while he removed his own, and then made love with thrilling, persuasive emotions such as Liz had never encountered with Neville.

They both slept afterwards locked in each other's arms, and it was only when Liz woke abruptly and saw it was already dark that the beautiful superb satisfaction they were both enjoying was disrupted.

'My God! Titus! What time is it?'

Titus struggled awake and switched on the bedside light. 'It's only a quarter past ten. Plenty of time.' He began kissing her again, obviously intending a wonderful repeat. For a few seconds Liz responded, but felt she had to get home, to Neville. Old habits die hard. She pushed him away.

'Sorry. No can do. Let me go.'

Titus relaxed his hold on her and studied her from head to toe, caressing her with his fine, sensitive hands.

'I don't want to leave, Titus. But I must.'

'It's been wonderful. Perfectly wonderful.'

Liz smiled at him, as she half-sat up ready for flight. She bent her head to kiss his lips. 'You've woken me up from a lifelong sleep. Did you know that?' Liz kissed him again, picked up her clothes from the floor and began dressing as fast as she could. 'I'll phone tomorrow. Right?'

Titus was sitting on the edge of the bed admiring the

elegant manner in which she was dressing, despite her rush. He loved every part of her, and admitted it willingly. 'I love every bit of you, from head to toe.' He stood up and kissed her, then walked with her to the door.

'Don't put the light on – someone might see you. You've nothing on!'

'Oh! I'd forgotten. Goodnight, my love.'

'Goodnight.'

But when she got home, Neville had company. Whoever could it be at this time of night? Help! Oh no. It was Peter's voice she could hear. She guessed, without looking in the mirror, that her love for Titus would be written all over her face. But there seemed to be nothing she could do about it.

'Good evening, Peter.'

Peter got to his feet. 'Good evening, Liz. I shan't be long with Neville.' Those penetrating blue eyes of his seemed to see through to her very core.

'Oh! Right.' Peter, she thought, had a subtle method of dismissal. At the same time she was grateful. 'I'll close the door, leave you to it. Can I get you a drink of some kind?'

But Peter showed her his glass of whiskey to indicate he was well catered for. So Liz closed the door without even acknowledging Neville. Must be church business, she thought, and went to make the coffee she hadn't had with Titus. She sat in the kitchen in the chair Titus had occupied at lunchtime, her hands wrapped round her coffee mug, and thought about him. How she would have loved to have stayed and slept in his bed tonight. But then Neville sprang to mind again, and she wondered what Peter was talking to him about in the study.

Peter had rung the doorbell earlier that evening. Neville, when he saw who it was, expected he'd come to discuss church finances, which wouldn't have been at all unusual except for the late hour.

But Peter had come to talk about finding him weeping in his car in Pipe and Nook Lane that afternoon.

'I know it's late,' he said, 'but I've been busy all day and this is my first chance. Perhaps I can help? You were very distressed when I saw you.'

Neville was horrified. 'So sorry, Peter, about that. Thought no one would see me. Just a bad moment, nothing that mattered at all. Not in the slightest.'

'Come, Neville, it was much more than any bad moment, and people's pain is part of my job description. Shall we talk?'

Neville didn't want to talk, but at the same time it would feel good to confide in someone he knew would never divulge a word of their conversation, no matter how tempted he might be.

Peter cleared his throat and opened their discussion by asking outright, 'Is it about Liz? Is that why you were so distressed?'

'You know, then.'

'I do. To be honest, most people do. Let's go and sit down.'

'In my study,' Neville said, leading the way. 'Whiskey?'

'Yes, please. I'll sit here, shall I?' He was too tall and broad-shouldered for the imitation Edwardian tub chair, but he sat down nevertheless.

Neville poured the whiskies, intending to sit at his desk to put some distance between them, then changed his mind and sat in the other tub chair, placing the bottle on the table between them.

Whiskey wasn't Peter's first choice but in view of what he'd come to say he hoped it might help him. 'It must be very distressing for you. I saw ... them at your anniversary party and guessed instantly what had happened.'

Bitterly Neville answered, 'They say they can't help themselves. That they should have met twenty-five years ago. That it's inevitable. But she's my wife. We're married to each other. What does he mean?'

'Love is a complicated thing. Have you ever been in love?'

Neville stood his glass down on the table with a sharp tap. 'Of course I have. I'm married. I must have been.'

'Oh, there's no *must* about it. One can marry and not be in love. One can think one is but one actually isn't.'

'You're talking in riddles now.'

'For me, loving and being in love means ...' Peter put the fingertips of both hands together and propped his elbows on the arms of his chair, while he thought about what to say first. 'Being willing to sacrifice anything to make the other one happy, at whatever cost to oneself. That your loved one is the beat of your heart, your all-consuming passion. That you belong to them and they to you. That without them you are only half a person, and to lose them for whatever reason is like death itself.'

Neville listened, kept intending to interrupt but didn't. Was this what love was then? He couldn't have been in love, then, because this wasn't how he felt about Liz. That was, if Peter was right. Being closer to God than most people, maybe he had higher expectations, higher ideals than ordinary men. He, Neville Neal, had never felt anything of that. Pride, yes. Pride that she looked good, that she was well spoken and belonged to him. Pride that she'd borne him two sons. For his part, he dutifully remembered birthdays and anniversaries, hence the diamond necklace. But was she the beat of his heart? His passion? If he lost her would it be like death itself? No, he concluded, that was for people who lived in a fantasy world.

'Well, to be frank, I don't know anything like that,' he said. 'It all sounds like romantic rubbish to me and nothing at all to do with real, everyday life. I've never thought like that at all. Ever.'

Peter picked up the bottle of whiskey and offered it to Neville. He shook his head, so Peter poured himself another double.

'Do you never wish it was like that?'

A longer silence ensued and it was Peter who broke it.

'I committed the most grievous act of unfaithfulness to Caroline when Suzy Meadows and I ... came together, but Caroline overcame it, because, despite the terrible distress of my betrayal, she quite literally could not live without me, nor I her for that matter. I'd no right to expect her to forgive me, still less had I any right at all to expect her to want to adopt Suzy's and my children, but she did, all because of love. So Caroline gave me the children she, herself, could not carry, and our love is stronger and more vibrant because of it. That is the kind of love I'm asking you if you have.' There was still no reply to his question, so Peter answered himself. 'If you haven't then you should let Liz go, if that's what she needs.'

Neville almost choked with anger. 'Let Liz go? Let her go without a fight? Just let her go, if that's what she needs. Are you mad? Have you lost your senses? The whiskey must have gone to your head.' He couldn't believe he was saying such things to Peter, the man to whom he'd always shown such deference. So he must have passion, somewhere buried deep.

'But why do you want to keep her? For what? She wouldn't have found love with Titus if she already had enormously satisfying love with you.'

Neville was stumped by Peter's logic. 'Why should she need to be in love? What happened to keeping one's promises? What about loyalty? What about being faithful? I've clothed her and fed her and housed her for twenty-five years. Does that count for nothing?'

Peter smiled a little ruefully. 'Not much where love is concerned, I'm afraid.'

'How can she love him more than me? That Titus Bellamy has done *nothing* to earn her love. They only met a couple of weeks ago, for heaven's sakes.'

'He's a charming man. Cuddly and warm, is how Caroline describes him, and he is. Widower, you know. His wife died in childbirth, I understand, and the baby, too. Terrible blow for him. Splendid husband material, Caroline says.'

Sarcastically Neville asked, 'Are you writing a job reference for him?'

Peter was dismayed by how obdurate Neville was proving to be. 'If you care for Liz you should care that she finds a good person to share her life with.'

'She already has a good person. Me! I don't care what he's like. He's not having her. She's mine, you see. I've spent thousands on her, on holidays, on clothes, jewellery, you name it. She *owes* me.'

Peter gave up trying. He got to his feet saying. 'It's late. I must go.' Gently and with great compassion, he concluded, 'Love, to thrive, needs to be freely given,

Neville, without counting the cost. Think about it. God bless you. Goodnight.'

The moment Peter's foot left the front step Neville slammed his extremely expensive, genuine solid oak door, and the sound reverberated right around the village. He listened until the echo had died away. He'd show Peter, and every person in Turnham Malpas, who had passion. He raced up the stairs two at a time ready to satisfy the passion he thought he'd discovered.

Chapter 12

Harriet, who always rose early to give herself time for half an hour of yoga before she began her day, was downstairs on her yoga mat halfway through her exercises when she heard urgent, discreet knocking on the front door. Who the blazes was it at 6.40 a.m.? Her yoga outfit emphasized more of her curves than she liked the general public to see, so she wasn't quite on top of things when she opened the door and saw who was there.

It was Liz, with a holdall at her feet. 'Can I come in?'

'Of course you may.'

She stepped over the threshold and fell into Harriet's arms.

'Liz! Liz! What on earth's the matter? What's happened?'

Her voice muffled by tears, Liz whispered, 'Can I stay for a couple of days? You've none of the children at home, have you?'

'Fran's here, that's all.'

'I could have a bedroom, then?'

'Of course you could.'

'Can I go to sleep right now?'

'Yes, if you like. Come on, bring your bag.'

Harriet took her upstairs, showed her the bathroom, put her holdall in Flick's old bedroom and, when Liz had finished in the bathroom, Harriet stood outside on the landing till she knew Liz had got into bed. Then she popped in.

'Would a whiskey or something help you to sleep?'

Liz shook her head. 'No, thanks, I need a clear head.'

'Well, we're getting up now, I've just heard our alarm. You stay put and I'll bring you up a cup of tea when I make the breakfast. If you're asleep I won't disturb you. I'll close the door, OK?'

Jimbo, who was stretching and turning over onto the warm patch Harriet had left, said, 'What's going on?'

'I don't know.'

'Well, I certainly don't. Who've you been talking to?'

'Liz.' Harriet sat on the bed trying to get her head together.

Jimbo emerged from the duvet. 'Liz? What does she want?'

'A bed.'

'A bed?' Jimbo considered this strange state of affairs and then asked, 'Has she said why?'

'No. But she looks ghastly. Absolutely ghastly. I don't think she's slept all night. She looks totally drained. And she's walking as though she's done twenty miles before breakfast.'

Jimbo put his not inconsiderable intelligence to the dilemma and came up with an answer. 'This Titus business — it's blown up in her face, hasn't it?'

Harriet disappeared into the en suite. 'Could be.'

Twenty minutes later, showered and dressed, Harriet tapped on Fran's door. 'Are you up, darling?'

Neither Jimbo nor Harriet mentioned that Liz was asleep in the house until after Fran had left to catch the

173

school bus. The cup of tea Harriet had promised wasn't needed, as Liz was fast asleep.

'She's absolutely spark out, Jimbo,' Harriet told him, as she came back downstairs. 'What do you suppose has happened?'

'The mind boggles. We'll have to wait and see. Can the girls get on in the kitchen without you for a while? Best if you're here when she wakes. I'm off to see these people about the wedding at the Abbey at Christmas. Our grade A menu, the casino with croupiers, the jukebox, the carriage and horses – you name it, Jimbo's organizing it. Three-tier cake but twenty-first-century design. Please note, my dearest … are you hearing this?'

'It's this morning I'm worrying about. December can take care of itself.'

'Oh, right.'

'Has Neville thrown her out after she spent a night of hot passion on Titus's sofa, do you think?'

'You've a very lurid imagination this morning. You need another half-hour of yoga to calm you down.' He laughed as he kissed her goodbye. 'Must be off. Promised to be there by nine and it's already a quarter past eight. Lots of love, Harriet, my darling, and good luck.' As he spoke he pointed a finger at the ceiling, and was glad he had a cast-iron excuse to leave the house.

What the hell had happened last night? Honestly, one lived in a quiet village so quaint it didn't even have street lighting or numbers on the houses, and yet all these things happened amongst seemingly sober citizens. Jimbo pulled away down Stocks Row and had to pause to wait for a car crossing in front of him. It was Neville Neal leaving for work in Culworth as he normally did. His driving was both fast and erratic, nothing like his usual precise style. Suddenly it struck Jimbo that maybe it hadn't been a night of passion on Titus's sofa that had brought Liz to their door, but something closer to home. Jimbo felt sick at the thought.

Harriet didn't hear a sound out of Liz until noon when she emerged from the bathroom, her looks only slightly improved.

'Something to eat, Liz? What do you fancy, the breakfast you missed or lunch?'

'Lunch. Please. May I use your phone? I forgot to bring mine.'

'Feel free. Use the one in the study; it's more private in there.'

While Liz was in the study, Jimbo rang Harriet on her mobile. 'It's me. Any news? Are you free to talk?'

'No news at all. Only just woken up. Are you coming for lunch?'

'Er ... er ... no. She'll find it easier to talk with me not there. I'll accept this luncheon invitation I've received, OK? I'll be back at about four.'

'Coward!' They both burst into laughter, then Jimbo said, 'Bye-bye' and rang off.

The two of them sat on the bar stools in the kitchen for lunch. They ate soup, rolls, cheese, biscuits and fresh fruit. Liz didn't speak except to say thank you, and neither did Harriet. It was the quietest lunch they'd shared since, well, since they first knew each other when Jimbo and Harriet were new to the village.

'I've given myself the day off, so if you need to talk I'm here,' said Harriet eventually. 'If not, that's fine by me. We can't pretend nothing has happened, can we?

Obviously something serious has. If you'd prefer, I won't tell anyone that I have you staying, OK?'

'Thank you, that's how I want it. I've spoken to Titus and he's coming to see me, if that's all right.'

'Of course it is. He's a lovely chap. Really sweet and kind, but with lots of backbone, too.'

A smile crossed Liz's face, albeit of the fleeting kind.

Harriet pressed on. 'I'm glad he's special to you. Everyone needs someone special.'

Tears brimmed in Liz's eyes. She snatched a tissue from the box on the kitchen worktop and rushed upstairs.

Titus arrived at four o'clock, then disappeared upstairs without the tray of tea Harriet offered him, and she didn't see him again until after Fran came home.

'Mum! What's going on? Who's here?'

'Why do you think someone's here?'

'There's a different smell in the house.'

Harriet swung round from the worktop and leaned against it. 'Liz Neal is here, sleeping, and Titus Bellamy has just come to see her.'

Fran, who took after her father for loving gossip, emptied her mouth of Blue Riband and asked, her eyes sparkling with fun, 'Really? Whatever for?'

'I shall be quite truthful with you, Fran.' Fran went on red alert. 'I honestly do not know why she's here. But she's very upset and has asked Titus to come to see her. That's all I know. On my honour.'

'Maybe he'll tell us when he comes down. Is he staying for dinner?'

'Not that I know of, but I shall invite him.'

They heard footsteps coming slowly down the stairs. When Titus came to stand in the kitchen doorway, the sparkle in Fran's eyes disappeared, because it was plain to see the gossip didn't appear to be fun. She said quietly, 'I'll go and start my homework, Mum,' and disappeared as quickly as she could.

Harriet looked up at Titus and began to smile, but that quickly changed to distress when she saw his expression. He raised a hand as though begging for understanding, and shook his head at her. Because she didn't know what to say, she handed him a glass of water. 'Oh, Titus. What the hell. Has he ...'

The fearful answer was written all over his face.

'Oh, God. No.' Harriet gripped the edge of the work-top to steady herself.

Titus drank some of the water and then placed the glass down. 'I'm going to find somewhere for her to live. Could she stay one more night?'

'Of course, no need to ask.'

'She's hiding. She doesn't want anyone to know where she is.' Titus stopped speaking and stood quite still with a hand over his forehead shielding his eyes. 'Oh, God. I don't know what to do.'

Instinctively Harriet went to put her arms around him to give him at least a little comfort.

The front door opened. It was Jimbo. 'Harriet?'

Jimbo arrived in the kitchen and stood looking at them. Eventually he said, 'Sorry about all this, Titus. How can we help?'

Titus and Harriet broke apart. Titus rubbed his face with his hands to clear his head and said, 'Liz needs some clothes. I wonder, Harriet, if you would go across the road with Liz and me to collect her things. I don't think she should go by herself.'

Jimbo answered before Harriet could. 'Absolutely

not. You never know what you might have to face. *I'll* come.'

'I don't mind, Jimbo.'

'*I* mind.'

'I've just said I don't—'

Jimbo bellowed, '*Harriet*! You are not going.'

'You've had a long day.'

'I will not allow you to go under any circumstances.' Jimbo signalled to Titus to hurry up. 'Have we got a key?'

'Liz has. I'll go and tell her.'

While they were alone in the kitchen Jimbo whispered, 'I know what I'm doing. I'll explain when I get back.'

Liz came down the stairs with Titus. When Jimbo saw the two of them together, sympathy for their situation enveloped him, causing him to say gruffly, 'We'll go in my car. It's too far for Liz to walk, and with all her stuff to carry.'

He reversed into the drive at Glebe House; that way they were much less in the public eye.

But the first thing to delay them was the fact that Liz's key didn't fit the lock.

Jimbo swore. 'He's changed the locks already. Round the back. Come on, Liz.'

He found that the kitchen window was not quite locked shut, but when he'd got it open he knew he hadn't a chance of getting through it. 'Sorry, Titus, this looks like your call.'

With a nimble spring Titus squeezed through, and was soon standing in the kitchen, unlocking the back door.

'You go up, Liz,' he said, 'and give me a shout when you've got what you need.'

When she'd gone upstairs, well out of hearing, Jimbo

looked at Titus and raised his eyebrows. He shook his head and raised his hands helplessly.

Jimbo needed to be told nothing more. 'So sorry. So very sorry.'

Titus said, with his lips almost tight shut, 'I could kill him – and me a pacifist.'

Jimbo ventured into the hall. It looked as though a bomb had dropped. Torn clothes were strewn everywhere and a mobile lay smashed to pieces alongside the hammer that had done the damage. Neville must have gone berserk.

They heard Liz calling and Titus disappeared up the stairs two at a time.

When they got back to Jimbo and Harriet's, Titus carried her things upstairs and left Liz to put them away.

Downstairs in the kitchen, he said to Jimbo and Harriet, 'I look after a flat for a friend on the other side of Culworth, while he works abroad. I've rung him and he says Liz can stay there for a while, but I'll have to go and look at the flat, collect any post, open the windows, see to the bed. He won't be back until September. That'll give us time. Thank you very much. I'll be in touch.'

Titus stood for a moment longer, as though knowing what he wanted to say but not being able to find the words. Finally he said, 'You know who your friends are at times like these. Thank you. She doesn't want people to know anything at all about what's happened. Wants to protect him, you see.' His voice became choked with his tears and he had to wait until he'd got control again. 'So, if possible keep mum ... she's determined about the nursery – to continue, you know – and hopes to begin again on Monday. Angie had to manage for today. Liz can come and go between ... between N-N-Neville coming and going from the office. Says it will help keep her sane.'

'Fine. That's a good thing. Leave her with us, and phone any time. Did she pick up her mobile from the house?'

Titus hesitated. 'No. It's broken I'm getting her a new one tomorrow. Goodnight.'

Liz stood at the top of the stairs and called, 'Goodnight, Titus.'

When he'd gone Harriet suggested Liz went to watch the TV in the sitting room. 'We've got our new one – big screen, surround sound. Go and enjoy yourself.' She gave her a gentle push, and Liz wandered off.

In the kitchen Harriet asked Jimbo why he'd been so angry and refused to allow her to go with Liz.

Jimbo perched on a bar stool, opened the biscuit tin, didn't like the digestives that were in there, snapped the lid shut, and finally satisfied her curiosity.

'I drove behind Neville all the way to Culworth this morning on his way to the office. How he got there without having a major accident I have no idea. You know what he's normally like – sedate, slow, every archaic hand signal you could imagine. But this morning he drove like a madman. He was terrifying. Twice he almost knocked someone down, and I lost count of how many times he had to swerve. I didn't want you to go in case, well, in case ...' He went to look out of the window. 'She couldn't bring her mobile because he'd attacked it with a hammer. A lot of her clothes were torn to shreds and thrown all about the hall and the staircase. Some photographs of her and the boys had been ripped apart, and their frames smashed. It was horrific.'

Harriet began to tremble. 'He always appears totally controlled as though nothing could ruffle his calm. No wonder Titus is so upset. What Neville did to her doesn't bear thinking about.'

'She hasn't told you anything then?'

Harriet shook her head. 'Jimbo, what if he comes to the door looking for her?'

'We'll make sure he can't get in. In fact, I'll go round right now and lock everything – windows, doors, garage up-and-over, and personal door. I'm starving, by the way.'

'I thought you'd had lunch out?'

'I did, but I couldn't eat much. Go and tell Fran not to open the door to anyone, please.'

In fact, they did have to open the door because Grandmama was hammering on it. At first they assumed it was Neville, judging by the noise level, but when Jimbo peeped through their spy-hole he saw it was his mother. Seeing as she'd declared she wouldn't speak to him ever again, he guessed they must be reconciled.

She didn't acknowledge him beyond a pat on his cheek as she whizzed by. Charging into the sitting room, she said, 'You won't believe it, but they've ...'

Her jaw dropped when she saw Liz. Instinct told her there was something very wrong because Liz looked so ghastly, so she didn't say what she would have said. Instead she smiled at her. 'What a lovely surprise you being here. You can be one of the first to hear my news. I have been working in collaboration with the Culworth police – and between us we have two antique dealers in the nick!' She plumped herself down in Jimbo's chair, intent on regaling them with the story.

But Jimbo said, 'Stop! Before you go any further, are you and I speaking?'

'Why, of course we are. Why shouldn't we be?'

'When I received this *severe wound*,' he pointed to the

nasty cut still evident on his forehead, 'you told me you were never speaking to me again.'

'Ah! Well, I was very angry at the time. But I've got something better to do than bear grudges. So give me a kiss. There, that's better. Where's Fran?'

'Just coming. She's making us a pot of tea.'

Rather too eagerly, Grandmama said, 'I'll go and give her a hand. We'll need an extra cup.' She sped into the kitchen, closing the door behind her. 'Fran!' she whispered. 'Why is Liz here?'

'I don't know, Gran. Not even Mum knows. But she's staying the night. She came before we got up this morning. Titus has been here, too.'

'Now he's what I call a lovable chap. Such a sweetheart, even if he has brought that damned market to Turnham Malpas. Have we got everything? The extra cup for me?'

Jimbo went to draw the sitting-room curtains, glancing out before he did so. He saw that Titus's car was outside the pub and Titus appeared to be walking towards Glebe House. Alarm bells rang. 'Liz, Titus is here and he looks as though he's intending to go to your house. Shall we sit tight?'

Liz grabbed the arm of the sofa and made to get up, but sat back down again. 'I can't dare to go back to the house with *him* there. I just can't.'

Grandmama put an arm round her shoulders and said, 'No need. I'll go.' She stood up. 'Come along, Jimbo, we may be needed.'

Jimbo hesitated. 'Look here ... I'm going by myself. If I'm not back in twenty minutes, get Peter to go to the house. Right? Not you, Harriet, nor you, Mother, nor you, Liz. Each one of you girls must stay here. That's an order.'

When Jimbo got to Glebe House he found the front door ajar. He stopped for a moment to catch his breath and to listen. He could hear Titus's quiet voice speaking reasonably, and no sound of Neville's at all. The study door was slightly open, and, so they wouldn't hear his footsteps, he walked carefully along the Persian runner, which went the length of the hall and right to the kitchen doorway. He could only hear snatches of phrases, or the odd word, and decided to stay out of the study and not interfere. Jimbo sat at Liz's kitchen table and waited.

It had all begun with Titus ringing the doorbell and Neville taking a few moments to get to the door. He was verging on being drunk, and when he saw who was standing at the door he reacted so violently that he slipped as he lunged at Titus, and needed a hand to save him from falling full-length out onto the path.

'Steady, Neville, take it steady. Here, let me help you.' Titus grabbed his arm firmly and piloted him back into the hall. 'Study, I think.'

Neville righted himself as they entered the study and, recognizing familiar territory, headed for the safety of his desk chair, although he needed Titus to steer him into it.

'I've come to see you, Neville, on behalf of Liz. What possessed you for heaven's sake? Mmm?'

'What possessed me? What are you talking about? What have I done?'

'Don't pretend you don't know to what I am referring. I'm talking about y-your b-b-behaviour to Liz last night, here in this house.'

People knew. Neville felt an explosion erupt in his head. Possibly the whole village might know about his actions. But if they thought he lacked passion all he'd done was show Liz he didn't. But that wasn't quite right, was it? Self-doubt made the explosion worsen.

For a brief second Neville could have torn his torturer apart, so angry was he that it was the despicable Titus Bellamy who was standing there confronting him.

Casually, almost flippantly, as though last night meant nothing, Neville answered, 'Passion, that's what. Peter came and talked about it, about love and what it means. So I did just that. I showed her passion, I showed her what it means, just as Peter talked about.'

'No, you didn't.'

'I did.'

'That wasn't passion, that wasn't loving. You damn well nearly murdered her!'

'I did not. She is *my wife*.' Neville threw back his head and laughed confidently. 'She won't be gone for long. Oh, no. She'll be back. She can't live on thin air. She can't ignore the money I provide.'

Titus firmly stated in a loud, clear voice, 'She isn't coming back.'

Neville, who'd been confidently swinging his chair from side to side, stopped to glare at Titus. 'You can read her mind, then? I think not. I haven't been married to her for twenty-five years without knowing her mind.' He rubbed his fingers together. 'Money! That's what makes the world go round. And I've got loads of it. She'll be back with her tail between her legs ... begging.' He appeared wholly delighted with the image of Liz penniless.

Titus grew angry. 'I'll say it again. Liz is not coming back. I'm finding her a flat. After what you've done to her she cannot come back. I won't allow it.'

Neville shot up from his chair, rested his hands on the desk and, leaning forward, thundered, '*You* won't allow it? You're not married to her, *I* am. What the hell has it got to do with you? I tell you what – *nothing*. Nothing at all. Get out of my house. Right now!'

When Titus didn't make a move to go, Neville rushed round his desk and squarely faced up to him, fists raised, his face the colour of a beetroot, breathing heavily.

Titus sat down and said nothing. As a pacifist he couldn't measure up and threaten Neville. He had to confront him with stillness, and match anger with gentleness.

It's difficult to threaten a person who is not responding to your anger. There's nothing to hit, nothing to vent your fury on when your opponent simply sits down, shoulders slumped, with his eyes downcast.

By now Jimbo had left the kitchen and was standing in the hall, prepared to step into the breach.

Neville screeched with frustration, 'Stand up like a man and take my challenge. Stand up, you coward. Stand up! Get out of Turnham Malpas and take your damned market with you! Do you hear me? And I want every penny of the money I lent you. *Every single penny!*'

But Titus didn't answer; he remained still and silent, avoiding Neville's eyes. He didn't care about being called a coward; when his principles were at stake he could be extremely stubborn.

There appeared to be an impasse. A heavy silence fell on the study. They were both so completely still they could have been figures in a painting, until Titus spoke, his voice so low he could just be heard.

'You may as well understand, after the terrible things you did to Liz last night, you have only yourself to blame that she's not coming back. It may be that she will allow me to care for her for the rest of her life. If I have that privilege then I shall cherish her and love her as you have never been able to. What you make of your life is up to you. What your sons will think of what you've done to their mother is something I would not like to contemplate. You've years of life left to live. Make the best of them.'

Then Titus stood up and walked out, too overwrought to show surprise at seeing Jimbo standing at the ready in the hall.

After he left, Jimbo watched Neville drop like a stone into his chair, lay his arms on the desk, drop his forehead on them and begin to rend the air with horrifying cries of grief. Sick at heart, Jimbo shut the door behind him and left Neville to his hell.

When he got home it was the least he could do to ring Hugh and Guy to ask them to go to their father's aid.

Chapter 13

No matter what the world has been up to, the sun rises each morning, and so, from first light, did the gossip in Turnham Malpas.

Where was Liz? they all asked themselves. She hadn't been at the nursery on Friday morning and poor Angie Turner had been left to cope, not knowing who to get to help her.

And why did Dr Harris go round to Glebe House at two o'clock in the morning? She was there for half an hour and then returned home. That was the truth because Maggie Dobbs couldn't sleep, had gone downstairs for a cup of hot chocolate to settle her nerves, and had seen her entering the house and about half an hour later leaving it while she, Maggie, was at the kitchen sink washing up her Royal Doulton hot chocolate cup and saucer. She was convinced she'd seen one of Neville and Liz's boys opening the door for her, but in the dark and not knowing them very well and them being so alike – like twins, they were – she couldn't honestly say.

The coffee morning in aid of the Scouts opened at ten-thirty, so those who hadn't heard the latest spent the first half of it craving whatever news they could pick up, and those who knew begged anyone they saw for more recent information. The most annoying bit was that Grandmama appeared to know the whole story but refused to tell. She never let on that rather infuriatingly for her she didn't know anything at all, but she made herself look as though she did. Grandmama longed for an update about last night, because Jimbo, when he got back from Glebe House, had closeted himself in his study ringing, *he said*, Hugh and Guy Neal, and when he came out he didn't explain, so in the end she'd gone home none the wiser. He could be, quite annoyingly, like his father sometimes, able to keep a poker face that gave nothing away. Nevertheless, she had a long morning ahead of her so there was hope yet. When she saw Caroline she called out, 'Caroline! My dear, what would you like? This apple cake was made by Greta Jones, this nutty thing by Evie Nicholls – heaven alone knows what's in it, though – and this was given by Miss Parkin. These fairy cakes were made by Sylvia, so you don't need me to tell you how delicious they'll be. This flapjack was given us by Kate Fitch; apparently it's a speciality of hers. Well, according to Old Fitch, who delivered it personally at some ungodly hour this morning.'

Caroline contemplated the cake stall, but she was too tired to make a choice. It wasn't just the half-hour she'd spent attending to Neville, it was the length of time she then spent answering Peter's questions and trying to get back to sleep again. She'd really no business dispensing sleeping tablets to all and sundry when they weren't her patients, but what could one do? Hugh and Guy had called her saying their Father was in desperate need.

They'd finally got him into bed, clothes off, pyjamas on, rambling and raving pathetically, begging for help. He clung to his sons, asking them to fetch their mother, which of course they wouldn't do. Then they'd got the tablets down him and gradually he became calm, closed his eyes and slept. Hugh and Guy had looked shattered. What help could she give them? There was so little one could say. Platitudes had no place in this situation, only plain, honest truthfulness.

'My advice, for what it's worth,' she had said, 'is someone must be here when he wakes up, because he'll feel appalling. By the look of the house something absolutely traumatic has taken place and he'll be in need of support.'

She hadn't been told what had happened, but she'd taken a guess, and felt unpleasantly sweaty and unclean at the thought of it. Poor Liz.

'Thank you, Doctor Harris, for coming. We'd no right to ask, but we didn't know what to do.' Hugh looked to be in shock, and no wonder, thought Caroline. Of Liz there was not a sign, but she had to ask. 'Your mother, does she need me to attend to her?'

'She says no ... thank you.'

Trying hard to cut through her muddled thoughts and concentrate on the cake stall, now Caroline heard Grandmama asking rather sharply, 'Have you decided?'

'I'll take the flapjack, the whole lot, please. How much is that?'

'All of it? There's rather a lot. Are you sure?'

'I'm sure.'

'Well, it comes to six pounds fifty. But I'm not having you paying that, it's far too much, so I'll give you a discount. Let's call it five pounds for quantity. All right?'

Caroline looked at her and said, 'No, it's for the church, so I'll pay full whack.' She looked as though she were about to say something else, and Grandmama paused helpfully, but in the end Caroline gave her the money, thanked her and went away. So she was still no wiser.

Then she spotted Peter coming in, looking first, as he always did, to see where Caroline was. He went across to where she was sitting.

'There you are, darling. Shall I get you a coffee?'

Caroline nodded her thanks.

'Caffè latte, cappuccino or ordinary?'

She looked up at him and was grateful for the love in his eyes. 'Whatever you're having.'

She felt so lucky, after what she'd guessed about Neville and Liz. She tried hard not to loathe Neville because she shouldn't ... but she did.

When Peter came back with their coffees, after numerous stops on the way to talk to people, she said, 'They're all wanting to know what happened.'

'We don't really know anything, do we? Except I feel responsible. I should never have said what I said. The man was too distraught to take any reasonable notice of my advice.'

'Hush! Walls have ears.'

Peter sat thinking for a moment and then added, 'When I've drunk this I'm going round there.'

'Are you sure that's a good idea? Hugh and Guy stayed the night, so he's got someone with him.'

The church hall was filling up and the buzz of conversation was mounting.

Peter left the church hall and walked up to Glebe House. Waiting for someone to answer the doorbell, he stood idly examining Neville's front garden. It was like a garden entered for an international competition. Not a stone or a weed to be seen; every plant and bush neatly manicured; everything behaving well. But at the same time somehow ... barren, which was ridiculous because it was filled with plants. But there was none of the tumbling luxuriousness of Caroline's garden, every plant thrusting for all available space.

His reverie was broken by the door opening. It was Hugh looking strained. 'Come in, sir. Please.'

'Your dad, how is he this morning? Caroline told me, you see, so I thought I'd better come.'

'Guy's taken him to our flat in Culworth. He's staying with us for a while. I've seen Mother this morning. She's going to the flat Titus has found, so that is that. Mother and Dad have separated for ever.' Wryly Hugh added, 'It's surprising how it hurts considering Guy and I are supposed to be grown-ups. But we can both see how good Titus is for her, and we're glad she's found someone to look after her. They're a good match.'

'But your dad, what's he going to do?'

'We don't know yet. Too early to tell. Thanks for your help, by the way. He said you'd been.'

Peter shook his head. 'I don't think I helped at all. I think I aggravated the situation, telling him about what loving someone means and not sensing just how stressed he was. I'm sorry about that.'

'It was inevitable. My mother's been unhappy for a long time. He'll come back here eventually. He just needs time away from everything. We'll attend to everything he's been involved in, with the church and such.'

'And the business?'

But Hugh clammed up then, became tight-lipped and uncommunicative, and Peter saw it was time he left.

'I'm just tidying up and collecting some clothes for him, and then it's a case of wait and see.'

'I won't delay you, then. Give him my best regards, and tell him he can call on me anytime. I'm here to help.'

They shook hands, and Hugh closed the door.

Once everyone realized that there was nothing new to pass on about the Big Neville Neal Mystery, the Anti-Market Action Committee set about organizing everyone for the protest the following Thursday. Willie had come up with the idea that a petition would be a good idea. He'd asked Sheila if he could borrow her clipboard and harried everyone at the coffee morning to sign his petition.

Curiously there were lots of people from Little Derehams and Penny Fawcett also present, as though by some uncanny bush telegraph they all knew something was brewing in Turnham Malpas. So Willie got lots of names on his list but also lots of rebuffs, as many of them didn't want the market to close. In fact, it almost came to blows when Willie told someone who'd rudely refused to sign that if he actually lived in Turnham Malpas he'd be signing in quick sticks. Then it did come to blows when he asked for the third time, just to be annoying, a big chap from Penny Fawcett known as Masher Murdoch, whom everyone made certain not to annoy – Willie got thumped in the eye for being aggravating.

Sylvia rushed out from behind the bric-a-brac, Evie from behind her embroidery knick-knacks stall, and between them, they gave a piece of their minds to Masher, who'd struck Willie so forcibly. Masher apologized, confused by the double attack, and hastened when Evie said, 'And on church premises, too. You ought to be ashamed of yourself.' It didn't help Willie's pain, though, and Caroline was called upon to administer medical help.

Caroline tenderly suggested it looked serious. 'Do you know, Willie, I think you'd better go to A&E.'

Willie, who hated hospitals with a virulent passion,

shuddered and refused to go. 'It'll be better when the bruising comes out. I'm not going.'

Caroline argued that she thought he'd cracked his cheekbone. 'It needs looking at. It must have been one heck of a blow.'

Sylvia backed this up. 'It was an almighty punch, believe me.'

'It was, but I'm still not going.' He held a handkerchief to his eye and walked off, his head beginning to spin.

When they got home Sylvia made an icepack from cubes of ice enclosed inside a freezer bag, and applied it to the bruising. He grumbled and moaned all the time, but by four o'clock that afternoon the pain was so bad he was begging Jimmy Glover to give him a lift to the hospital.

As they sat in the back of Jimmy's taxi holding hands, Sylvia said to Willie, 'This knocks you off the list for the protest on Thursday.'

'It does not. I shall be there manning the barricades.'

'You will not. If I have to tie you to the bed, you're not going. When you know Masher used to do bare-knuckle boxing, why did you ask him to sign the petition *three* times?'

'Bravado, I expect. I shall be there on Thursday, though.'

But his resolve weakened when the triage nurse took his homemade bandage off and gently pressed the big black and blue swelling which used to be his good eye. The other eye was waiting for a cataract operation.

On the Wednesday night there was a final meeting of the Anti-Market Action Committee in the Royal Oak, with Willie in the chair. Newly out of hospital, he had had his cheekbone set and, despite feeling distinctly odd and needing Sylvia to read his notes, he was fully prepared to whip up enthusiasm. By the time he'd finished his opening speech they were all right behind him. It was, thought Greta Jones, as she watched Willie bang on the table and raise a clenched fist in his passion, almost like that rallying cry by that king at Agincourt. What was his name? Willie spurred them on with talk of ridding the village of the market – and Titus Bellamy. 'Look at the damage he's caused!' He lowered his voice and said, 'And all this business with Neville and Liz Neal would never have happened but for him. Let's get rid of him, I say!'

A dissident muttered from the furthest table, 'It would have happened anyway with or without Titus. Who'd want to be married to that cold fish? No wonder she looked elsewhere.'

The meeting was abruptly brought to the verge of turning into fruity gossip about Liz and Neville, but Willie caught up his rallying cry once again and all was saved. The upshot of the meeting was an increased enthusiasm for getting rid of the market and a conviction that their plan of action would succeed.

As Vince Jones and his Greta walked home arm in arm, Greta suddenly said, 'It was Henry the Fifth! Of course!'

Vince, steering her away from tripping over the edge of a new footpath round the wall by the school, said, 'You do witter on. Henry the Fifth, what's he got to do with anything?'

'Willie's speech, it was just like his. Old Mr Browning, you remember him, he did it with us the year we were fourteen and leaving school. He went on and on about patriotism and such. Brilliant, he was. That's how Willie was tonight. I say, that black eye after the operation looks bloomin' painful, doesn't it?'

'That'll teach him to mess with Masher Murdoch. I understand Old Fitch wants the market to stay. Says it's a good thing for the village.'

Secretly Greta was half-inclined to agree, but having nailed her colours to the mast she didn't want to give in now.

They had cocoa and went to bed, setting the alarm for 5.15 a.m., so they had time for breakfast before they left for the protest.

Thursday morning saw a host of villagers preparing themselves just after first light. Dressed in their gardening clothes, they carried bottles of water, some food, their placards and, above all, stout hearts. As planned, they organized three cars to block the Culworth Road, after letting Malcolm through with his milk float. The bin men they could ignore, for they were lucky if they turned up before three o'clock. But they had genuinely forgotten that a major part of Jimbo's deliveries were due in the village by nine o'clock.

Colin Turner had the bright idea of blocking the car park with some great lumps of concrete he'd found discarded by the side of Royal Oak Road. He'd placed them at dead of night so no one could object to his bright idea.

Just after 6 a.m. the first big van trundled along the Culworth Road and drew up in surprise.

Leaning out of the cab, the driver shouted, 'What's up?' It was the stallholder who sold the meat. 'It's market day, I want to get through.'

'Sorry,' shouted Willie Biggs, 'the road's blocked.'

'I can see that, but I bet you can't with an eye like that. Who hit yer? An angry van driver like me?' He roared with laughter, and a few of the protesters had to smother their grins. 'Just a little space will do. I can easily squeeze past down this left-hand side. My van's not as big as it looks. A free piece of best steak for anyone who 'elps to move this ramshackle car that's blocking my way. A foot'll do it.'

But with Willie at the helm not even the promise of a piece of best steak would make them move. The butcher used some rather coarse language but cheered up when the greengrocer arrived with a screech of brakes and an angry fist.

'What's all this, then? I thought you liked us coming.'

'No, we don't,' shouted Willie, waving his arm to indicate how steadfast everyone was.

The greengrocer got out and held a whispered conversation with the butcher, by standing on the van step and reaching his head almost inside the cab. Without another word the two of them managed to reverse out of their predicament and trundle off.

The protesters cheered, thinking they'd won the day. But ten minutes later they heard a shout of triumph and saw the meat van and the greengrocery lorry gliding triumphantly alongside the village green followed by several other vehicles. Each of them had caught up pieces of bushes and plants from the gardens and fences they'd driven over in their determination not to be defeated. One in particular had a whole lupin, torn up by its roots, sticking out from a wheel arch. It had never occurred to the protesters that anyone with anything bigger than a bicycle could possibly squeeze down Royal Oak Road, and they were livid at their disregard of its possibilities.

Vince Jones, already regretting his enthusiasm at the

meeting last night, threw down his hat and jumped on it. 'How the blazes 'ave they got along that narrow road?'

Ron Bissett added, 'They must have driven onto people's gardens. No other way. And what about that bad corner everyone complains about, where Granny Stacker lives?'

Maggie Dobbs swore the lorry must have been spirited through. 'Bet old Granny Stacker's been out waving her stick at 'em.'

'She'd be fast asleep.'

'Not her. She reckons she's past needing sleep.' Maggie packed her breakfast back into her holdall saying, 'Well, might as well eat this lot at home,' and left the field of battle, thoroughly disheartened.

Vince was so angry he hauled a can of beer out of Greta's goodie bag, flicked the opener and began drinking.

'Vince! At this time in the morning! Take our car down there and block Royal Oak Road as well.' But even as she shouted Greta saw another stream of vehicles had found their way down it and were now pouring into Stocks Row, and everyone had to admit that their foolproof scheme was a dismal failure.

Willie hid tears of frustration behind his handkerchief. His eye hurt like hell and he felt ridiculous into the bargain. What a waste of effort. All the flyers and the posters and the boards they'd made! They'd been rousted, trounced, beaten – nay, woefully beaten – and Willie felt humiliated. So much for his magnificent victory. And Greta Jones thought about Henry the Fifth and was glad that at least *he* hadn't been beaten after he'd roused his troops.

★

Disconsolately they wandered home, hiding their placards as best they could. Expecting jeers from the stallholders who were now briskly setting up, they got nothing except embarrassed or sympathetic looks as they went by. That came as some measure of relief, but Willie hadn't finished fighting yet, and went home scheming how he could get the better of them all, including Titus Bellamy. He was surprised to hear a knock at his door about half an hour after they'd arrived home. And there he stood, the man of the hour. Titus.

Sylvia was all for keeping him out, but Willie wouldn't have it. 'Let him in, Sylvia, and put the kettle on.' When she didn't look as though she would do as he asked, he added, 'Please.'

So there they were with Titus Bellamy, the man of peace, seated in their small living room drinking tea and eating thick slices of homemade bread, toasted and buttered and topped with a generous portion of Willie's home-produced honey. There was a silence while the sticky part of their impromptu breakfast was passed, and neither Sylvia nor Willie chose to speak.

Titus wiped his hands on his napkin and said, 'In one way I'm glad you didn't manage to stop the market this morning. It's the joy of my heart, is this market here in Turnham Malpas. Not one of my other markets thrived so well in the early weeks, and none of them is as success-ful as this one is going to be. It would be an awful pity if I had to close it.'

The pain in his eye and the early hour of his rising caused Willie's bile to rise. 'We don't want your damned market here, not a single one of us wants it. You're a nuisance, a damn blasted nuisance, and we want you gone. So pack up this morning and just ... *go*.'

Titus's face grew sad and he asked gently, '*No one* wants my market, then?'

Willie had to pause and decide between exaggerating, and thereby telling lies, or being truthful.

'Jimbo, perhaps, with his gateaux, or Evie with her wools? Or Jimmy with his taxi bringing people in from Culworth?' Titus spoke quite gently to Willie, not wishing to hurt him any more than he had been by his magnificent protest scheme collapsing about his ears. 'Or old Mr Stubbs from the Big House taking the money at the car park entrance?'

'Well, that's another load of bother we could well have done without. His daughter Pat was adamant he shouldn't do it because of her being Jimbo's group catering manager but he insisted. Wanted something to do instead of sitting home feeling useless. He finds it a right chuckle despite his arthritis. They had endless rows about it. But it's the beggars that come from outside on their bikes, and those thieves – they're the main problem. We're not used to it in our village. Never had no reason to lock our doors and our windows on a summer's day before. Now we do, for fear, yer know. It's not right.'

'Can I let you into a secret? Just between you and me, Mr Fitch has had a discussion with the police and there are going to be extra officers in the village on Thursday mornings for a few weeks, proper police officers and some of those community police. I don't know how he's managed it but he has. I tried and got nowhere at all. He rings up a few people and before we know it the place is swarming. The magic of knowing the right people.'

Willie grunted. 'You're naive. It's not so much knowing the right people, it's his *money*. A donation to the

Police Benevolent Fund and hey presto! The magic has been worked.'

Titus smiled at Sylvia. 'If we get our own way, who cares? At least someone benefits, and what more admirable cause than police orphans? Mmm?'

'*I* care.' Sylvia made herself sit bolt upright before she boldly remarked, 'I don't specially want a market here in Turnham Malpas. Causes too much upset, so it's no good coming here with your quiet persuading talk. I'm not taken in with it, even if Liz Neal is.' That last phrase sprang out of her mouth before she knew it, and she wished she hadn't said it, then she decided it had needed saying.

Titus sat back in his chair. 'Ah! Liz. My dear Liz. I wondered when someone would bring her name up.'

'It needs bringing up. I mean, where is she? Not at Glebe House, that's obvious. Is she dead? We know about murder in this village, you know, we've been through it twice in the last twelve years. It's very upsetting. Sharon from the Royal Oak, and poor Jenny Sweetapple only last year. So where is Liz?'

'Liz has moved out because of Neville, not because of me.'

Sylvia's eyebrows were raised and he knew she didn't believe him. But there was no way she could be told the truth.

'I've taken her to a place of safety, and that's all I can say. She's doing the nursery still, so please, if you see her, don't question her, because she's suffering so much over the matter. And if anyone wants to know, we're not living together, much as we'd like to.'

Sylvia blushed with embarrassment. She hadn't meant for Titus to say that, her being eternally conscious of when she and Willie had lived together for a few months before they married.

'I'm sorry.'

Titus shook his head. 'Don't be. You see, we love each other, and it breaks my heart that it's all such a terrible mess. Now, Willie,' Titus stood up, 'I've kept you long enough. I reckon a couple of aspirins and a lie-down would do you good. Thanks for the tea and toast, Sylvia. I might make a habit of it. It was delicious. I'll see myself out.' He shook their hands and quietly drifted away, leaving behind a strange, almost disconcerting silence.

Sylvia put a glass of water and two aspirin on the table beside Willie. She said dreamily, 'It's as if he's never been, he's so gentle. Like a spirit that comes to earth but only now and then.'

The pain of Willie's eye didn't allow him to feel such sentimental thoughts, and he roughly declared she'd better not talk about Titus like that. 'Don't be daft! Next you'll be saying he's Jesus come down to earth.'

Sylvia was angry. 'For goodness' sake, I will not. He's not *that* pure, at least where Liz is concerned. I wonder what *has* happened there, with Neville.'

'I'm off to bed. Remember, what he said here,' pointing an angry finger at their new hearth rug, 'was private. Don't go spreading it about.'

'Do I ever?'

Thoughtlessly Sylvia volunteered that she might have a look round the market while Willie had a sleep.

Willie's headache had grown worse and he only managed a grunt as he climbed the stairs. If he'd felt better she'd have had the sharp edge of his tongue. Going round the market indeed. Such disloyalty. Willie fell asleep only after he'd ruminated for ten minutes about the morning's fiasco. It was so shaming, them finding a way down Royal Oak Road. He'd go and have a look to see how much damage they really had caused to people's gardens and fences. Then he fell deeply asleep, missing all the excitement of yet another tumultuous morning in the market.

Chapter 14

Many of the customers in the market hadn't heard about Willie's momentous effort to stop the stallholders getting into Turnham Malpas. So far as they were concerned, everyone was in their place and their stalls open for business at eight-thirty as expected. What they hadn't noticed were two cyclists with large backpacks cycling by merrily, *innocently*, drawing no attention to themselves. They propped their bikes up in Dicky's bicycle rack and wandered away, looking for all the world as though they were sightseeing, which, in a way, they most certainly were.

The cyclists slipped down behind the school, crossed Church Lane and came to the front of Glebe House.

'Are we doing the right thing? Coming 'ere this morning when it's so busy?'

'Yes! This is the time to steal when there's so many people about. Or'nary day and we'd stick out like sore thumbs. They'd all remember us.'

This Glebe House looked an enticing prospect, so they turned sharp left on to the side path and down the side of the house. One of them linked his hands while the other put a foot on them and then sprang over the side gate, landing athletically in the back garden. He silently unlatched the gate and his companion followed him in.

They found the kitchen window still slightly open, as it had been when Jimbo and Titus gained entry that dreadful night.

What an amazing stroke of luck! Their technique was to take some things of value but not all, which meant that often the owners didn't realize for weeks that valuable items had been stolen. Small but good was their motto. Not for them big bronze statuettes, or large paintings; they were all too bulky, too noticeable. So they raided the safe, which, to experienced thieves, was easy enough to open. It didn't take long to find the key – they knew every conceivable place people chose for their safe keys – and removed Liz's jewellery, which included the twenty-fifth anniversary diamonds, a gold necklace, a string of pearls and some good costume jewellery, just right for their purpose. Then they closed everything up as though the safe had never been touched. Experience taught them that one minute spent closing a cupboard or a drawer – or, in this case, a safe – and putting the key back where it belonged, delayed the discovery of the theft. They moved on to small ornaments, to the antique carriage clock, the silver cigarette box and the antique solid silver grape scissors. Then they looked at each other and acknowledged they'd got enough.

Moving next door, to Miss Parkin's they got the back door open, but as soon as they surveyed the kitchen and the sitting room they shook their heads, knowing through experience they'd find nothing in this cottage. They also drew a blank next door at Bel Tutt's.

Eddie, who was a lapsed religious fanatic, never ever stole from a church on principle, fearing heavenly retribution of some unmentionable kind, so they bypassed the Church by walking down the back, past the little wicket gate in the back wall, behind the church hall and then on to Willie Biggs's house.

Sylvia had gone, as she'd said she would, to walk round the market, and Willie was upstairs sleeping as he hadn't slept since Masher Murphy thumped his eye.

The back door was unlocked, so they just wandered in. But there wasn't much to choose in this little cottage – just an old 22-carat gold gentleman's watch, which had belonged to Willie's granddad, in its velvet pocket in the sideboard drawer, and a lovely solid silver locket belonging to Sylvia's great-granny, kept wrapped in a silk handkerchief in the same drawer and never worn. It would be a while before they realized they'd been burgled.

The next house in the row was the Rectory, and again there appeared to be no one at home, so they carefully prised the back door open and wandered in, automatically listening for sounds of occupation just in case they were mistaken.

But when Eddie saw Peter's study and the rough-hewn wooden cross on the wall by his desk, he shuddered. 'No! Out. Go on, out. Don't touch a thing. He's a vicar or a bishop or somefink. Hell fire! Get out quick.'

Eddie raced out through the back door, vaulted the back gate and squatted down with his back up against the stone wall in Pipe and Nook Lane, sweating with fear.

Tone, his mate, followed him closely, his backpack, badly strapped on, banging against his kidneys as he ran. When he got his breath back he said sharply, 'You're enough to scare the living daylights out of me. You're a fool. I could tell that was a place for goodies, ornaments and that. There'd have been rich pickings there and not half. Anyway, you got your breath back?' Eddie nodded. 'Right then, we'll stroll nonchalan' like to our bikes and hop it. With you in this state, anything could happen.'

So they stood up, dusted off the seats of their trousers and endeavoured to look casual.

Perhaps they made themselves too obvious and tried too hard to blend into the crowds milling about in the road by the Royal Oak, but Mac (on duty for market day) took one look at them and their backpacks and quietly followed them.

Eddie, growing more nervy and furtive by the minute, turned his head to see if they were being followed and spotted Sergeant Mac taking a lot of interest in them. He took a flying leap for his bike, wobbled a bit, got his balance, and then began pedalling away like mad. Tone, not quite so quick, also took a flying leap but missed and fell in the road. Then he picked himself up, got back on the bike just as Sergeant Mac's hand was within a whisker of grabbing his saddle.

'Stop!' bellowed Sergeant Mac.

But he was too late. The pair of them had disappeared at some considerable speed down the Culworth Road.

A hue and cry grew, but it was all to no good. Sergeant Mac was fuming.

'Who was it?' a helpful member of the public asked. 'Someone you knew? What've they done?'

'I don't know, but they were up to no good.' Sergeant Mac swore under his breath. Damn and blast, he thought. Of course, they'd chosen the right day for thieving, with everyone so busy and the village so noisy, no one giving a thought to their homes. He was sure they had been thieving. After twenty years in the Force he could almost smell thieves, and they smelt. He decided to ring to Culworth Station, provide a description, and tell them to keep their eyes open. Especially around Mervyn's pawn shop. They'd probably go straight there to get rid of whatever they'd stolen if his hunch was right.

Of course, the suggestion that burglars were in the area spread like wildfire, and more than one sped home to check, including Sylvia. As she dashed down Church Lane she tried to remember if she'd locked their front door. Had she? Or not? But the front door was locked. She had.

She crept in so as not to wake Willie and, to her relief, saw that not a thing had been disturbed. Even the aspirin packet and the empty glass were still there on the table. Not a drawer was opened, nor a chair out of place. She checked that her EPNS milk jug and sugar basin belonging to her mother were still there in the china cabinet. Yes, they were. Then she went in the kitchen and decided to open the back door to let some fresh air in and found it unlocked. Drat it!

Sylvia decided she wouldn't worry Willie when he wasn't well. Obviously no one had been in, because nothing was disturbed. Anyway, she'd only been gone half an hour.

The police in Culworth were at pains to catch the thieves, but Mervyn's shop, though watched throughout the day, yielded nothing.

There was an altercation going on by the butcher's van. Masher Murphy, dispatched by Mrs Murphy to get some steak for his supper, was challenging the butcher about the freshness of his meat.

'I reckon this in't fresh. More like last week's meat masquerading as this week's.'

'Are you questioning the freshness of my meat? I tell you, it's the best in the county. Fresh as fresh, it is. You smell it.'

'It's a very funny colour for fresh meat, is that. Not even fresh enough for my mastiff. I should have brought him along to test it, but he'd turn his nose up at it.'

The butcher, already upset by the struggle to get onto the green in the first place, couldn't take any more of Masher's lip. Not knowing his history, the butcher, from inside the van, leaned over his meat display, shoved Masher on his shoulder and shouted, 'I wouldn't sell meat to you if I had a van full and you were my only customer!'

He immediately regretted it.

For Masher, who had a long reach, returned the push. The butcher, Bryan, reciprocated with all his strength, except this time he almost shot head first out of the van, and finished up lying on his meat display. Masher laughed loudly and long, but hadn't bargained on Bryan's tough edge. He gathered his resources, pulled himself up from his meat display, pushed past his wife, who'd begun screaming and couldn't stop, and raced out of the van. Then he tripped on the top step and fell out onto the green, catching the back of his head on the bottom step as he fell. Blood poured out of the cut and he sat moaning on the ground with the blood sheeting down the back of his T-shirt. His wife, our Bet, screamed, climbed over her husband and rushed around the van to accost Masher. He was 6ft 2in and big with it; she was 5ft 1in and built like a doll. She pounded him with her fists and, being at heart a gentleman, Masher didn't even try to push her away, but stood like a statue taking her punches, laughing like a drain. Soon she ran out of energy, so Masher picked her up and carried her to the meat van door, stood her on her feet, patted her head and walked away.

This didn't solve the butcher's plight: he was still seriously covered in blood. Jimbo rang for an ambulance, and suddenly what had been a laugh turned into an incident. Sergeant Mac took out his notebook and made a note. Masher declared the butcher had struck him first and that he was acting in self-defence. A witness, namely Jimbo, agreed Masher was quite right.

'Full name?'

'Declan Ignatius Murphy. Number seven, Bracken Drove, Penny Fawcett. Aged fifty-nine.'

Mac took his telephone number and promised to be in touch.

'See,' said everyone, 'we *do* need to get rid of this dratted market.'

Titus had had a worrying time that morning. One extra stallholder had turned up and there was no space for him; the rest of the stallholders were angry about the Culworth Road being blocked off and how hazardous it had been getting through the narrow Royal Oak Road – little more than a cart track, they declared, and what was he doing about it? And then the fight. Poor old Bryan had been carted off to A&E. Our Bet was really upset.

Titus eventually escaped to the village hall to meet Liz after nursery.

His heart lifted the moment he saw her. There was a hint of her beginning to look like her usual happy self and his worries about the market fell away.

'Liz! My darling.' There being no one else in the hall, Titus hugged her and kissed her cheek.

'Titus, you've had an exciting time, haven't you? I've been hearing all about it from the mothers.'

'Devastating, but it's all gone away now I'm with you.' He held her close and felt all the familiar feelings for her rising in his heart. She was the best antidote for trouble anyone could hope to have. He just wished he could hold her and share a bed with her every day of his life. But she'd said no most emphatically, and he had to abide by that. 'Any news on the Neville front?' He didn't really want to know but at the same time he did.

Liz stood back from him. 'He's at Hugh and Guy's flat. Still not going out. Still not been to the office. Still refusing to mention my name. But he's eating and sleeping, conducting proper conversations and answering questions about the business. So I suppose that's all a plus.' Liz smiled brightly at him. 'Let's go to the Wise Man for lunch.'

'Great. I need to bank the money while we're out, so that means popping into Culworth, OK?'

'Of course.' Liz finished locking the nursery cupboards, put the dustpan and brush back in the kitchen, gave a last check of the room, picked up her bag and took out the key to the main door. Titus watched her movements, every one so precise, so elegant. She moved, he thought, almost like a ballet dancer, smoothly and with poise, and she was always so attractively dressed. He was so lucky to have met her. So lucky. He adored her in a way he had imagined he would never adore another woman after Marie. She, Marie Margaret Bellamy, had filled his heart and his mind, and now he was experiencing that same uplifting joy with Liz.

Finally they were both standing outside with nothing to do but get their lunch. Liz gave him a wonderful smile and Titus felt his heart lurch. He would have loved to kiss her there and then, but they'd both decided not to give any demonstrations of affection in public – there was already enough gossip about them – although he could see in her eyes the promise of a kiss, and his heart thudded.

The Wise Man was almost too busy for people in love

and they ate quickly, glad to escape to the solitude of Liz's car. Before she turned the ignition key she kissed him. A long, savouring kiss that excited them both. 'I really intended to go home – Glebe House, that is – to get some more clothes and bits and pieces, but I can't get in without asking Neville for the key.'

'Don't fret. I can climb in through the kitchen window as I did before.'

'Ah! I'd forgotten that. I won't linger. I don't *want* to linger. In fact, I don't want to go at all but I must. I want nothing of me to remain in that house.'

'We'll park in Pipe and Nook and go in through the back garden. The fewer people who know what you're doing the better. Then I'll pick my car up and we can go our separate ways.'

'Of course, yes. I've got some big carriers in the boot.'

'Let's go, then.' Titus stroked her hand, which rested on the gear-stick. She released her hold and let him take her hand to his lips and kiss it. 'Love you very much indeed.'

'Snap.' Liz laughed and then said, 'Turnham Malpas, here we come!'

Titus managed to reach the bolt on the garden side of the fence. It opened easily and the two of them were soon in the back garden, with Liz's car parked in the road. Titus squeezed through the kitchen window again, and opened the back door for her. To Liz it felt odd, very odd, this house that was no longer her home. It was tidy – obviously the boys had been in and cleared up the mess Neville had made in his roaring temper – but Liz felt quite peculiar walking up the stairs that had been hers for so long. Her foot crunched on something, which stuck into the sole of her sandal. She stopped to get it off and found it was a small piece of the mobile phone Neville had smashed. It touched her heart more than she had expected, perhaps because she'd loved using that particular mobile. The sparkling red casing had made it feel so up to the minute, so very much hers.

Damn Neville. Damn him. How could he have done what he did to her, with such cruelty and vicious, systematic violence? Her insides stung painfully at the memory. To have had those wonderful couple of hours with Titus earlier in the evening and then to have the memory of them totally scrubbed out by Neville's supposed passion was soul-destroying. She'd get her things, every piece of clothing out of every drawer, every cupboard. She'd rid herself of him *for ever*. Divorce. The whole thing. Everything.

Titus shouted up the stairs, 'I'll bring the bags down when you're ready.' Then he went to sit out in the garden to enjoy some peace, so he didn't hear Neville parking his car in the drive and opening the front door.

One day, Neville thought as he got his key out of his pocket, he'd have to come back to live here, and he found he didn't relish the thought. But he would. He'd make himself come back to live in it, like a normal human being. Key in lock, door shut softly as always, and into his study. The familiar comfort of this room that was so much his own made him feel he could have stayed and not gone back to the boys' flat. But when he thought about it Neville shuddered. This big house was so full of memories ... No, he couldn't, not all by himself. He'd get his clothes, as he'd intended, and go back to the flat. It was safer there, with no memories. Neither good nor bad.

Then his head jerked up. Had he heard a noise? Was Liz in the house? He trembled with shame at the thought. No, of course not. Just the house creaking. But then he heard it again. In the kitchen? The kitchen window overlooked the garden, and he saw ... Titus ... comfortably ensconced in one of their smart garden chairs, for all the world as though he lived there. His scalp prickled with alarm. Surely he hadn't moved in? How *could* they? He'd changed the locks. That devil, though, with his quiet ways, his gentle manner, he could do anything. Upstairs creaked again. Footsteps – footsteps he recognized. Liz's rapid steps criss-crossing their bedroom floor.

He crept up the stairs, one foot placed carefully after the other, crossed the landing, remembering to avoid that creaking floorboard – he'd kept intending to have that screwed down – and there she was. He stood in the open doorway, watching her. She had her back to him emptying her wardrobe, putting clothes into huge smart bags from the fashion boutiques she patronized. Neville's top lip began to curl. Titus wouldn't be able to afford those clothes. She was worth it, though – she always looked so good. Just as she did now, classy and smart.

He stood admiring her even now. Was it only admiration? Or was it ... love? Why had he never acknowledged that word? The more he watched her moving about, the more the idea came to him that he'd smothered all the good feelings he'd ever possessed in his desperate need for recognition, for power, for money, for success. And he knew now that he'd thrown away that good side of himself in one crazy, devastating night of what he'd called passion.

For her to see him there so close to ... where it had all happened would terrify her all over again. She'd faced enough of him that night, she wouldn't be able to take any more. Best to leave without her knowing he'd been watching her, because he knew he was being sly, watching her so covertly. Far away at the back of his mind he thought about Peter's concept of love and wished he possessed it. The beat of your heart?

Neville crept quietly down the stairs, silently unlatched the front door and went out, shutting it behind him. Then he drove away. He'd collect the rest of his clothes another day.

Titus came into the house, needing to get away, because even in the garden he could feel Neville's presence. He called up the stairs, 'Are you ready to leave, Liz?'

She answered him emphatically. 'Yes.'

Chapter 15

The following morning, when Liz went to open up the nursery, she found a sealed envelope, addressed to her, pinned to the church hall door. She recognized the handwriting. It was Caroline's, and the note was asking her to call for a cup of tea that afternoon if she was free. She'd be home about three. A talk with a close friend was just what Liz needed.

The afternoon was quite mild after a week of changeable weather so they sat in the garden as they had done that last time at the beginning of her troubles. That seemed months ago, yet it wasn't. Caroline had somehow found time to bake biscuits, and what with the china tea set covered in a spring flower design and the stunning garden full of flowers, Liz decided to enjoy herself for a short while.

'I'm in love, you know. First time ever.'

'Well! That's an outstanding opening sentence. I'm glad to hear it.' Caroline smiled. 'With whom, might I ask?'

'Titus Bellamy, of course. Who else?'

'Oh! I see. I saw Neville's car outside your house yesterday afternoon ... and I kind of wondered.'

Liz sat bolt upright, shocked. 'Yesterday afternoon? What time?'

'Let me see. That tea OK? Not too strong? About half

215

past two. I was coming home from the practice. Yes, about half past two.'

Liz felt terribly sick. Neville must have been in the house when ... 'Was he sitting in the car?'

'No one was in the car. Why? Liz, are you all right? You look quite strange.'

'If you knew what that man did to me that night you wouldn't even ponder if he and I had got together again. No, we haven't, and we never will. I shall never get over it.' Liz spoke with her teeth clamped together as though still in pain.

'I'm so sorry. I was thoughtless.'

Caroline's lovely, compassionate face spoke volumes to Liz, and she almost began to tell her something of what she had suffered, but clawed it back just in time. 'I think you must be wrong because Titus and I were in the house about then. I was collecting every single piece of clothing I own, every single piece. It's all over, and I'm suing for divorce.'

'Oh! Well, perhaps I've got the time wrong. Yes, it probably was later than that because I'd called in the Store for a few things.' Caroline hurriedly changed the subject by asking Liz what her flat was like.

Liz didn't answer her immediately. Instead she took one of the biscuits and had eaten half of it before she replied, 'Have you asked me here to ply me with questions? Find out what you can? Get to know the nitty-gritty? Is that it?'

Caroline was stunned by her attack. 'You know me better than that! I just thought you had no one to talk to, and that it might help. I'm sorry.'

Liz burst into tears. She'd no tissue with her, so Caroline

passed her one. Liz muttered through her tears, 'I'm so sorry.'

'No, it's me who should be sorry. You have a good cry if you want. I don't mind.'

So they sat together in the pale sun amidst the beauty of Caroline's garden silently endeavouring to make friends again. Gradually the tears ceased, and Liz blew her nose and felt better.

'It's all been so awful,' she said eventually. 'The only thing I have to hold on to is Titus and how much he loves me. Then in the night I panic because how can he love me as he says he does in such a short space of time? How is it possible? It isn't sensible, now, is it?'

'*You* fell in love with *him* in the same space of time, though.'

Liz wiped her eyes, caught Caroline smiling gently at her and began to laugh. 'You're right. Absolutely right. Oh, dear. I never thought of it like that. What it is to have a friend with common sense!'

'Peter and I felt like that when we met. He had this appalling cold and sore throat, looked about ninety-five years old, and had come to the surgery for medical help. We fell in love immediately, but neither of us would admit to it because we both thought it couldn't possibly have happened. But it had.'

Peter, who had dashed home for an afternoon cup of tea before sick visiting in Penny Fawcett, appeared in the garden now. He pulled out a chair and joined them. 'Hello, you two. I don't know. Here am I working my fingers to the bone, and I come home to find my wife and a dear friend of hers, lounging in the sun with nothing to do but laugh.'

Caroline got to her feet. 'We're just ready for more

tea, so I'll make another pot and get you a cup so you can lounge in the sun like us.' She stroked Peter's head as she passed his chair, and he grabbed her hand and kissed it. Liz, at the sight of such happiness, wept again. As Caroline made more tea, Peter stayed silent until Liz had controlled her tears once more.

'I'm so confused,' she said. 'I can laugh and cry at the same time. I'm so envious of you and Caroline. Can *you* tell me what to do?'

'I might be able to put forward some points of view but I can't tell you what to do. Only you can do that. I take it that it's definitely all over between you and Neville?'

Liz nodded, not trusting herself to speak.

'I feel very sad about that. Marriage is such a good framework to build one's life around, but if all the trust and the delight is gone then there's nothing left to build upon, and it might as well be cast aside. Caroline and I love each other more today than when we married. We're so lucky.'

'We all envy you.'

Peter looked her straight in the face and she saw tears brimming in his eyes. 'If you feel you would have that with Titus then all I can say is go for it. It's not what a man of the cloth should be saying, of course. You know the usual high-minded blurb – you made vows, made promises, work at it, get some counselling. But your boys are old enough to cope so it's not as if you're tearing small children apart – then I would advise differently. But for me, when one experiences deep love one wants everyone to have it. And in your case, unspeakable things have taken place between you and Neville, so, yes, go ahead and find love in as dignified a manner as you can.'

He smiled almost apologetically at her, and Liz, deeply

moved by the sincerity of his words, leaned across the table and kissed his cheek. 'Thank you for saying that.' She gave him a second kiss on the other cheek just as Caroline arrived back with the fresh tea.

She raised an eyebrow at the two of them. 'Have I come back too soon? I wouldn't like to be guilty of interrupting something.'

The three of them laughed together. Then Caroline poured the tea and they chatted about this and that until Peter, looking at his watch, said, 'I should be gone. See you, Liz.'

He kissed Caroline on her forehead and left.

When the sound of his footsteps had faded, Liz said, 'What a lucky woman you are. I'm certain Titus will give me what you have – real love and security, caring and consideration – and Peter says I should go for it. What do you think?'

'What can I say? He should follow the usual path of persuading you to make a fresh start with Neville, but being Peter … he says what he feels is for the best for you.'

'I'm going, before I make a fool of myself again, and to tell Titus I'm his as soon as. Thanks for the tea and the advice, Caroline – it was just what I needed.'

Liz gave a brief wave and left.

After such a lovely, reassuring afternoon at the Rectory, having her own opinions of what she needed to do to put her life straight confirmed by Peter and Caroline, she felt much more confident.

But it all fell into shattered fragments when, to her horror, she found a hand-delivered letter from Neville on the doormat as she stepped inside the flat. She felt overwhelmingly nauseous. What shocked her most was that he obviously knew where she was. How else could the letter have got there? Liz thrust it down on the hall table and refused to look at it. Ignoring it, she thought, in an unbalanced way, might make it go away.

Her hands shook as she took her jacket off, and as she pottered about the flat, tidying things she should have tidied before she left that morning. The electricity bill had come for the owner, and some useless junk mail, which she threw in the bin. Still that damned letter sat on the hall table. The temptation to tear it into little pieces and throw it away overcame her, and her trembling hands began to do just that. But something stopped her. Twenty-five years of allegiance couldn't be dismissed in a moment. She had to know what sick thing he'd written.

My dear Liz,

Although you didn't know it, I watched you yesterday afternoon as you were packing your clothes at Glebe House. I saw once again the beautiful girl I married. Such class, such style. I'd forgotten.

I have always imagined I presented that beloved house of ours to you as a tribute from a husband to his wife. In fact, I know now that it was a tribute to myself and my success. That journey to success destroyed all the natural feelings I should have had. All that good side of me was drowned by my frantic, overleaping search for power. Watching you yesterday afternoon made me realize Titus hadn't stolen you from me. I, with my own efforts, had already lost you.

I intend selling the house, with your agreement, and sharing the proceeds with you. A divorce, I think, will be the best thing. If that's what you want I shall agree to it, then that Titus Bellamy can claim you as his own. I want the whole of the divorce to go smoothly without any bitter acrimony, and whatever is decided I shall agree to without question.

You know where the keys are for the safe. Rescue your jewellery; it is yours for ever. I don't know how you got into the house, but I enclose a new key to the front door of Glebe House. If ever, in the future, you are in desperate need, tell me and I will help in whatever way I can.

Sincere good wishes to you, Liz, now and in the future.
Neville

Liz thought she'd done all her crying already today but as she folded Neville's letter, great tears rolled down her face. If only, she thought, he'd spoken of all this before, perhaps they might have managed to stay together. But she'd grown to hate that house. He was right; it was a tribute to him, an opportunity to flaunt his wealth and success. She didn't want that kind of tribute anyway.

She'd go right now and get her jewellery this minute. No time to waste. While she still dared. While she still felt angry and determined and full of confidence. Tomorrow she'd sell it all — somewhere, somehow — and use the proceeds to live on until the divorce went through and she and Titus could marry. There was that dear Victorian necklace with the four little owls sitting on a twig, and the silver Art Deco one with the pink enamelled flowers that Neville's mother gave her before she died. Just how vindicitive she would have been in the present circumstances Liz couldn't imagine. She'd have called her daughter-in-law all the names under the sun, because, of course, in her eyes none of this would have been Neville's fault.

Liz snatched up her bag, locked the flat door and headed straight for Glebe House. Thank God she'd never have to see it again after today. Why had she not thought of taking her jewellery while she was packing her clothes?

Just showed how confused she'd become with all this trauma.

This time Liz parked her car in the drive and let herself in with the new key Neville had sent. The safe was in Neville's study. The keys ... Surely she hadn't forgotten where they were hidden? Neville changed their hiding place on a regular basis. She paused for a moment to clear her head. Ah! That was it. Yes, of course. It was the small bookcase behind his desk.

The door of the safe sprang open and Liz opened the drawer kept specially for her jewellery. In the first instance she thought she'd opened the wrong drawer, but no, the other one was full of legal papers, deeds and such. She had got the right one. It was ... *empty*. Empty? Her head exploded with horror. What kind of a cruel joke was this? All the kindly stuff in the rest of the letter, all the acknowledgement of the break-up being his fault and then ... *this*. How low could he sink? Was he sitting laughing to himself in the boys' flat? She would have rung him there if she'd been confident that she could be coherent. He was a slimy toad. She was well rid of him.

Liz rang Titus, and the whole sad tale was sobbed out over the phone. He was horrified. Then he said, 'Listen here, no, no, listen to me for a moment. OK. He appears to have done a very hurtful thing, but that letter sounds very sincere to me, and for Neville to be genuinely sincere it shows he's trying hard to improve himself. No, I don't think giving you a key is a spiteful trick. Hush, let me finish. But I don't want you having it out with him; that can cause nothing but trouble. Drive to Culworth police station and tell them you've had a burglary. I'll drive there from here, and we'll meet so I can back you up.'

There was no reply so Titus waited. He heard a few

more sobs and then Liz's voice saying, 'If I do that it will work either way, won't it? We've either had a burglary or he's taken possessions which are rightly mine?'

'Exactly. Drive carefully. Do you have photos?'

'Yes.'

'Insurance policies?'

'Yes.'

'Bring them with you. Take care. See you there.'

They both stood on the pavement outside the police station feeling as though they'd been stripped bare. The stupid smirk on the constable's face when they declared what their problem was expressed what everyone else would think: that one of the three of them was guilty of the theft, for insurance reasons more likely the two of them, and they were declaring it to the police to cover their tracks. She could have slapped his face for him. Didn't he recognize they weren't that kind of people?

'A drink, Liz, as of now,' Titus said. 'Don't talk about it, just let it all slip away. I will not allow that oaf to upset us.' He steered her into the nearest pub, sat her down and asked what she would like to drink.

'A vodka and tonic, please.'

'Won't be a moment.'

Liz watched him waiting his turn at the bar, and was thankful for his calm approach. She'd never actually seen him in a temper and wondered what that would be like; he was always so calm and strong whenever she was with him. She couldn't imagine him being angry.

Titus placed their drinks on the table and sat down. 'Your good health, my darling.'

'And yours.'

She waited until her drink had begun to calm her

223

nerves. 'When I read his letter I honestly thought that he'd regretted everything and wished he'd behaved differently, but this ...' Liz shook her head in disbelief.

'We don't know the whole story, do we? It could be there's been a burglary. Remember that kitchen window we found so useful when you wanted your clothes? A burglar could have got in that way. We don't know, so let's not be too hasty.'

'There was no sign of burglars.'

Titus smiled. 'They can be very clever; they could have been in and out in minutes, leaving not a single trace. It's inexperienced teenagers who enjoy leaving a mess. Don't worry, darling, we'll get it sorted. Are you happy staying where you are?'

'I was until he found out where I was, but I'm not going to let him worry me.'

'All you have to do, Liz, is to make sure who is at the door *before* you open it.'

Liz nodded.

'If you know it's time for the postman, say, you've still got to check before you open the door. Remember that. I'd much rather you were with me.'

Liz thought about the conversation she'd had with Caroline and Peter and how much she felt the need for love like theirs, but she shook her head. 'Absolutely not. I've got to get my head sorted out before I take such a permanent step. I'm in such a muddle, you see, about everything. My emotions are see-sawing up and down like crazy. I don't know what I *think* half the time. Anyway, the boys are coming round tonight for a meal, so I shan't be alone.'

The next day Liz went back to Glebe House after nursery

to wait for the police officers, who were coming to see the safe. It was only then that she noticed the antique carriage clock, a wedding present from Neville's grandfather, was missing from the sitting-room mantelpiece. She began looking around and discovered the silver grape scissors, a wedding present from Neville's great-aunt had also gone from the big silver dish on display on the sideboard. A further search revealed that the silver cigarette box, which had belonged to Neville's father, had also gone. So they *had* had burglars. Unless ... Neville had taken those as well, as they were from his side of the family ...

By the time the policemen had gone Liz was in turmoil. They both appeared to intimate that either she, her boyfriend or her husband had stolen the missing articles. All of them had reasons for doing so. All had had the opportunity. And there were no signs of forced entry to indicate burglars. After all, they said, on her own admission her boyfriend had been in the house alone while she was upstairs packing her clothes. The prospect of Titus being a thief was staggering.

It had to be Neville. Who else? Suddenly she felt so angry and so convinced he was guilty of the theft that she decided to confront him, eyeball to eyeball, face to face, and have it out. He'd still be slinking about in that gorgeous flat belonging to their sons, no doubt.

Neville answered the door immediately, looking as though he was ready to go out.

'Oh! Liz. What is it?' He looked her up and down in a critical fashion. 'Money?'

'No.' She studied his looks. He appeared pale and ill but she didn't care. 'I thought you wanted an amicable divorce.'

Neville led the way into the sitting room and offered her a chair. 'I meant what I said.'

'It can hardly be called amicable when you've taken my jewellery. I was relying on that for income.'

'What do you mean?' Neville looked puzzled.

'All my jewellery in the safe has gone. And the grape scissors, the carriage clock, and that cigarette box of your father's.'

'Are you certain?' Neville looked agitated.

'Of course I am,' Liz snapped. She stood up to make herself look as though she intended toughing it out, which she did.

'Well, *I* haven't taken them. I might be the devil in-carnate according to everyone in Turnham Malpas but that is something I haven't done. Honestly, Liz, I have not touched your jewellery or any of the other things, I really haven't.'

'Why can't I believe you? You've half-lied about things for years.'

'As God is my judge, I am telling the truth.'

Liz bent over to put her hands on the arms of Neville's chair and looked closely into his face. She knew instantly that he wasn't lying. 'So we *have* been burgled.'

'Have you told the police?'

'Of course, but they say it could be you or Titus who's taken them, or me.'

Neville's face screwed up in that well-known accusing manner. 'It'll be him. While you were upstairs packing he came in from the garden and took the lot. The thieving, scheming, layabout. I—'

Liz gasped. 'So you *did* see me packing, just as you said in your letter.' She shuddered at the thought. 'Did you watch me from the landing?'

'Well, yes, I did. I'd no idea anyone was in the house but then I heard you walking about upstairs and saw Titus sitting in the garden. You were a long while, he'd plenty of time.'

'But you were there, you would have seen him come into the house.'

'I left before you did. I'd only come to collect some clothes, like you. I watched you and thought what an idiot I'd been letting you slip through my fingers so easily. If I'd loved you properly you wouldn't have wanted him. But I didn't. So you found Titus. I'm so sorry, Liz.' Neville reached out his hand and touched her arm so sympathetically that she felt a measure of distress for his predicament. Poor Neville.

Liz drew in a deep breath. 'So it really is a proper burglary.'

'Leave it with me, Liz. I'll go higher up the chain and get something serious done about it. Have you time for a drink?'

At that moment Hugh and Guy came in. Once they'd greeted their mother with delighted surprise, Neville suggested they had a meal together. He nearly added 'for old times' sake' but decided not to. 'Here in the flat, or out in a restaurant. Mmm? What do you say?'

Hugh and Guy jumped at the chance to avoid cooking in the flat, so Neville found a jacket and the four of them went out to eat. Neville took them to the smart restaurant he'd found objectionable that night Liz had prised him so unwillingly out of the office. Liz didn't comment on the fact but felt amazed at the change in him.

No one watching the four of them would have imagined for one moment that Neville and Liz were divorcing. They appeared to be having a pleasant family meal together, but beneath all the jollity they were all putting on a front to keep the atmosphere pleasant for the sake of the others. The boys were very aware that their father had changed and their mother was on a knife edge.

When Neville decided to talk to the boys about the divorce, Liz almost shrivelled into a pathetic blob at the thought of him speaking out on such an intimate matter.

'Your mother and I are very sorry that matters have reached the stage when we both want a divorce. What I don't want is to have the two of you feeling distressed about it. We both want an amicable settling of our affairs and don't want either of you to be harmed in any way. We're selling Glebe House, but that doesn't leave the two of you homeless, obviously, as you own the flat. I might ask for a few more weeks' accommodation while I find a property, and then I shall set about making our business into the kind of company you are both willing to work in.' Neville lowered his voice. 'My mole will be getting the elbow, and I shall cut down on my property investments, so there will be no need to come into contact with him at all.'

Guy leaned closer to Neville and said quietly, 'Kevin's known to be vengeful, Dad, he's very capable of a hatchet job.' He sliced the air with the edge of his hand to emphasize his point. 'He's earned a lot out of you in the past, and he won't take kindly to being elbowed out of the cut and thrust.'

'Guy, Kevin may think he's the sharpest knife in the box, but he'll never get the better of *me*, I can assure you. He's a very small pawn in the game.'

Liz recollected Kevin's foxy slyness and, to her surprise, found herself worrying about Neville. But what was she doing here? Divorcing him? Or getting back together with him? 'I've got to go,' she said abruptly.

She pushed her chair away from the table with such decisiveness that it tipped over, making a terrible clatter on the tiled floor. With a flushed face she apologized, just as Neville got up and stood her chair back on its four legs. 'Liz! Are you all right?' The change in him was unnerving. She'd expected him to snarl because she'd drawn attention to them, but not tonight. She simply did not know this new Neville. Could he have changed so much in such a very short space of time? When he asked if she was well enough to drive home, Liz snapped, 'Of course I am.'

'Well, then, at least let me escort you to your car. This time of night, you know.'

'There's no need. Thank you for the nice meal, Neville. Bye, boys, I'll be in touch.'

But he did go with her, taking her elbow as they walked through the almost deserted multi-storey levels of the car park. Liz had difficulty preventing herself from shuddering at his touch.

Neville muttered, 'Never noticed what a grim place this is. It's almost asking for a vicious gangland film to be made here, isn't it?' He turned to see her reaction to his flight of fancy, with a smile that almost reached his eyes.

'You're right there.' Liz took in a deep breath and muttered, 'It's no good, you know, you're not getting me back. Under no circumstances. You shot your bolt that night when ... you ... did what you did. There is actually a word for it but I can't bear to use it. You were brutal, and you don't know what an effort it was for me to have a meal with you, or even to have you holding my elbow as you are now.'

He let go of her immediately and his step faltered. When eventually he spoke his voice was barely audible above the sound of their footsteps on the concrete. 'I didn't imagine I would, no matter how hard I tried. I've done too much damage ... that night ... I can never apologize enough for my behaviour. But I'm trying harder to be a better person than I was. And I mean what I say about Kevin Smickersgill. I shall finish with him. I can't ruin him, because after all, I've played a part in his crime so to speak, encouraged him in fact, so that wouldn't do. Goodnight, Liz. Thanks for coming with us tonight. Guy and Hugh will have reason to be proud of me ... and you will be proud, too. It matters, you know. Goodnight, Liz.' She felt his lips tremble as he landed a brief kiss on her cheek. Then she opened her car door, got in and drove away.

When she arrived back at her flat, Titus had left a message on her answerphone which she knew would restore calm to her swirling thoughts.

Of course she wasn't going back to Neville. The very idea made goosebumps come out all over. She checked her e-mails and found just one. It was from Titus.

Chapter 16

Darling Liz,

You're out. I wonder where? Bad news, I'm afraid. My friend who is loaning you his flat is coming home to England. He has had an emergency operation in Uganda after a serious car accident and is returning by air for further intricate surgery in England. His mother is intending to live with him in his flat to help him. He will require it on Friday. So sorry, darling. I had hoped you were safe for a good while yet. Of course you know there will always be a home for you Chez Titus if that is what you wish. Ring me when you get this message and we'll see what is the best for you to do.

Your Titus.

Liz sat staring at the e-mail for a good five minutes before she rang Titus. Somehow everyone she used to rely on had gone out of kilter. Neville at his worst she knew how to deal with; the new Neville she didn't. Now she was becoming suspicious of Titus. Was this just a ruse to get her to live with him? No, that wasn't like Titus at all. Of course not.

She dialled his number.

His first words reassured her. 'Firstly, Liz, you must understand I am not expecting nor am I asking you to come to live with me. I know you're not ready for that ... unless it is your dearest wish, that is.'

'Thank you. You see, I need to rid myself of one life before I take up another. Can you appreciate that?'

'Of course I can.'

'When you called I was having a meal in a restaurant with Hugh and Guy and ... Neville. I went to the boys' flat to see Neville and challenge him.' She heard Titus gasp. 'I know you think I was stupid, but I was so wild I had to confront him. I asked him straight out and he said it wasn't him that took the jewellery. I believe him. Titus, where shall I go? I feel abandoned.'

'Liz, Liz, you're not abandoned, I'm here for you.'

'Thank you. Yes, I know you are. I won't make a decision right this minute. I shall be strong and brave in the morning, which I'm not now, as I've been through too much tonight. Just too much. Goodnight, Titus.'

But Liz slept in the next morning, and only arrived in Turnham Malpas for the nursery in the nick of time. She hated starting the day on the wrong foot. She felt that it put her out all the rest of the day and now, because of her bad start, she still hadn't decided what to do.

She needed some groceries so she called in at the Village Store after nursery. Only Tom and Bel were working, but she had a chat with them both and then selected her shopping.

She carried her purchases to her car and found Neville standing beside it waiting. The sight of him jolted her and she wished she could run away, but she marched on regardless. 'Are you stalking me?'

'No. How are you, Liz? Thank you for eating with us last night. It was a pleasure.'

'What is it now, Neville?'

Liz looked more closely at him. How casually he was dressed: no tie, a short-sleeved shirt, shorts. *Shorts?* Heavens above. He was almost unrecognizable.

'I've come to find you to say that if you need somewhere to live, then I would be pleased if you would live in Glebe House, temporarily, until we find a buyer. Just a thought, you know.'

His idea exploded in her head. 'Oh, no! You'd be there like a shot and I'm not having it. No, definitely not. You've no rights to me at all, not after what you did.'

'I wouldn't. Believe me. It works two ways, you see. It would mean there'd be someone living there when we were trying to sell it – which we shall, of course, it's very desirable – and you would have a nice home in the meanwhile. I'd pay all the expenses – cleaner, gardener, utilities. You can move in tomorrow.'

It was extremely tempting. Her own surroundings, not another session of adapting to an unfamiliar place, near the nursery, near her friends. 'Yes, but ...'

'Well, yes, there is a but ... I will not tolerate Titus Bellamy living there. In fact, it's on condition that he doesn't set foot in the place.'

'And neither will you?'

Neville nodded. 'Neither will I.'

'I'll let you know tonight. I still have the new key so that's no problem. On your honour you won't harass me? I mean it, Neville, you're not to come anywhere near me.'

'I won't. But it has its advantages you living there, hasn't it?'

'Just go, otherwise people will begin to think we're getting together again, and nothing could be further from the truth.' Having stored her shopping in the boot, Liz opened the driver's door. Then the thought hit her like a missile. 'How the blazes do you know I need somewhere to live?' She turned round to see his reaction and found him so close their bodies were almost touching. Liz leaped back. 'Well?'

Neville spread his hands to indicate his innocence. 'I just thought there was no need for you to be paying rent for that flat, when you can live rent-free in your own home.'

'It doesn't feel like my home. It's always been yours. You might *say* you built it and furnished it as a tribute to me, but it was actually a tribute to you, and don't deny it. I was daft enough to fall for it.'

Neville did have the grace to look suitably humbled, although the unaccustomed look didn't improve him in her eyes.

'However, I'll move in if I decide to without reference to you. After all, as you say, it is *my* house, too.' Liz got in the car, remembered something else she needed to say so wound down the window. 'I wouldn't sleep in our bed. Too many ... ghosts. Too much ... horror.'

As she drove back into Culworth Liz was overcome by a terrible feeling of being strangled, or smothered or some such. She became short of breath, and it seemed as though there was a heavy weight pressing down on her head. She pulled in to give herself time to recover but it didn't work, so she drove the rest of the way concentrating 150 per cent on her driving, because she was terrified she might have an accident through lack of concentration.

Once inside the flat she poured herself a glass of brandy for medicinal purposes and lay down on the bed afterwards trying desperately to relax. After about half an hour she fell fast asleep and didn't wake for four hours.

When she got up she felt much improved, hungry and clear-headed. Of course she wasn't going to move into Glebe House. Not likely. She'd been stupid even to give it a moment's thought. She'd move into a little guest house she knew in Culworth for a few days until she'd found a holiday flat on the outskirts of Culworth to rent for a few weeks, and not let Neville know. Fact was, how the devil had he found out she would be in need of accommodation when she herself had only just found out? Was it a coincidence? Could it have been? It was almost as if her phone was being tapped. Liz shuddered. She'd watched too many spy thrillers on TV, that was her trouble. Of course it wasn't tapped. Was she going mad?

However, after that Liz decided not to use the flat landline but always her mobile – she'd just bought a new one – and rang Titus to tell him.

'I'm sure you're wrong,' Titus said. 'I mean, how could he have the phone tapped? It does sound odd, though.'

Liz told him her new mobile number and then said, 'For a while there I was thinking of moving back into Glebe House, but I've come to my senses. At least here or in a guest house he hasn't got a key. At home I would be conscious that he might walk in at any time. But he's changed. When I saw him this morning he was wearing shorts and no tie. He was almost unrecognizable. Do you think he's *really* changed, inside?'

Titus heard alarm bells ringing and didn't like it at all. He changed the subject. 'It's the market tomorrow. We'll go for a picnic. I'll get the food and things from the stalls, and we'll treat ourselves to a happy hour. If you want to stay in a guest house, by all means do so. If you like, I can store your excess belongings for a while. That's not me moving you in. Just a kind gesture. OK?'

'Right. I'll move tomorrow afternoon, after the picnic. Lovely idea. I'm looking forward to it. See you after I've cleared up from nursery, my darling.'

There was no demonstration that market morning. The protesters had lost heart, Willie in particular, so there had been no more rousing speeches, just a quiet acceptance that the market was there to stay. It was another brilliantly bright morning, with an azure blue sky and just the occasional bird swirling around, catching the thermals. Fran's cats lingered by the meat van in the vain hope that a tender lamb chop might mistakenly leap off the display, and a busy crowd of punters charged about looking for bargains.

Instead of using their bikes, Eddie and Tone had come in on the morning bus. It was packed with market-goers and they were scarcely noticed, dressed as they were in summer gear – shorts, T-shirts and open-toed sandals – and carrying shopping bags, not backpacks. They looked quite different from the last time they'd visited Turnham Malpas on market day. Their last 'shopping trip' had been highly successful because not a word had they heard from the police or anyone else about it. Apart from the diamond necklace, which they were still having difficulty selling on, everything else had brought good prices and they were hoping for a repeat of their last visit.

They drifted around the stalls, picking up trifles here and there but never actually purchasing anything, just looking as though they would buy something any minute now, and, at the same time, keeping an eye on the houses around the green. By mutual consent they wandered down the path to the church hall, slipped over Willie and Sylvia's fence, then over the fence of the newly occupied house

236

that had been Andy and Jenny's – which, by a quick look through the back windows, appeared to have nothing in it but a few sticks of dirt-cheap furniture – and into the back garden of Sir Ralph and Lady Templeton. The back door was locked but Eddie, an experienced locksmith, had it open in a trice. Imagining that the cottage was empty, they began walking cautiously through the immaculate kitchen, without even a bill laid on the worktop waiting to be paid, and to the door of the sitting room. They stood very quietly in the hall for a moment listening for sounds of occupation, not knowing that Sir Ralph was in his study and Muriel fast asleep in bed upstairs, as she had spent most of the night walking about the house unable to sleep.

They were dazzled by the number of treasures on display. They collected one here, one there, again making sure they didn't leave gaps which would draw the owners' attention to their losses.

The furniture! Well, they'd have been delighted to pop that into their shopping bags too, but regretfully ... Tone set off up the stairs and went straight into the main bedroom. He got the shock of his life when he saw Muriel asleep in bed, and froze when she turned over in her sleep. Her left hand was resting on the top of the sheet and he saw her magnificent engagement ring. Could he possibly slip it off her finger without disturbing her? Her hand was very bony. Perhaps the ring was more loose than it used to be. He tiptoed across the carpet, onto the sheepskin rug on her side of the bed, listened to her slow, deep breathing and, reaching out, took hold of the ring. He wriggled it very slightly to see just how loose it was. It was, and she hadn't moved a muscle. Poor old girl, poor old thing, like a bag of bones laid there. Despite his sympathy for her he slid the ring carefully over her arthritic, swollen knuckle, passed just below her fingernail, then it was off and in his shopping bag, and Tone was down the stairs tugging at Eddie's sleeve and pointing to the back door. The two of them got out just as they heard someone knocking on the front door.

It was Grandmama with a message for Muriel. Well, Ralph would deal with it, but they were all polite and pretended that Muriel still had all her faculties, which she patently hadn't. Apparently Ralph's bell was not working and he hadn't heard her tapping on the door, so Grandmama set off to go round to the back door and there, in full view, were Tone and Eddie making their escape across the garden and into Pipe and Nook Lane.

Mobile phone at hand, Grandmama dialled Mac. Within moments he was at her side still clutching two lamb chops he was buying from the meat van.

Grandmama was handed the chops, and Mac set off after Tone and Eddie. They'd headed the wrong way down Pipe and Nook, turning up past the Rectory instead of the other way into the Culworth Road, which would mean them having to escape into Rector's Meadow, now filled with parked cars. Granddad Stubbs, perched comfortably on the chair Barry Jones had made specially for the job, sized up the situation as he saw Tone and Eddie racing up followed by Mac, and, as they rushed through the gateway, he stuck out a foot. Tone tripped and then Eddie, very close behind, tripped over Tone. Mac, who kept very fit, had them both by the scruff before they could get to their feet.

'Got yer!' bellowed Mac. His problem then was to hold on to them, as they wriggled and squirmed, trying to evade his grip. As luck would have it, Barry Jones arrived just then with Granddad Stubbs's morning coffee in a thermos.

Between the three of them they managed to control Eddie and Tone, though with difficulty. After all, they weren't going to allow themselves to be arrested on the one morning when they'd got such a good haul so easily. But Mac rang for assistance and a police car was there within minutes, having just dropped off a witness in Penny Fawcett.

Grandmama, worried now about Ralph and Muriel, tapped on the back door. Getting no answer, she tentatively went in. The silence in the house was unnerving but she progressed into the hall, dreading she might find the two of them lying bloodied somewhere, having been coshed by the burglars.

But when she tried Ralph's study door all she found was Ralph fast asleep, his head resting on his desk. 'Ralph, dear, it's Katherine Charter-Plackett. Is everything all right? Where's Muriel?'

At the sound of Muriel's name, Ralph raised his head from the desk and stared blearily round. 'Muriel? Muriel? She's resting in bed.'

'I'll just go upstairs then and make sure she's all right.'

'She's fine, thank you, there's no need ...'

But Grandmama was already on her way up the stairs and was soon in the bedroom. Relieved to find her unharmed, Grandmama patted her hand and said, 'It's all right, Muriel, just me making sure you're OK. And you are, aren't you? I'll be back in a minute.'

Muriel looked confused but nodded her head. Katherine went back downstairs to talk to Ralph. Back in the study Ralph had pulled himself together. 'So sorry, Katherine.

Muriel's been up a large part of the night – couldn't sleep, you know – and I must have been catching up. Sorry about that.'

'Don't you worry. We all need a power nap sometimes.'

Ralph smiled. 'Is that what they call it nowadays?' Ever conscious of good manners, he asked if she had a message for him.

'Well, I did, but now I need to tell you about something else. I'm wondering if you're all right because I surprised what looked like two burglars coming out of your back door.'

Ralph stiffened with apprehension. 'Two burglars? You must be mistaken.'

'No, I'm not. Mac's just gone to catch them, but they're too far ahead of him. I don't think he'll have any luck.'

'What about Muriel?' Ralph asked anxiously.

'She seems quite unperturbed. She's just waking up.'

Ralph sat down. 'I'd better see what they've taken.'

'Maybe nothing.'

But when Ralph went into the sitting room to check Muriel's ornaments he knew immediately that things were missing, although the chances of Muriel knowing what had gone were very slight.

Down the stairs came Muriel crying, 'Ralph, Ralph, it's gone.'

Ralph shook his head at Grandmama behind Muriel's back. 'Nothing's gone, my darling, you've been asleep and you're all mixed up. See, we have Katherine here visiting. Had we better get dressed?'

'No, not till I've found it. I must find it. I wonder where I put it?' Muriel wandered aimlessly about, lifting things, opening drawers, taking books off the shelves and searching behind them. 'I don't understand it.' She scowled at Katherine. 'Did you take it?' she asked.

This came as a surprise to Grandmama, and she tried hard not to reply sounding indignant. That would never do. 'No, Muriel, I didn't. Whatever "it" is.'

Ralph whispered, 'I'll distract her, she'll soon forget.'

Taking Muriel by the arm, Ralph guided her back upstairs calling out, 'Thanks for visiting, Katherine.'

Grandmama decided that Ralph must be almost as muddled as Muriel, for he appeared not the slightest bit concerned that he'd been burgled. Unable to work out the complicated keys and locks on the front door, installed to keep Muriel in, Grandmama went out via the back door and bumped into Mac rushing back.

'We got 'em,' he announced. 'Both of 'em. They're the same ones that stole from Glebe House. I recognize 'em. Right, I'll go in and speak to Sir Ralph.'

'You'll have to leave it for now. He's trying to get Muriel bathed and dressed, so he could be a long time. Give me five!' She held up her hand and Mac held up his, and they slapped them together in triumph.

'We make a good pair, don't we?' Grandmama laughed.

Mac agreed. 'They could sack that lot in Culworth and just pay you and me!'

He roared with laughter and so did Grandmama in a most unladylike manner. She felt that she'd justified her existence this morning and no mistake.

Mac said, as he took possession of his two lamb chops, 'I might need you as a witness. I'll let you know.'

As Grandmama went home, her heart broke for Muriel. Dear, dear Muriel, who'd been such a stalwart of the village all the years she'd been there. She remembered the times Muriel had tried to keep them all behaving like ladies, for instance, when the WI had suggested sponsored skinny-dipping as a fundraiser. Now it seemed that only Caroline's Beth could get through to her. More than once Grandmama had seen Beth taking her for a stroll round the Store as part of her Girl Guide badge work, making sense of Muriel's wanderings and treating her with such respect. Surprising how the young can have such empathy with the old, but then that was all part of Beth and what she'd inherited from her father. As for poor Ralph, at his age he must be exhausted caring for her full-time as he so obviously had to do. It was pride that kept him going and not asking for help.

She'd go round to find Jimbo and tell him of her exploits. But, of course, he was on his gateaux stall, taking in the money like there was no tomorrow with no time for idle, non-productive chatter. So Grandmama went instead to find Harriet. Now *she* would be interested.

They had a chat in the back kitchen seated in two chairs provided for the staff, drinking iced ginger beer and munching some homemade marble cake, which sold well in the Store.

'... So I rang Mac's number – I have his private line, you see – and he was round in a moment and off after them.' Grandmama's eyes filled with tears.

'Why, what's the matter?'

'It's Muriel. She's definitely lost her marbles, believe me. She had something on her mind that was lost and she asked if I'd taken it! Me, of all people! Mind you, she didn't know who I was. So sad, isn't it?' She gently wiped her eyes so as not to smudge her discreet mascara, and said, 'Ralph must be worn out. Well, I'm going now to look round the stalls. I loathed the idea of the market at first for Jimbo's sake, but now, well, it does seem to have some good things. All due to Titus, of course, he maintains a good standard. And I don't think it's made inroads into Jimbo's takings after all, has it?'

'No. In fact, last Thursday the takings were up.'

'Talking of Titus, what's the situation ... you know.'

'Well, Liz is having to move out of the flat today because the owner's coming back from abroad. I offered her a bed but she doesn't want to be in Turnham Malpas, too many memories, so she's going to a guest house till she finds somewhere nice to rent.'

'You see, I can't believe that Neville would be capable of something ... well ... less than pleasant. Always appears to be such a gentleman, though rather cold, if you get my meaning. Do you know what happened?'

'No, Katherine, I don't. Only Neville and Titus know, beside Liz, that is. Whatever, she's well shot of him.'

'Well, sometimes I wish I'd done that very thing, divorced Jimbo's father and got rid of him once and for all, but I adored him so, and Jimbo was too young to be fatherless. I kept hoping he'd come home and stay but he didn't – well, not until he was dying. So gracious in the face of death, you know. Harriet, if ever I go like Muriel, will you bump me off before I become an embarrassment to myself and everyone? I'd hate my grandchildren to see me completely barmy.'

Harriet could see that her mother-in-law needed a sharp word or two. 'You're getting very maudlin, Katherine, and it's got to stop. Finished your ginger beer? Then you'd better buzz off before I find you a job to do.'

It was then that they heard the cataclysmic roar of motorbikes approaching Turnham Malpas, dozens of them pouring down the Culworth Road and onto the village green. The noise was unbearable. They emerged from the Culworth Road at full throttle. It was the horrifying sound of their triumphant shouts of laughter as they poured onto the village green, which chilled everyone to the marrow.

Chapter 17

The crowd of bikers diverged and sped down the alleyways between the stalls, revving and thudding about, caring not one jot who or what they toppled. Pedestrians were entirely at their mercy. The smell of diesel, the rubbery reek of screeching tyres, their triumphant shouts of laughter, the screams of the terrified punters, the furious, futile protest of the stallholders and the crash of the stalls and the canopies made Turnham Malpas appear to have descended into hell. It seemed to last for hours – hours of pain and fear, of shock and terror.

In fact, the devastation lasted only minutes, but in that time substantial items of food were stolen, and Bryan the butcher broke down in tears when he saw his beautiful joints of meat being kicked and thrown everywhere.

Having had their fun, the bikers roared off as quickly as they came, waving stolen produce from the stalls, whirling pieces of the striped canvases around their heads, swiping plates and dishes from the food stalls, even taking great bites out of Jimbo's gateaux and throwing them down in the dust as they swirled away. They left behind a scene of total destruction.

There was a moment of silent shock as the bikes stormed off, then came the wails of distress from the stallholders, howls of protest from the customers, cries of pain from the wounded – and there were quite a few of those – and general confusion. From the Royal Oak came Mac, who'd been in the gents' when the bikes had arrived. He flung up his arms in despair. Then Grandmama was at his side, breathing heavily, and holding a list of motorbike numbers under his nose.

'See, I've taken these down,' she panted. 'Some but not all of their numbers. So you've something to get on with.' The writing was uncertain but then she had been distraught at the time, not to mention knocked and nudged as the bikes streamed by.

Mac thanked her profusely, trying hard to focus on the list and relieved he'd look efficient to that lot in Culworth. So, what had happened to the extra officers he'd been promised? So much for Mr Fitch and his promises. If Sir Ralph had arranged it, they would have been here. A single bobby couldn't possibly have controlled what they'd experienced. Thing was, he'd an idea they were part of a different motorbike gang from those bikers he'd arrested last time. Why? he asked himself. Why? For fun, that's what. For them, it was one great big joke. Damn them.

Titus Bellamy was speechless. As a man of peace he was appalled at the vicious glee with which the bikers had destroyed his living and those of his stallholders. He stood with his head in his hands, trying to hold back his emotions as best he could. He gasped for breath, as though his lungs had gone into cramp. The initial opposition from the villagers was as nothing compared to this, for now the opposition was life-threatening. One unconsidered step and someone could have been killed by a motorbike, such was their speed and fury. He gasped for breath again, sucking in great draughts of air in an effort to control his speaking voice before he rang the police. He pulled his mobile out from his trouser pocket, dialled nine, nine, nine. Got through, but found he couldn't say, 'Police, please!' Felt the enormous pressure of something storm-like building up in his chest. He clutched his shirt-front in an effort to still the raging. Tears welled in his eyes. Still the pain escalated. He rubbed his left arm to bring it to life again, tried breathing deeply and slowly, but still he couldn't stop this gigantic beating taking control of him.

Silently Titus called out, '*Liz*!' He had to see her one last time. Just once! His darling Liz.

Then she was there. Her hand on his arm felt like a balm to his raging pain, but it didn't still the excruciating pain in his chest. Gratefully Titus looked into Liz's eyes, then he slumped to the ground at her feet.

Liz tried to stop him falling but she couldn't, and went down with him onto the grass.

Kneeling beside him, she screamed, 'Titus! Titus!'

Titus could hardly hear her for the roaring in his ears.

He struggled to say her name.

Strove to kiss her lovely lips, so close to his own.

Mumbled nonsense.

Then the searing pain overwhelmed him, his heart stopped abruptly and he lay dead at her feet with her arms around him. Liz moaned and howled her despair, she hugged him, stroked him, begged him to stay with her but the desolation in her heart told her it was all in vain. Her beautiful, dearest, sweet Titus was gone forever. Her finger trailed along the line of his lips, she bestowed tiny kisses around his mouth, gently shut his staring eyes still so full of pain it seemed, she kissed his temples, smoothed her thumb along his eyebrows, rubbed his loving gentle hands, hoping to bring life back to them. Life! Yes! Of course! She'd *breathe* life into him. Liz pumped his chest and breathed forcefully into his open mouth until she was giddy from the effort, but there was no response.

Caroline, helping to look after the injured, came upon them both. At a glance she summed up the situation and knew exactly what must have happened. Tenderly, she pushed Liz aside and knelt beside Titus, held her fingers to his neck to search for a pulse, and tried herself to return him to life.

After a few minutes she took Liz into her arms.

'My dear, it's all too late, I'm afraid. There's no response at all. My dear Liz, I'm so sorry.'

In the midst of the chaos the two of them continued to kneel beside Titus, one giving comfort, the other paralysed with shock. It was a grim, silent circle of pain, totally detached from the rest of the hectic pandemonium.

Liz lifted her head from Caroline's shoulder and whispered, 'How can he have died? We love each other so much.'

'That's how life can be.'

'What kind of a God can do this to us? What kind?'

Because she couldn't think of a single word of comfort when faced with a question like that, Caroline too began to weep.

That was how Peter found the two of them on his way back from a visit to Penny Fawcett. Horrified, he leaped out of his car and joined them on the grass. He questioned Caroline with his eyes, and her answer was to shake her head in helpless despair. He encircled the two of them in his arms and rocked them both, murmuring words of comfort, at the same time shaken to the core by Titus's sudden death.

248

Caroline took off her cardigan and laid it respectfully over Titus's face and chest.

Liz shouted, 'No! No! Don't shut him away, please don't shut him away.' Tearing off the cardigan, she bent to kiss his lips again and again, but she was horrified to discover they were unresponsive and just beginning to lose the body warmth of a human being, and finally she realized that he was dead and gone ... never more would those wonderful, tender hands caress her, those gentle, questing lips of his touch her body. No more would she feel his sweet breath against her skin, nor would she lay her head on his chest and feel the very beat of his dear, kind heart. Great, passionate tears rolled unceasingly down her cheeks. Why hadn't she died with him? Why didn't she fall on his chest this very second and put an end to it all? Why couldn't she have a heart attack right now? With the sun beating down on the pair of them, side by side, out here. Not even Peter's words of blessing could reach the thick, impenetrable wall of her grief.

The ambulance came, called for by no one knew, and took Titus away. How Caroline and Peter managed to get Liz from the place outside the school where he'd died to the Rectory they didn't know. It was a nightmare journey. Anyone less well built and less fit than Peter wouldn't have been able to do it because Liz was a dead weight. They were constantly stopped by horrified villagers, who didn't know that Titus was dead, and they fell back in dismay when they learned the truth.

'Have you any sedatives in the house?' Peter asked Caroline.

'None.'

'None?'

'None at all.'

'Painkillers?'

'Yes.'

They laid Liz on the sitting-room sofa, not able to face getting her up the stairs. Instead of howling with pain she'd become too exhausted to make any effort to express her grief, and lay quite still in her own desolate world. Caroline knelt beside the sofa holding her hand. She tested Liz's forehead. 'She's in shock, and very cold. We need a blanket.'

'I'll get one.'

'Top shelf. Our wardrobe. The Scotch plaid one.'

'Right.' Peter raced up the stairs two at a time, glad to be of use and feeling that for once in his ministry he was at a loss for words. What could you find to say to someone who lived for twenty-five years with the wrong man, then found her soulmate, and, in a single, shattering second, lost him? Not a single, damn word. He put the rug against his cheek and relished its comfort for a moment. God help him ... and more so, God help Liz.

Chapter 18

At six o'clock that evening Peter opened the Rectory door for the umpteenth time that day and found Neville Neal standing there. A Neville Neal he hadn't seen before. His hair was lank with sweat, his cheeks were sunken, his skin was grey, his lips were trembling and his clothes were creased.

'Liz. Is she still here? I asked. No one knew.'

'Yes, she is. Come in.'

'Will she see me?'

Peter shook his head. 'I don't know. She hasn't spoken since we brought her here. I'll go and ask.' He disappeared into the sitting room.

Alex crossed the hall. 'Hello, Mr Neal. Isn't it terrible about Mr Bellamy?'

Neville studied the question. Ever since he'd heard about Titus's death he'd wavered between absolute delight and crippling shock. His own life had dropped several gears just as Liz's had until the whole world had gone into slow motion. 'Even sadder for Liz, my wife.'

'Yes, of course. Good of you to come.' He turned to climb the stairs.

Neville watched him go. So like his father. Lucky man. Neither Hugh nor Guy looked like him.

Peter came back into the hall. He nodded towards the

sitting room, inviting him in.

Neville wiped his face with his handkerchief, slicked down his hair and softly walked in. When he'd last seen Liz she'd been so radiant with love for Titus that he'd felt jealous of the man. He was appalled by her appearance now. She looked gaunt, pale-faced, and were those white hairs he could see? Surely not, not so quickly. She appeared to have sunk into the cushions as though she were too heavy for them.

'Liz. I've come.'

At the sound of his voice she sprang up, her face glowing with pleasure. 'Darling! Darling!'

He went to her side. 'Liz. Liz.'

For a moment she looked confused, then the terrible truth seemed to dawn that it was Neville and not Titus, and she fell back onto the sofa as though dead.

Neville, so blinded by his own distress, wasn't aware of the mistake she'd made, and he enveloped her in his arms, raising her from the sofa so he could kiss her and hold her tight. 'I'm so sorry, darling, so sorry. I'll look after you, for as long as you need me. Poor Titus. It must have been a heart attack, you know. Nothing could be done. You tried, I'm sure. You're being so brave.'

She was so heavy to hold, but hold her he did until his arms were in agony and he had to put her back down again. She hadn't objected to his embrace, he thought. She obviously needed his sympathy.

He called out, 'Peter? Are you there?'

Peter and Caroline had been standing in the doorway waiting in case Liz reacted badly to Neville's presence, and they were surprised when she didn't.

'Yes?'

'The best thing we can do is to take her home,' Neville

announced, coming out into the hall. 'Everything is familiar there.'

But Caroline, being a woman and a doctor and therefore more astute about the strange reactions bereaved people sometimes had, insisted she remained where she was. 'I'm sorry, Neville, but she's staying here. Just in case. She's better with a doctor around.'

He mounted a protest. 'But she needs me.'

'I don't think she knows anyone at the moment. She's so badly shocked.'

Seeing the sense of Caroline's argument, Neville said determinedly, 'Very well, then, I'll stay here with her, if you don't mind. I'll go home and get her night things and I'll sit up with her all night. Believe me, I will. If anyone can comfort her I can.'

He spun on his heel and marched out of the Rectory.

When the door closed behind him Caroline whispered to Peter, her voice thick with unshed tears, 'She thought it was Titus, you know. She'd no idea it was Neville.'

'But I thought it looked as though she knew him.'

'Well, I'm telling you, when she realized it wasn't him, it was as if Titus had died twice. Now, brandy, I think, and we'll see if she can sleep a little. That's what she needs.'

Alex came down the stairs. 'Is he coming back?'

'Hello, darling,' Caroline said. 'Yes, I think so.'

'How's Liz?'

'Prostrate with grief.'

Alex peered round the sitting-room door and went in to see her. Caroline watched as he stroked her hand and talked softly to her. She saw yet again how much like Peter he was, with his compassion and inner strength, which had taken him through the troubled time in Africa.

Liz opened her eyes, saw it was Alex and gently stroked

his cheek. 'Thank you,' she said, and closed her eyes again.

She stayed like that until Neville came back, by which time Peter, Alex and Caroline were drinking hot chocolate in the kitchen.

Neville called from the door, 'Has she woken yet?'

Caroline answered, 'Not really. I've put a blanket for you, Neville, on the other sofa. If you need anything from the kitchen during the night, please help yourself. I've also left the brandy on the worktop there. If she needs some, feel free.'

'Thank you. I'll say goodnight. Thank you for all you've done.'

'It's a pleasure. Just sorry it's in such awful circumstances.'

Neville grunted and disappeared into the sitting room.

In bed, snuggled up against Peter, Caroline asked him if he thought Neville was imagining that his moment had come to get Liz back.

'Possibly. I'm so upset with the grief of it all I can't think straight. Such a lovely chap, Titus.'

'I know, so am I. I tried, how I tried, but it was already too late to revive him. There wasn't a flicker of life in him. But perhaps if I'd tried another minute or two ...'

'Don't think along those lines. You'll crucify yourself. You did your best, with no equipment. If he'd been in hospital maybe ...'

'I don't think so, Peter. The heart attack must have been colossal. He had no vital signs at all. But let's face it, it was those bikers who killed him.'

'Being the kind of man he was, he must have been devastated at what the bikers had done, not just for himself but for his stallholders, too.'

'They were doing it just for fun, weren't they? It certainly sounded like it. So cruel, their laughter. So cruel.'

'That's certainly the end of the market.'

'Considering the trouble it's caused, perhaps it's as well.'

'Maybe, but everyone did enjoy it, didn't they?'

'Yes, they did. Poor Liz. I can't imagine what she'll do or if she'll ever get over this.'

'I don't think she will get over it. The shock, the unexpectedness of it. It's dreadful. What a day.'

They both fell silent, wrapped in their own thoughts.

Eventually Peter said, 'Goodnight, darling. Aren't we lucky, you and me?'

'Yes, we are.'

The two of them had not been disturbed during the night and had slept well, but the moment Caroline opened her eyes the horror of yesterday immediately filled her mind. She sat up abruptly and leaped out of bed, hastened into the bathroom, showered and then dressed and went downstairs.

It was only half past six but she opened the sitting-room door to see if either Neville or Liz was awake. Liz was, but Neville slept soundly.

'Caroline. It did happen yesterday, didn't it? Titus. You know.'

'Yes, Liz, it did. That's why you're here.'

'But Neville, what's he doing here?'

'I don't really know. Said he didn't want to leave you alone and he'd sit with you all night.'

'Where's Titus? I want to see him.'

For a moment Caroline wondered if Liz thought he hadn't died. Then she realized what she meant, and

255

cleared her throat while she thought how to phrase her reply. 'Well, as you can expect, Titus is ... well ... he's at the hospital, in the ... mortuary. You see, with it being so unexpected ... they'll have to find out why. You see.'

Liz uttered the words 'post-mortem' as though they were the most repulsive, disgusting words in the English language. She visibly shrank from the whole idea. 'Not that. Please not that. Looking at him and cutting him up. Can I stop it?'

'It's the law. I assume he'd no previous history of heart problems?'

'I don't know. Haven't known him long enough. He never said. Damn the law. Damn, damn, damn it. Not my dearest, dearest Titus, please not.' Liz writhed with the pain of it all. The absolute crushing pain of her loss.

'I'll ... I'll ... make a pot of tea.'

'That's right. A pot of tea, it'll put everything to rights.'

The scathing mockery in Liz's voice floored Caroline. 'I'll do it just the same.'

She escaped to the kitchen and began to organize the breakfast.

After a few minutes Neville came in wearing a flamboyant dressing gown. 'She won't let me touch her.' He sounded indignant.

'She really doesn't know what she's doing.'

'But I'm determined to do what's right. Take her home to Glebe House, attend to the arrangements. Someone will have to do it. Save her the trouble. Has he any relatives?'

Caroline shrugged. 'I've no idea.'

She set a tray for Liz to eat her breakfast in the sitting room. It didn't seem right for her to breakfast with Beth and Alex. Their emotions were still so fragile after Africa, and they were only fourteen.

'Here. Take this in for Liz,' she said. 'I've given her a warm croissant and butter, although I'll be surprised if she can eat anything at all, after the shock. If that doesn't suit, let me know what she prefers.'

'She needs to eat; I'll see she does.'

'Please, Neville, tread very carefully. She's bereaved.'

'She isn't bereaved,' he snapped. 'You'll be calling her a widow next, which she isn't. I'm still alive and kicking. Look!' With his arms outspread he indicated his live presence.

'She's lost her soulmate. That's how it feels to her, anyway.'

Neville raised his voice, 'Caroline! That kind of sentimentality is ridiculous.'

He'd forgotten it was half past six so Peter would be going out for his morning routine and had heard every word.

'In this house, no one speaks to Caroline with such disregard. My wife has done all she can for Liz. One more outburst like that and I shall physically turn you out.'

'I apologize. I beg your pardon, Caroline, and yours, Peter. It's the stress. I'm worn out with it. I've been awake most of the night. She's been sobbing and calling his name.' They could hear him grinding his teeth at the thought. 'How would you feel about that, Peter, if it was Caroline calling out another man's name? Eh?'

He marched out with the tray, leaving the two of them seething.

'I'm going for my run, it might make me feel better,' Peter said. 'Don't take any more claptrap from him. I'm not having it. Bit late now to begin caring. It would never have happened if he'd been a good husband to her in the first place.' Peter placed a kiss on Caroline's forehead as he was leaving. 'I'll cut my run short just in case. What's more, I'm not having him staying here, OK? Liz, yes. Neville, no. If he asks, you say, "I don't think Peter would want that." Right?'

The day following Titus's death it rained, and was very cold for a summer's day. Caroline knew Peter was dreading taking the funeral service. Neville had tried to take charge of the details of it, and there'd been a real struggle for Peter to insist that Liz's wishes must be taken into account.

Finally Neville had accepted that Peter was right, but with little grace. 'She doesn't know what she's doing. *I* know what needs to be done. Neat and short and without the heart-rending pathos so often initiated for someone for whom most people at the service haven't any feelings at all. After all, who of the people attending will want to shed a tear for *him*. He was pathetic.'

Finally, Peter, to his chagrin, lost his temper. 'Titus was ...'

Neville interrupted with ... 'Titus was a pathetic idiot, he'd never make progress either in his boring business nor anything else he put his hand to ...'

'I think, Neville, you could put on a postage stamp your knowledge of Titus Bellamy. I have learned that he read history at Oxford and later became an astonishingly young professor of history there and was well respected in his field. Unfortunately he had a breakdown and had to leave. That was when he turned to running organic markets. His funeral will be conducted in the manner that Liz requests. She wants a celebration of his life not a dreary, sad affair. And a celebration it will be. If you're not willing to go along with that then don't bother turning up.'

Neville had been taken aback by the news of Titus's scholarly background, but the knowledge gave him even greater grounds for disliking him. After all, he'd had what Neville had always deeply envied, a doctorate from one of the most prestigious universities in the world. He was even more horrified to hear what Peter said next.

'There will be several highly distinguished people from Oxford coming to pay their respects and, of course, journalists and photographers.'

Neville grew angrier. So this loathsome predator who, with less than the flick of his finger, had taken his wife from him, was to have plaudits and praise even at his funeral. It was the final bitter pill. Momentarily, at first, he'd felt slight sorrow for Titus, but now it was replaced by bitter fury. And to boot, Titus had won Liz's love, which he, Neville Neal, had once enjoyed and had now lost. But perhaps there was a chance to win her back now the man had damn well died, and it was a chance he'd take with both hands and *win*, so long as he played his cards right.

'Of course. I didn't know. I'm sorry. Of course Liz must have what she wants, a celebration of his past, full of joy and light, very appropriate for a man of his merit. Truly fitting.'

'Good. That settles it.'

'Do you think it would be appropriate for me to sit with Liz at this service? We're not yet divorced, though we shall be. Should I, do you think, just in case it's too much for her?'

Caroline, not convinced by Neville's apparent change of heart, said, 'That's for Liz to decide, isn't it?'

Neville patted her arm. 'Of course, you're quite right. When the funeral is over I shall take Liz back to Glebe House. After all, it is her home. She can't stay here for ever. I'm living there again, you see.'

Peter, sensing that Caroline was about to boil over at the suggestion, laid a quiet hand on her arm. 'Yet again, that's for Liz to decide.'

The problem was Liz found it intensely difficult to make decisions because she was so completely empty of every-thing. It was as if someone had drained away all her faculties – her brain, her innards, her appetite, her bodily strength, her will, the very zest of her – and left behind a weak and useless empty shell. But still they would keep asking her for decisions, and she'd nothing left of her with which to make them. She felt the need to lean on someone, and was grateful for Peter's strength, Caroline's loving common sense, and, above all, Neville's kindness. He was so different, so considerate, so attentive to her every need. Had he truly had a metamorphosis, like a caterpillar changing into a butterfly? Or was it only a pretence? Well, for now she'd lean on him until she was more able to cope, and she'd go through the motions of believing in this butterfly until her strength came back to her, if ever it did.

She turned over and lost the duvet on the sitting-room floor. I might as well get up, she thought. She needed her breakfast. Breakfast. Cereal and toast and hot coffee. Yes. That's what she'd have. Liz slipped on a dressing gown of Caroline's and went into the downstairs loo to freshen up her face. Who was this woman looking at her? My God, she thought, that's me! Oh, Titus, I'm so glad you can't see me now. Still, you wouldn't mind, because you love me for what I am, and how I love you, so very much. Liz stroked her cheek and imagined the hand she saw in the mirror was Titus's beautiful, slender hand, and she remembered the times she'd held it and enjoyed those fine-boned fingers caressing her.

The cold water from the tap surprised her and brought her back down to earth. That hand of his would never touch her again, and she might as well get used to the idea. Pain of an unimaginable kind passed through her from head to toe. Where was Neville when she needed him?

He was in the kitchen with Peter and Caroline, scoffing his breakfast, looking robust, healthy and, what was worse, thoroughly alive. He'd no *right* to be alive.

Taking his cue from Peter, Neville got to his feet when she went into the kitchen.

'Good morning, Liz.'

'Good morning, Peter. I've come for my breakfast.'

Caroline made no comment, even though she knew she'd already eaten her breakfast, merely said, 'What would you like?'

'I see you've got coffee. I'd like that and then some hot toast with butter. Please. Oh! And some cereal.'

Neville pulled a chair out for her. 'There we are. You do realize you've ...'

Caroline shook her head at him and he stopped.

Neville argued to himself that there was no point in not letting her know she was behaving ridiculously. He tried another tack. 'I'll get you fresh underclothes, shall I, from the house?'

'All my clothes! Where are they? I should have taken them out of that flat.'

'I've done it for you, my darling. I emptied the flat last night and gave the owner your keys.'

'Thank you, Neville. You are so thoughtful. Could you fetch me a dress or something, too, from the house?'

'Of course, it'll be a pleasure.'

He came back with her clothes and put them in the sitting room. When she went to dress she found he'd brought her very newest, smartest underwear and a frock more suited to a royal garden party. He walked into the sitting room just as she'd got the underwear on.

'Sorry! My word, Liz, that looks good.' For one miraculous moment he actually felt serious lust for her. At that moment he could have ... the new, unaccustomed brightness in his eyes told her exactly what his thoughts were.

When she was fully dressed, Liz went close to him and said, 'Never. *Never*. OK?'

Startled by the rough determination in her voice, Neville asked abruptly, 'Are you staying here or going home?'

'Home.'

'With me?'

Liz weighed this up in her mind. Standing so near to her, he could feel each breath she took. He'd never been more aware of her than at that moment. He'd bide his time. She was too raw right now, but it would only be a matter of time ...

'My own bedroom.'

Disappointment almost overrode his new-found consideration, but he answered sweetly, 'I wouldn't have it any other way.'

'Thank you, Neville.' She automatically reached out to stroke his cheek by way of thanks as she would have done had he been Titus, and instantly recognized he wasn't Titus and never would be. She had to get to grips with reality. But all that love, all that wonderful love, taken from her in one appalling moment ... However would she live another day, never mind a week, a year?

'Neville, I want to go to the mortuary to see Titus. Will you make arrangements for me, please?'

'It's not safe for you to drive. I'll get my keys and take you.'

When they came back neither of them was able to say anything at all. Liz went into the sitting room and Neville sat brooding on one of the rocking chairs in the kitchen, rocking gently to and fro, and then sometimes rocking furiously. Caroline had gone to take a surgery and Peter was in his study working on his plans for the funeral.

Dottie, having finished her cleaning, was about to leave, and very glad indeed she was to be doing that. The sooner this funeral was over the better it would be for everybody. Caroline had given the twins money to go into Culworth so there hadn't been anyone available to talk to. Before she left she knocked on the study door to speak to Peter.

'Rector, I'm sorry to be troubling you, sir, but I've come to say I'm off now. I've done what the Doctor asked, and I'll be here tomorrow as usual.' Dottie hesitated, then closed the door so no one could hear her and added, 'I've no business saying this but I am: he's got a different agenda from you and the Doctor. Be warned.'

Peter smiled. 'I believe you're right. I'll keep a keen eye on him.'

'Can anyone go? On the day?'

'Of course.'

'He was a very lovely man. I liked him very much. Very genuine. Which is more than ...' she nodded her head in the direction of the kitchen, 'you know.'

Chapter 19

On the evening of the day of Titus's funeral there was the usual crowd of people in the bar. Seated at the table with the old settle were Vera and Don, Sylvia and Willie, Jimmy and, for a change, Dottie Foskett. Jimmy, in a rare mood of loving the whole of the human race, had got in the first drinks and was giving them out when in through the door came Grandmama Charter-Plackett. Sylvia waved, and she came over to join them.

'Don't worry, Jimmy, I'll get my own drink, and the next round is on me.' She bustled across to the bar to order a gin and tonic. 'Georgie! How's things?'

'Weary after all the people who'd been to Titus's funeral came in for a post-funeral feed and a knees-up. I had thought they'd have had a wake at Glebe House but they didn't ...'

'At Glebe House? Come on, Georgie, Neville's hardly likely to have a knees-up for his wife's lover in his own house, is he?'

Georgie clapped her hand to her mouth. 'My God! Of course not, I never thought. They kept their romance so low-key I'd almost forgotten about it. She's back, you know, living in Glebe House.'

Grandmama had just taken her first sip of her drink when Georgie's innocent remark made her splutter it down the front of her top. 'Are you sure? After ... you know.'

'Well, that's it. I *don't* know. Do *you*?'

Grandmama fitted her not inconsiderable bosom onto the bar top and, leaning close to Georgie's ear, whispered, 'I don't know for certain, but the story is ... he ... *raped* her that night she left him and went to Jimbo's.'

Georgie made a great effort to control her voice but she didn't succeed. '*Raped* her! He never! *That* cold fish. Just goes to show.'

Those who hadn't heard quite correctly soon had it relayed to them by those who had. The bar fell silent, except for Don, who said loudly, 'I'm surprised at Grandmama letting on like that. With her class she should know better.'

Vera blushed bright red, Sylvia fixed her eyes on her drink, and Jimmy said, 'So the truth will out, it seems.' Willie, shocked to the core by such revelations almost before Titus was cold in his grave, muttered something indistinguishable and took a long drink of his home brew. What was this village coming to? He recollected that Arthur Prior at Wallop Down Farm was an illegitimate cousin of Ralph's, and not everyone kept to their own beds even in what was described as the Good Old Days, but that wasn't rape, now was it? More like mutual good fun in the haystack. What Neville had done ... well, that was awful.

Grandmama never arrived at the table with the settle. She got waylaid by eager gossips wanting to know all the latest news.

'Well,' said Dottie, 'that is disgusting, I must say, and him a pillar of the church. Really disgusting. Poor Liz.'

'But going back to live in the house where it happened! How can she?' Sylvia whispered.

Dottie tapped the table with her forefinger. 'She's got nowhere else to go. The flat she was renting, well, the chap came back for medical treatment after a nasty car accident wherever he was abroad, so she had to leave, and it all happened the day Titus died. So, apparently,' she drew a deep breath, 'she's back in Glebe House and so is ...'

'Yes ...?'

'Neville.'

They'd seen him going in and out of Glebe House but never guessed he was sleeping there. Well, of all things. Would you believe it? There was a silence for a few moments while they all digested the implications.

Sylvia asked where Dottie had got the information, suspecting it might be from the Rectory.

Indignantly, Dottie refuted such a suggestion almost as it took wings. 'Like you, Sylvia, working at the Rectory, anything I hear there I don't divulge.'

'So-o-o ...?'

'From overhearing Jimbo and Harriet talking when they'd forgotten I was there cleaning, and that's the truth.'

Vera nudged Dottie and winked at her.

Dottie winked back and asked, 'It's all right talking about it, but do you give poor Liz a thought? I certainly do. That's dreadful what he did to her.' She felt a change of subject was needed, so rooted about in her handbag and came out with a gilt-edged card.

Vera tried peeping over the top of the card to find out for herself. 'What's that, Dottie? You're full of surprises tonight.'

'You'll all be getting an invite. I've got mine early 'cos I happened to be there cleaning when the invites came from the printers. Take a butcher's.'

It was eagerly passed round, and a few people sitting near tried to have a butcher's, too.

'Two weeks Friday. Eight p.m. Well, isn't that lovely? Opening of the Old Barn. Well, we've waited long enough. It's seems like months since they started renovating it.'

Dottie casually mentioned she'd been in to have a look round when she'd been helping Jimbo unload a never-ending stream of boxes of table linen.

'What's it like?'

'Beautiful. Transformed. Still medieval, you know – can't get away from it, can you, in a place built back then. For weddings and big parties, mmm-m-m. All them oak beams, magnificent they are. Can't believe they could build like that all those years back. You can have it with small tables for four or six, or do a kind of medieval banquet with the tables in long lines and benches. Such good taste, it is.' Dottie bunched her fingers and kissed them. 'That building, combined with Jimbo's food – no one, and I mean no one, will be able to resist. He'll make a mint, he will. He's already got it booked for several events before it's quite finished. Anyway, you'll all see it when you go. He's got fairy lights in all the trees as you drive up, and he switched them on for me. Course it was daylight, but I could see it would be lovely. And the ladies' loos! They could win a prize they're so beautiful: pale turquoise, dark turquoise and white tiling from floor to ceiling, and great big mirrors, with hand creams and a choice of perfumed sprays and soaps and such for anyone to use.'

Sylvia got her diary out and wrote in the date and the time. 'That'll be a night to remember and not half, though could anything beat that champagne race meeting for the Africa fund?'

They all agreed nothing could beat that.

Vera asked if Dottie had any more explosive news to tell them, 'cos if so, would she wait till Don had got the next round in? They might be in need of alcoholic support after hearing it.

Dottie tapped the side of her nose and winked at them all.

Vera got to her feet. 'Go on, Don, I'll come with you, and help carry the drinks. Dottie, not a word till I get back.'

Quietly Sylvia commented that it was wonderful how Don had improved since that fall. 'Never thought he would.'

'The brain can take years to mend, you know, or not mend at all. Can't expect too much. I mean, after all, he was always a man of few words *before* his fall.' Willie nodded knowledgeably. 'He's not quite A1 at Lloyds but not far off.'

Don came back carrying a tray of drinks, followed by Vera putting the change in her purse. He sorted them out, remembering all by himself exactly who wanted what. When he'd sat down and taken his first sip of orange juice he looked up at Dottie and said, 'Well, then, what is it?'

'What's what?'

'Your big news.'

'Oh! That.' She wasn't nearly as reluctant to tell them as she sounded. 'It's just that I've got a job with Pat Jones, helping out when they have an event on at the Old Barn.

I shan't be waiting on, just hurrying about giving Pat a hand in the background. She's got a new uniform to wear; not dressed like a waitress, more like management. She's a slave driver, is that Pat.' She sounded annoyed, but the smile on her face was lovely to see.

'Well, Dottie, here's to your new job.' They all clinked glasses and drank to Dottie.

'Congratulations!'

'Well done!'

'All grist to the mill, eh!'

'They say the tips are excellent.'

'At last I shall have money to spare, for the first time in my life!'

'Good luck to you, Dottie,' Don said, meaning every word.

'There're a few jobs going still.' Dottie looked round the table but thought not one of them could fit in quite as well as Dottie Foskett. 'What with this new job and my house all done up – the builders say they'll be finished by next weekend – I shall be sitting pretty.'

When Grandmama finally joined them, their talk turned to the position Liz Neal found herself in, and they speculated on her future.

'None of us knows, and we are not likely to. But believe me, if he'd done that to me he'd have been out on his ear in quick sticks,' Grandmama pronounced loudly.

'We haven't seen much of you lately. Have you been away?'

'No, I've been assisting the police with their inquiries.' For one wild, unbelievable moment they all thought she meant the police had hauled her in for questioning, and sat stunned. Grandmama looked round at their faces and began to laugh. 'Not because they suspected *me* of anything. I was helping them because I saw the burglars leaving Sir Ralph's.'

'Whew!' said Don. 'That's a relief!'

'Did you know they actually took Muriel's engagement ring from her finger as she lay asleep in bed?'

'That beautiful sapphire? My God! The cheek of it. Stealing from a poor old lady who doesn't even know what day it is.'

They digested this piece of information, and Dottie asked, 'Have they got it back for her?'

Grandmama nodded. 'Oh, yes. They confessed what they'd done, couldn't do any other. I'd seen them leaving the house, you see, and Mac caught them as they were escaping, so they really couldn't say it wasn't them. And they were carrying all the stuff. So, between us, Mac and I have caught *both* sets of burglars. When they've been sentenced Muriel's ring and her ornaments will all be given back as will all the other stolen property, including my silver snuff boxes. Blinking good job the market's finished with. What with the bikers and the burglars … mind you, the bikers have only been fined not imprisoned. It was two chaps called Tone and Eddie who took your stuff, Willie. I feel quite sorry for them. The bikers, on the other hand, did an awful lot of damage, to say nothing of indirectly killing Titus.'

Indignantly Willie shouted, 'Sorry for them? They need horsewhipping, never mind sorry for them. Stealing my grandad's watch – twenty-two-carat gold it is – and Sylvia's solid silver locket. Disgusting. To think they'd been poking about in our belongings. They deserve all they get.'

Grandmama retorted, 'Perhaps if you'd been treated like they were when they were children, you'd not have spent the last thirty years comfortably working as a verger in a lovely backwater like ours. They didn't have a chance.'

Willie slapped his glass of home brew down on the table and said, 'Comfortable? Comfortable? I worked bloody hard at my job. In summer every hour God sent, believe me. At everyone's beck and call night and day, locking up, unlocking. Believe me, it was no soft job.' His face flushed and his eyes sparked anger, and for one terrible minute he thought he might be going the same way as Titus, because his heart was thumping and he felt if it went any faster ...

'Now, Willie,' Grandmama laid a quiet hand on his arm, 'you *know* I didn't mean a thing about your job. But you have to admit it was peaceful. After all, *your* customers didn't answer back.' She smiled as sweetly as Grandmama could ever do, and Willie's heart began to slow.

From the dining room Police Sergeant MacDonald and his wife came into the saloon bar for a drink to finish off their evening.

'Come and join us, Mac.' called Grandmama. 'Move up and make a space, all of you.' So they did and Don collected two spare chairs from other tables for them and Grandmama dug in her purse and got to her feet.

'The drinks are on me, you two, what would you like? Home brew for you Mac, eh? and Mrs Mac?'

In that precise speech she suffered from, Mrs Mac said, 'I'll have a gin and orange please, if you'll be so kind.' She gave everyone the benefit of her sickly ingratiating smile, which made their flesh creep as it always did.

When they'd got settled with their drinks Mac asked if they were glad the market was finished with, saying before they could answer, 'I must say I am, it brought too much attention to Turnham Malpas, far too much.

271

That was what caused it all. Before, a stranger would have stood out like a sore finger, so to come to the village in broad daylight to burgle would have been a stupid thing to do.'

Willie interrupted him. 'Absolutely, I agree, and with the bikers there wouldn't have been anything to spoil, would there? But a village green full of stalls and loads of people, a right target and not half. And what fun I 'spect they thought.'

Mac put his homebrew down on the table, 'Exactly, that's what they said, "we did it for fun." Unbelievable. Absolutely unbelievable.' He shook his head in despair. Mrs Mac, only accustomed to speaking pleasantries in public, indignantly offered an opinion, 'Pity they've nothing better to do, they should be in prison for what they did.' They all nodded in agreement with her comment and then something happened that they had never expected in all their wildest dreams. The main door of the pub opened and two people entered. A deep, scandalized silence filled the bar.

There'd been plenty of times in the long history of the Royal Oak that a full bar had whooped with joy or fallen silent at the news of some event or other – Henry V's victory at Agincourt, when a queen of England had been beheaded by her king, Nelson's victory at Trafalgar, the end of the First World War – and tonight was no exception. Tonight's news may not have been included in the national archives, but in the history of Turnham Malpas it scored highly.

Liz was dressed all in black, but Neville wore shorts, a T-shirt and open-toed sandals. Liz was drained of all colour, and looked as though she were sleepwalking. Neville had a spring in his step and quite a flush to his cheeks.

272

When they reached the bar it was Neville who ordered their drinks. 'Two gin and tonics, Dicky, please.'

He motioned to a table which had just been vacated, and, looking as though Neville was twitching her puppet strings, Liz walked across to it and waited for Neville to pull out a chair for her. She sat down heavily.

Neville smiled and nodded as he squeezed past the tables on his way back with their drinks, but got few smiles in return. What were they thinking of? The night of the funeral! Liz looked so ill it seemed to everyone she'd be following Titus to the churchyard within days. Had Titus's death deranged the pair of them?

All eyes were on their table. Everyone saw Neville persuade her to clink glasses with him and have a toast to someone or something. To Titus possibly? Then Neville began speaking to her in quiet tones so that not even the people on the table next to them could hear, try as they might. But Liz appeared oblivious to his every word.

Through gritted teeth Neville said angrily, 'Smile, for God's sake, woman, smile.' Liz managed a fleeting grimace. For a brief moment he wondered why he'd insisted on bringing Liz out for a drink. To prove to everyone Titus wasn't the love of her life, merely a casual friend? To prove he, Neville, still owned her? That she was still his wife? To dominate her? To restore the status quo?

All of those things, and more. He'd show 'em he was no longer a cold fish. The whole blasted pack of lily-livered, self-righteous nosy parkers could go to hell, and that included the Rector, who, Neville suspected, could see right through him. Keep talking. Look normal.

Though the conversation level rose a little, the camaraderie of a usual evening in the pub was gone. Quite a few people left with subdued goodbyes. Those who stoically hung on couldn't find it in their hearts to behave normally. Grandmama loudly declared she was leaving. She made a point of walking by their table and paused beside Liz. Taking her hand in hers, Grandmama gently kissed her cold cheek. 'Anytime you need to talk, my dear, you know where I am.'

Then she stalked out. That cold fish had a lot to answer for. His outrageous behaviour absolutely shocked her, because it was so obvious that he'd made her go out for a drink when it was the last thing she wanted to do. Grandmama stormed back to her cottage, glad she could call her home her own and didn't have some man dictating to her. She could have her hot chocolate with marshmallows tonight, and wallow in her indulgence with no one to question it.

Willie whispered, 'I'm off home. TV must be better than this. It's like a morgue in here.'

Sylvia agreed, remembering she still had some gin left over from her Christmas bottle and a fresh bottle of tonic Willie had bought last week in the supermarket, so she'd make do with that. Willie paused to purchase a bottle of home brew to take out, and they trundled home.

'I want to say this here and now,' she turned to face Willie just as they passed the Rectory, 'if you go first,' she gestured up to the sky, 'heaven forbid, I want you to know *I* shan't be in the pub the night of your funeral, looking as though I haven't a care in the world.'

Willie pondered on her devotion to him and agreed if she went first neither would he. They'd just kissed to confirm their faithfulness to each other when the Rectory door opened and out came Peter with the rubbish ready for tomorrow morning's collection.

'Goodnight, Rector,' Willie called out.

'Oh! Hello. Sorry. I didn't see you there.'

'That's all right, sir. We've come home early because we're that disgusted.'

'Disgusted? What about?'

'Neville. He's brought Liz into the pub for a drink. It's downright unseemly. She looks like death.'

Sylvia piped up, 'That man is not right in the head. Believe me. I was nearest and I *heard* him whisper, "Smile for God's sake, woman." He's cruel.'

Peter straightened up from putting the black bag down on the step. 'I'll go in and have a word with Caroline, see what she thinks. I'll have to do something about that. Thanks for telling me. Goodnight, God bless.'

'Goodnight, sir.'

Caroline was horrified. 'So what's happened to that charming husband who was giving her every consideration, mmm?'

'I thought Sylvia using the word "cruel" was absolutely right. We should never have allowed her to go and live with him in Glebe House. We must have been crazy to do so. He completely hoodwinked us.'

'But he did appear to have changed, didn't he? And it seemed to be what she wanted, which I must admit I found surprising at the time. Maybe he brought it about by bullying her when she wasn't in possession of her senses.'

Peter stood looking out of the window. 'I'm going over there to see how the land lies.'

Before Caroline could suggest he should be very careful what he said, Peter was out of the door and marching off to the Royal Oak, walking so quickly his cassock was swishing about his ankles.

He deliberately opened the outside door as gently as possible and walked in just as softly. The convivial atmosphere one was normally greeted with was missing, but there sat Neville at a table in the very centre of the bar, chattering away to Liz as though he hadn't a care in the world.

'Good evening, Rector. What can I get you, sir?' Dicky, who was wary of the atmosphere this evening, felt an incident of some kind was about to happen, which he fervently hoped wouldn't.

'I'll have a half of your home brew, Dicky, please.'

Peter leaned on the bar counter, paid Dicky, placed a foot on the brass rail and turned to face everyone. There was a small chorus of greetings and then the bar went quiet again. He toasted them all and sipped his ale.

'This ale gets better and better, Dicky. I always thought Bryn's ale was good but I do believe yours has the edge.'

Then Peter walked across to Neville's table and asked if he could sit down. Without waiting for Neville's approval, he pulled out a chair, sat on it, put his drink down on a beer mat and addressed Liz first. 'My dear Liz, how are you?'

She answered so softly he had to bend forward to hear her. When he looked closely at her he was appalled by the tortured look in her eyes.

'Thank you for this afternoon. The service was beautiful, so right for T ... T ... Titus. I'm not right, though. I'm desperate. Completely desperate. I don't know what to do about myself.'

'It will take time, it's been such a shock for you.'

Neville said, 'Speak up, darling, I can't hear.'

But she didn't. If anything, her voice went even quieter. Liz grasped Peter's hand. 'I don't want to live ... at Glebe House. But he compels me.'

'I see. Where would you like to be?'

There was a long pause. 'He thinks I'll stay married, but I shan't.'

'Where would you like to be? Your best place. Where is it?' By now both Peter's hands were clasping hers.

Neville felt his dominance waning. 'I wish the two of you would stop whispering. Don't you know it's bad manners to whisper in company?' Cheerfully he added, 'I'm her husband, don't forget. No need to keep Liz's secrets from me.'

Peter asked her again where it was she preferred to be.

'Anywhere will do. Just anywhere.' She released a hand for a moment so she could find a handkerchief. Having dried her eyes, she repeated, 'Anywhere.'

This time Neville heard her, and he swore, using words he didn't know he knew. Peter was shocked. At the sound of Peter's gasp Neville said them even louder and grabbed hold of Peter's wrist. 'She's my wife. What do you think you're doing? You may be wearing your God get-up but it doesn't intimidate me. In the past, I've accorded you respect you didn't deserve, but no longer. Let go of her. Do you hear me?'

Peter tried to release Liz's hands but she clung to him and unless he hurt her by prising her fingers from his hands he couldn't let go.

Neville, still gripping Peter's wrist, grew wilder. 'Liz! I insist you let him go. He's a nothing. He can't protect you from me. Do you understand? He has no influence on either you or me. We can look after ourselves without his help.'

Dicky's heart sank. Like everyone else, he was caught up in the drama. Horrified by Neville's attack on Peter, it was beyond his imagination to think about what might happen next. All of it was so totally unjustified.

Then Neville stood up, and so did Peter. 'Get out, Peter, and leave us to lead our own lives. We don't need you to soft-soap us all, smooth over the cracks, and put life back in its place, still less to provide some kind of spiritual dummy to keep us content. You're a waste of space.' His voice was getting louder and louder, more forceful, more scornful, more bruising, and when he struck out at Peter they all gasped.

Liz screamed. Neville put his left hand over her mouth, and aimed a further blow at Peter with his right, raining abuse as well as blows upon him. Surely to goodness Neville had gone raving mad? Liz, terrified by Neville's fury, forced his hand from her mouth and fled for safety behind the bar counter, where she hid behind Dicky, sobbing.

Peter didn't retaliate. He stood quite still and took everything Neville threw at him.

Realizing how futile it was becoming, Neville roared, 'You! You preaching God from that pulpit! What a mockery! What a sham! What an overweening attitude from someone with your sin on their shoulders! Don't think we none of us know who bore your children. It most certainly wasn't that well-educated, smug, self-satisfied, over-confident, patronizing wife of yours, was it? No, you were taking liberties, extreme liberties, with a member of your own congregation whose husband was dead but not yet buried.' Neville roared out the words, totally possessed by his fury.

At that moment, Dicky, at a loss as to how to deal with this problem, rang the bell for last orders, hoping to break the spell. At exactly the same moment Peter brought his arm back, clenched his fist and caught Neville a right hook on his jaw which clamped his teeth onto his tongue. Never in his life had he hit someone with such force and such pent-up anger, and immediately Peter was bitterly ashamed of himself. But that slur on Caroline was more than he could take.

Georgie, returning to the bar from upstairs where she been sneaking a quick break, found Peter rubbing his hand and Neville Neal, crouching against a table leg, his shirt-front soaked in blood, desperately trying to catch what blood he could with his handkerchief, and totally oblivious to the uproar in the bar.

'Eh! What's been going on? That's an awful lot of blood there. What caused it? Someone thumped him one?' Georgie asked innocently.

There was a note of triumph in Dottie's voice as she said, 'It's the Rector what did it.'

Amazed, and at the same time secretly delighted, Georgie said, 'The Rector! Well, that's news – and no more than Mr Neville Neal deserves. Drinks all round on the house.' There weren't many in the bar so it wouldn't be too costly an exercise, Georgie thought. 'Should we send for an ambulance, do you think?'

'So long as it comes from the lunatic asylum, because that's where he belongs,' shouted one of the customers on the point of leaving, but coming swiftly back inside at the thought of missing a free drink.

There were more troubled minds trying to snatch sleep in the village that might than for long time.

Caroline lay awake, concerned about Peter.

Liz, tucked up in the little bedroom under Grandmama

Charter-Plackett's thatched roof, felt more secure than she had since Titus died but was still unable to sleep.

Neville was under sedation in Culworth Hospital now they'd managed to stem the blood pouring from his mouth; he slept but then woke to screaming nightmares.

Most troubled was Peter. He had betrayed the very essence of his ministry and honestly believed he would never recover from it. Striking another human being simply because his finer feelings were being insulted? He, a supposed pacifist, taking such an action? Titus Bellamy would have stoically remained silent and unmoved, but he, Peter Alexander Harris, had reacted in the worst possible way. Peter cringed to his very soul and, at 6 a.m., after an almost sleepless night, he rose, dressed and went to pray in church.

Caroline heard him go but didn't attempt to stop him. He was best left to sort it out by himself. She'd never liked Neville, try as she might, and now she knew why. At bottom he was evil, cleverly covered up with all the false polish of an educated chap, so much so that he believed his own opinion of himself and had lost sight of truth and honesty. Poor Liz. At least she was safe with Katherine, but what next for her? If only Titus ...

Caroline heard the children getting up and decided to do the same. There was no point in lying idle thinking terrible thoughts.

'Where's Dad?' asked Beth as she munched on her muesli.

'Gone for his run.'

Beth glanced at the clock. 'He's late.'

'Got a lot to think about. He'll be back when he's ready.'

When Alex had finished his breakfast, without

mentioning that his intended bike ride had an objective, he picked his bike up from the back garden path where he always left it and set off to look for his dad. He knew the exact route he took because when he was small his dad had helped him to understand map-reading by showing him the route on an Ordnance Survey map, and pointing out the places Alex knew.

He found his dad seated on a stile looking out towards the beautifully tended rolling acres of Nightingale's Farm.

'Dad?'

All he got was a nod of acknowledgement.

Alex stood in front of Peter, wondering how to break his silence. 'Is it something to do with Mum?'

Peter hesitated and then shook his head.

'What then?'

'I struck someone an outrageous thump last night and he had to go to hospital. I can't forgive myself. I may have broken his jaw.' He showed Alex his bruised knuckles.

Intrigued, Alex asked, 'Whose jaw?'

Peter muttered grimly, 'Neville Neal's.'

A broad grin spread across Alex's face. 'Well, he must have deserved it; you wouldn't have hit him otherwise. I bet there's more than you would like to do the same, though I can see why you're ashamed about it. You gave me a sense of perspective about Africa, when I killed the s-soldier, you know. Somehow you explained away all the guilt. I know I'm not grown up, but perhaps I can do the same for you? After all, Dad, you didn't kill Neville, did you? It's not m … murder like I did, just a well-deserved thumping for raping Liz.'

Peter looked up at him intending to discuss further the words Alex used to describe the Liz incident, but his voice stopped in his throat for, surprisingly, he saw in front of him a youthful version of himself, looking him straight in the eye with a deep, unmistakable compassion. Suddenly their roles were reversed. This time it was Alex giving his father some badly needed comfort.

Peter almost wept. 'You could be right.'

'And as you always tell me and everyone else, God forgives a penitent sinner, and you sound thoroughly repentant to me.'

'Indeed. You're right. Thank you for that, Alex.'

Together they walked all the way home and, as they passed the Royal Oak, Peter paused. 'You know, I first met Titus here. He was sitting outside. I'd just started my run and he caught my eye. We exchanged a few words. Even then he impressed me, just something about him. That's how it is with some people. He made a lasting impression.'

Alex replied, 'He was a very nice, genuine man. I liked him very much. Poor Liz Neal, to lose him like she did.'

The two of them stood for a moment silently picturing Titus on the bench and regretting their loss, then Alex began to head home, pushing his bike. Peter followed him, feeling better in a curious way. Back at the Rectory Alex flung down his bike on the back garden path, and the two of them went into the kitchen where Alex ate a second breakfast with his dad.

A Brief History of the Village of Turnham Malpas

The earliest recorded mention of the village of Turnham Malpas is in the Domesday Book, first published in 1086. This book is a record of all the landowners, with their possessions, and the towns and villages of England in the early years after the Norman invasion. The Book records that the main landowner in the district of Turnhamme Maelpass, was Sir Guy Bernard de Templetonne. The name suggests he is a Norman knight who came from France with William the Conquerer, whose idea it was to catalogue the fine detail of the land he had invaded in 1066.

It mentions that the house Sir Guy owned in Turnhamme Maelpass was the largest in the area and that all the lands surrounding it, including Ha'penny Forester, Little Derehams and Derehams Magna, were owned by him. The records show that Sir Guy had forty head of cattle, thirty pigs, fifteen horses, a large herd of sheep, numerous chickens, geese and ducks, and a large number of indoor servants, villeins and serfs all bound by custom rather than law to their lord of the manor. Sir Guy gave his loyalty to King William I.

Almost three centuries passed before any matter worth

recording happened in Turnham Malpas. In the year 1349 it is known that an itinerant traveller came to the village and slept under the Royal Oak Tree on the village green. He washed his clothes in the pond, hung them out to dry on the Royal Oak, stole food from the Inn and one night wrung the neck of one of the geese belonging to Sir Richard. He made a fire and cooked it for all the world to see right there on the green.

Sir Richard intended to hang him for the offence, but the small prison house in Little Derehams (now restored) was already occupied so he was put in the stocks on the Green to keep him secure until he sentenced him the following day. However, the morning after the offence, out of compassion, Jake Bigges, verger at the Church, went to give the prisoner an early morning pot of ale and loaf of bread, and noticed that the traveller was showing all the symptoms of the plague. Terrified, the villagers released him from the stocks and beat him with sticks to make him leave the village. Two days later in the field behind the church he was found dead and was buried where he fell. Within days the plague was claiming its next victim and the next and the next. Derehams Magna suffered the worst, with every single occupant dying of the plague. In consequence it became a ghost village. Eventually the cottages crumbled away and many years later were raided for stone and disappeared completely except for a few humps of walls, long covered with grass; they can easily still be seen by a persistent investigator in a field at the bottom of Shepherds Hill where once Derehams Magna almost joined Turnham Malpas. At the time a third of the population of England died, so the disappearance of a village was a comparatively common occurrence.

The rector was one of the first to die so, as there was no

one to conduct a burial service, all the victims were buried outside the church walls in a communal grave. In recent memory this plague pit was investigated by the county archaeologist, one Dr Gilbert Johns, and the remains of the victims were given a Christian burial service and laid to rest in a communal grave within the churchyard. To this day the villagers still avoid walking close to where the plague pit was, as indeed they have done right through the centuries, convinced that the area is haunted.

The death of this itinerant traveller is remembered annually and the village holds a ceremony on the last day of June every year commemorating the event; everyone dresses in medieval costume (handed down from generation to generation) and the rector of the day wears a devil's costume complete with horned headdress, then is miraculously revealed wearing a white cassock, to represent the promise of new life and the defeat of the devil so that the villagers can look forward to another year of peace and plenty. This ceremony has been held without a break for almost seven hundred years.

The church, completed in 1249, with numerous additions over the centuries, is a thriving community. Since the disintegration of the village of Derehams Magna and the lessening of the influence of Little Derehams and Ha'penny Forester (now called Penny Fawcett) it has been the only church for the three villages.

A visit to the church of St Thomas à Becket is highly recommended. It houses the tomb of a Templeton knight with his ankles crossed on the back of a small terrier, and the villagers claim the tomb to be haunted, though no evidence of this has been documented. Flags carried into battle by the regiment commanded by several Templetons over the centuries are displayed along the sides of the church nave. The regiment was disbanded in 1855 after the end of the Crimean War so the flags are very old. Also there is a beautifully crafted board made of English oak listing all the rectors of the church since its beginning. The incumbent recorded for the years 1519–40 is Geoffreye Le Sage, who strongly resisted the decision to make Henry VIII head of the English Church in place of the Pope and, fearful that the rich silver plate belonging to his church would be destroyed in the Protestant uprisings or stolen by the King's own men, hid the church silver in the cellar in Turnham House, the large newly built home of Sir John Templetonne.

Hiding the church silver in Turnham House occurred for a second time in 1940, when the invasion of England by the Germans during the Second World War seemed imminent. The then rector the Reverend Simon Whittaker-Cosham carried the silver to Turnham House in the dead of night in his Austin 12 where it was secreted inside a cupboard which was boarded over and panelled to match the room it was in. The silver, hidden during the war, during which both the Rector and Sir Bernard Templeton died, was not discovered until the early 1990s when the current owner Henry Craddock Fitch was having alterations done to the house. He disputed the ownership of the silver, though it was obvious it belonged to the Church from the engravings on it. The villagers rose up and in a calculated show of solidarity demonstrated their disapproval of his decision to sell it and keep the money for himself. Eventually Mr Fitch realised he was up against forces that even modern business practice could not overcome, and graciously returned the silver to the church. It is now on display in the church on high days and holy days.

The beginning of the Civil War in 1642 brought strife to Turnham Malpas. Sir Ralph Templeton was a Royalist and recruited volunteers among his tenants to fight on the King's side. This was not what the majority of the villagers wanted. They saw the arrival of Oliver Cromwell as a means of sweeping away ancient practices which would enable a freer and more benign administration to become a reality – one more in keeping with the newly embraced Protestant faith of the village. Victor Gotobed organised the Roundhead opposition and there were several local and very bloody skirmishes, after which the two opposing forces each linked up with their main armies at the battle of Winchester, where the Roundheads beat the Royalists and occupied the city. This left the Royalist cause of Turnham Malpas in disarray, and with the loss of so many of his supporters Sir Ralph Templeton disbanded his forces and retired to the village to await the result of the Civil War. Descendants of Victor Gotobed were still living in the village in 1914, as were the descendants of Sir Ralph Templeton.

Early in 1698 the Whitehall Palace in London, residence of English monarchs since Henry VIII, was burned down. Distressingly, Sir Tristan Templeton, in an attempt to raise his stature in the eyes of King William III, was at the palace to beg an audience with him. When news of the fire reached Turnham Malpas there was immediate consternation. If he had died, who then would own Turnham House? Who would be their Lord of the Manor? His wife of a few months was distraught. When they learned of his certain death in the fire, and with no body to bury, the village grieved. As for the succession, seven months after his death a boy was born to his widow, resulting in a collective sigh of relief; the Templeton line would continue.

During the Napoleonic Wars three of the young men of the village decided to sign up with a local infantry battalion. They were Stephen Gotobed, Nathaniel Glover and Saul Wright. Nothing was heard of them for over seven years, partly because not one of them could read or write, until Saul Wright returned at the end of 1815. He had lost a leg but not his ability to spin a yarn. According to a plaque on the south side of the chancel in the church Stephen Gotobed and Nathanial Glover had lost their lives saving that of Wellington at the Battle of Waterloo.

To the glorious memory of Stephen Gotobed and Nathaniel Glover, young men of this parish, who died with glory serving their King and Country.

At Waterloo they bravely commandeered a captured French horse, mounted it and the two of them raced with the greatest speed after His Grace who had become isolated from his General Staff in the furore of the battle. They fought off a small group of French cavalry who, seizing their chance, intended to kill the Duke with the greatest ferocity. Nathanial Glover and Stephen Gotobed heroically fought to the death in defence of their leader and died together, brothers on the battlefield, as the victory trumpet call sounded. These two humble English soldiers, sons of this village, displayed bravery above and beyond the call of duty.

May they rest in peace. Anno domini 1815

Though the plaque is still there word has it that they died in a drunken brawl outside a bawdy house in Islington having deserted only a year after joining up. The real hero, one understands, was Saul Wright himself, who lost a leg at the Battle of Leipzig while attempting to rescue a friend who had been seriously wounded. He lived to a ripe old age. Having been banned for life from the Royal Oak Inn for insulting behaviour, he was most often to be found outside sitting on the bench waiting for someone to take pity on him and buy him a drink. To this day the bench is always known as Saul's bench.

The size of the village increased notably during the nineteenth century. Greater prosperity, houses built down Shepherd's Hill and a long stretch of houses down both sides of the Culworth Road increased the numbers in the village. During this century the only village to have a shop was Turnham Malpas, so when the idea of a school was mooted by Sir Tristan in 1852 it was built in Turnham Malpas, giving the village even more prominence. The school was built with due consideration for all the modern requirements of education at the time and has served the villages faithfully ever since. The celebrations of its one hundred and fiftieth year were well attended. Nothing but the serving of the villages' educational needs is seen in the school logbook, faithfully kept by each succeeding headteacher. One shattering event, though, was the murder of the headmaster's wife in 1990 by an ex-pupil. The tragedy reached the headlines of national newspapers and put Turnham Malpas very definitely in the news. The murderer, a young woman of some eighteen years, kept an elderly person hostage in her own home for twenty-four hours until she decided to make a break for it. Climbing a wall, she slipped and fell on the carving knife she'd taken with her for self-defence, and she died before anyone could help her. A generous local benefactor has kept the school very much at the leading edge of computer education by providing and updating the equipment available to the pupils. This has led to several of the pupils making excellent careers in IT.

The visit of the Prince of Wales (later Edward VII) to the village in 1887 as part of the celebrations of the Golden Jubilee of his mother Queen Victoria has been recorded in great depth by the Museum in Culworth: copies of menus can be seen, pictures of the Prince with the day's shooting 'bag', and a walking stick purported to have been left behind by the Prince. He stayed at the Big House for two nights and attended matins at the church on the Sunday morning (note the plaque commemorating his visit). Some uncharitable local leaders spread the word that Sir Tristan Templeton was trying rather too desperately for a dukedom or some such, in fact the Prince had invited himself for the shooting (it being August) and to sample the renowned cooking of Sir Tristan's French chef.

World War I brought death to the village as to almost every town and village in the country. The family worst hit were the Glover family; there were five boys and three girls living with their parents in one of the tiny cottages right on the Green. (A descendant of the Glovers still occupies the cottage). The eldest four boys got their call-up papers and were drafted to France in a matter of months. In the space of three weeks all four of the boys had been killed. Other families lost a son here and there but none was so deeply affected as the Glover family. Rumour has it that the four Glover brothers had extracted, by force, a pound each from the charity fund which the Rector administered, and over time the villagers began to suspect a charity-fund curse. The rector at the time died when his carriage overturned, the verger's daughter died of scarlet fever, the verger committed suicide and in modern times the bank manager died of a heart attack while attempting to clear up the fund account. Peter Harris, the current rector, came close to death in a traffic accident because, they said, he was contemplating how to use the accrued money for the benefit of the church. Due to the fierce opposition of the villagers to the use of the money in their village, the accrued money was finally given to charity.

Over the years there have been several attempts by both the council and private individuals to put in street lighting and a one-way system for the road around the village green. But these ideas have been fiercely resisted and despite a major initiative by the council at the end of 1999 to bring the village into the twentieth century, never mind the twenty-first, it is still without street lighting, without a one-way system for the roads, without part-time traffic lights and without numbers for the houses. The Post Office attempted to introduce numbering to ease the work of the local postmen but this was rejected; consequently the village houses still have only names, not numbers. The Post Office even pointed out the confusion of Orchard House and Orchid House within yards of each other, to no avail.

In more recent times the Village Green came to prominence when an entrepreneur discovered a very old charter in the county archives, originally written in 1305, which gave permission for a market to be held on the green each Thursday from half past eight until one p.m. When it was originally established the market was a valuable addition to the livelihood of the occupiers of the surrounding villages, who could bring their excess garden produce to sell. However, when the plague struck the villages so catastrophically in 1349 the market was no longer viable and was stopped. The restarting of the market caused massive opposition in the village, but, worse, attracted outside invasions from thieves and troublemakers. Finally, through tragic circumstances, the market ceased, and peace once more reigns in the village.

If this brief history has intrigued you, hunt around in the village, see the remains of the plague pit, the ancient gravestones at the church, visit the old inn, now the Royal Oak Public House, sit on the green and feed the geese, descendants of the geese owned by the Templeton family for centuries, call in at the village store to buy souvenirs and some of their fine home-produced foods, but most of all talk to the people who live here. Everything that happens in the world takes place on a smaller scale in this wonderful village. It is an up-to-date, feisty village that has weathered all the storms the world might bring to its doors, but is still here, always looking forward and indeed sometimes leading the way, full of tradition, engaged in century-old feuds, but bound together by history and tradition.